"Carolyn, Tu...

Brett's hands fell firmly ~~on~~ ~~her~~ ~~and~~ ~~he~~
turned her so that she could not avoid facing him.
"Look at me."

Carolyn looked up into the depths of his dark,
intense gaze. She felt as though her every secret
desire was being explored. "Brett, I . . ."

"You wanted me that night up in the mountains."
His arms slipped from her shoulders and wrapped
themselves around her in a fierce embrace. "You
want me *now*."

His lips possessed hers; then he lifted his mouth,
breathing rapidly. "You do, don't you? You want
me as much as I want you."

JANE CONVERSE

is one of Silhouette's more prolific authors,
having published more than sixty novels under
various pseudonyms. She lives in California, but
travels extensively. Some of her recent trips
include Hawaii, Mexico, and Japan.

Dear Reader,

Silhouette Special Editions are an exciting new line of contemporary romances from Silhouette Books. Special Editions are written specifically for our readers who want a story with greater romantic detail.

Special Editions have all the elements you've enjoyed in Silhouette Romances and *more*. These stories concentrate on romance in a longer, more realistic and sophisticated way, and they feature greater sensual detail.

I hope you enjoy this book and all the wonderful romances from Silhouette. We welcome any suggestions or comments and invite you to write to us at the address below.

Jane Nicholls
Silhouette Books
PO Box 177
Dunton Green
Sevenoaks
Kent
TN13 2YE

JANE CONVERSE
Mist of Blossoms

Silhouette

Special Edition

Published by Silhouette Books

Copyright © 1982 by Jane Converse

Map by Ray Lundgren

First printing 1983

British Library C.I.P.

Converse, Jane
  Mist of blossoms.—(Silhouette special edition)
  I. Title
  813'.54[F]   PS3553.O544

  ISBN 0 340 33580 7

Printed and bound in Great Britain for
Hodder and Stoughton Paperbacks, a
division of Hodder and Stoughton Ltd.,
Mill Road, Dunton Green, Sevenoaks,
Kent (Editorial Office: 47 Bedford
Square, London, WC1 3DP) by
Richard Clay (The Chaucer Press) Ltd.,
Bungay, Suffolk

Dedicated with much love
to the L.V.S. and M.M.O.M.
who made this book possible

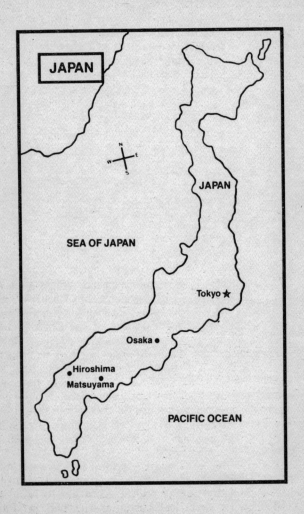

Chapter One

It was one of those late-February rains that are actually welcomed in Los Angeles, but Carolyn Chandler could have done very well without it. Darting from the parking lot to the doorway of the sleek Beverly Hills building that housed Macklin-Durham Talent Management, she imagined what her hair would look like, drenched by the sudden downpour. She had wanted to look her best for this luncheon date with Jennie Macklin. And there was always the slim possibility that Jennie's now-famous brother would be in town. Not likely, though, Carolyn thought. Since Brett's rise to superstardom, he was always either on tour or performing in Las Vegas.

Fortunately, her design portfolio had a waterproof cover. Riding the elevator to the sixth floor, Carolyn half-wished that Jennie hadn't asked her to bring the collection of theatrical costumes she had produced while taking the fashion-design course at one of San Francisco's most prestigious art schools. Her hope of becoming a costume designer belonged to the never-never-land of impossible dreams—like her infatuation with Jennie's older brother. Weeks of trying to get past secretaries at film studios and production companies had convinced Carolyn that she would be wise to shelve her overly ambitious dream. Tomorrow she would start looking for another newspaper job. At least she was qualified for that by her B.A. in journalism and several years of experience.

She did not have to introduce herself to the ultrachic young receptionist. As Carolyn stepped into the spacious, ultramodern waiting room of the talent-management company that was half-owned by Jennie's husband, her old friend was waiting for her. "Car*rie!*" she exclaimed, giving her an exuberant hug. "Oh, I'm so glad you're early. I'm starved! Not that I need another pound, but look at *you!* You look like a fashion model. Oh, I *hate* people like you!" Jennie's declaration of hatred was accompanied by another embrace.

She hadn't changed in the four years since they had seen each other last. Jennie might be married to an important figure in show business, she might own one of the most impressive houses in Bel Air, and she might be the sister of *the* Brett Wells, but she was still the same outgoing, unpretentious nonstop talker Carolyn had known as a child when they grew up next door to each other in Escondido. They could have been back in the rural avocado-growing town now, laughing and exchanging little-girl confidences.

Jennie, still slightly overweight, her now expertly styled hair still looking as though pixies had taken to it with a pair of scissors, rattled on and on, as though they had just met in the grove that separated their simple stucco houses.

"I've made reservations at the Bistro," Jennie said. She tapped Carolyn's portfolio. "I'm dying to see this, but let's have lunch first and catch up on gossip."

They were near the door to the impressive offices when they were interrupted, first by Jennie's husband, a quiet, affable man Carolyn had met once before when she had served as Jennie's bridesmaid, and then by Ken Macklin's partner, a sandy-haired man in his forties.

"Right after lunch," Gavin Durham said, after he had been introduced to Carolyn, "would you have a few minutes to help me? I'm counting on you to know what to do, Jennie."

Jennie's huge brown eyes widened. "Now what?"

Her husband excused himself, and then Gavin said, "It's my right-hand lady, Alice. Seems that she's not going to Japan with us."

Jennie scowled. "She's got to go! You can't do without an appointment secretary to help with publicity."

"Her husband's put his foot down," Gavin Durham said. "After all, they've only been married a few months, so you can't blame the man. And Alice, God love her, says she's not about to jeopardize her marriage for a four-month trip to cherry-blossom land. She's one of the rare individuals in this town who puts her husband before her career."

"Could we run an ad in the *Times?*" Jennie suggested.

"Sure," Gavin countered facetiously. "And have every female over sixteen in the Hollywood area storming our doors. I have enough troubles now, getting this tour together."

"You wouldn't have to mention that the job involves going out of the country with Brett," Jennie said.

"Sooner or later, every applicant would find out," Gavin replied. "And assuming that only half the women who applied were insanely in love with Brett, we'd be going out of our minds. Think about it, Jen. Find me an efficient assistant, and make sure she's married or otherwise committed to a man."

Jennie shrugged. "Give me a few hours, Gavin. I'll try to think of somebody."

Shortly afterward, at a table that was usually delegated to Hollywood VIP's, Carolyn expressed her curiosity about the sudden vacancy. "It doesn't sound like much of a problem to me," she said. "I imagine there would be hundreds of available candidates for the job."

Jennie sipped at her Manhattan. "Oh, sure. But we've learned the hard way that on a tour, you've got to screen your personnel very carefully. For example, the roadies—people who handle lights and sound and equipment—can't be drinkers or dopers. Enough headaches on a tour without *that*. And female employees—oh, boy!" Jennie rolled her brown eyes ceilingward for a moment. "If they're too old, they can't stand the pace. If they're young, we're asking for emotional problems."

"They fall in love with Brett?" Carolyn asked the question as though the thought were preposterous, but she understood. She could empathize. She understood all too well.

"You said it," Jennie replied with a mock sigh. "In fairness to my brother, they aren't encouraged. But he can't help being . . . what's the word, charming? He's warm and friendly with everybody. It's part of his stage presence to make every woman in the audience feel special, as though he's singing his love songs to her, and her only. Then they're in a foreign country, living in high style, going to press parties and meeting a lot of glamorous people. Aren't many young girls who don't get carried away. Alice Reynolds was ideal. Insanely in love with her husband. And she's always looked upon Brett the way I do. As a talented big brother."

"Sort of the way I've always seen him," Carolyn lied.

Jennie nodded. "Right. How could you feel romantic about a lanky guy next door who splashes mud on your new dress? Remember that day, Carolyn? Of course, there were times when he was a big help. The time you fell off the playground swing. And the night we both needed a date for the senior prom and he showed up in Escondido to visit. Remember?"

Remember? The night was indelibly etched in Carolyn's memory. She had designed and made dresses for herself and for Jennie—gossamer confections of silk and chiffon. Yet, neither of them had been asked to the prom, partly because it seemed that there was a shortage of male seniors who cared about going at all, partly because the others had always seemed too immature to cultivate. And then Brett, who was already beginning to make a small splash in the musical world, came home unexpectedly to visit his family, accompanied by Ken Macklin, his manager at that time. Jennie had prevailed upon them to serve as escorts.

What a glorious evening it had been! And how Carolyn had glowed with pride when the bandleader asked Brett to join them for a few romantic ballads! This incredibly handsome rising star was *her date,* and she had basked in the envious glances of every girl in the ballroom.

Afterward, during breakfast at an all-night local coffee shop, there had been a long, serious discussion of their respective ambitions, their hopes for exciting careers. And before Brett had said good night at her parents' door, Carolyn had slipped easily into his arms for a long and thrilling kiss.

Brett's kiss had lingered on her lips along with his parting words: "Let's always stay in touch, Carolyn." But staying in touch had meant nothing more than an exchange of Christmas cards, and letters from Jennie that sometimes ended, "P.S.: Brett says to say *hi.*"

If Jennie was even faintly aware of the impact of that momentous evening, she gave no indication of it now, only pausing for breath while their waiter served their crabmeat crepes and salads. "This is one tour on which Brett and Gavin can't afford any problems. Brett's not just going to Japan to do concerts, you know. He's going on location to make his first film."

"How exciting! I suppose it's a musical?"

"Uh-huh. Gavin says the script is an update on *Madame Butterfly*. Actually, it's just an excuse to feature Brett singing about twelve new songs he's written. With a glamorous, exotic background. Gavin's his personal manager, you see. He's responsible for Brett's material and production and personal appearances. My husband's the business, contract and money guy."

"And you?" Carolyn asked.

"I'm the all-around troubleshooter who has to worry about aggravations. Like having Gavin's assistant tell him she can't go to Japan for four months. On two weeks' notice. Brother!"

Jennie changed the subject then, saying she was anxious to look at Carolyn's new dress designs and recalling the days when they were ten or eleven and Carolyn had made glamorous wardrobes for their paper dolls, using construction paper and crayons. "You always had a flair for fashion, Carolyn. I was a little disappointed when you majored in journalism. And then you took those dull jobs, covering social events for that small-town paper up North. And that . . . what was that P.R. job you had for a while?"

Carolyn made a wry face. "I was promoting a new brand of spaghetti sauce, for one thing. That only lasted five months. My heart just wasn't in it. But I stayed with it long enough to save up tuition for art school. For all the good that training's done me. There just aren't many openings in the theatrical-costume field. And I've had no practical experience."

Jennie reached across the table to give Carolyn's hand an encouraging pat. "Stay with it, hon. Talent will out. Look at Brett. Talk about choosing a field that's hard to crack! And look what he's done." She smiled. "Of course, he happened to fall into the hands of two terrific promoters. Ken and Gavin believed in him and they've engineered his career. In return, Brett's made our agency."

There was small talk about their respective families after that. Yes, Carolyn's folks were still operating their tropical-tree nursery. They missed living next door to Jennie's and Brett's parents. Mr. Wells had died of a heart attack two years ago. Brett had since bought a veritable mansion for his widowed mother in La Jolla, and she spent most of her time going on cruises. Carolyn swapped "whatever-became-of" stories for a few more minutes before she asked, "What did Gavin Durham's assistant do? I mean, what's expected of his assistant on a tour?"

"Trying to keep up with him." Jennie laughed. "He comes on as very low-key, but Gavin's a dynamo." She paused to reflect. "What did Alice do? Oh . . . arrange for promo appearances, like TV one-shots and press parties. Interviews. Answering local fan mail that comes to Brett's hotel. It's a little of everything. Hectic, but interesting if you have steel nerves and a constitution like Superwoman. The job pays very well, but anyone who can stand Gavin's pace deserves to make good money."

"I've got the energy," Carolyn offered tentatively. "And I've done promotional work. I know how to write press notices." Jennie was staring at her with an incredulous expression, and Carolyn decided that she was being presumptuous. She managed a short laugh.

"Of course, I haven't promoted superstar singers. They're not the same as spaghetti sauce, are they? And I don't speak Japanese, so I'm not even suggesting . . ."

"Suggesting that you'd want to fill the opening?" Jennie tapped a hand to her forehead. "Heaven forbid! Not that you'd have to know Japanese. Overseas television and press people all know English."

"Then . . ." Carolyn summoned up the nerve to say, "I *am* looking for a job, Jennie. You know I'd give it my best shot. And going to Japan . . . I can't think of anything more exciting."

"Nothing exciting about being a small cog in somebody else's machine," Jennie said tersely. "You have a great talent of your own to promote. I wouldn't want to see you being just another flunky on Brett's tour."

Disappointed, Carolyn shrugged. "Maybe I'll go to work writing up weddings and club-officer installations for some other small-town paper."

Jennie's eyes narrowed. "You weren't seriously thinking about . . . ?" She answered her own question. "I guess you were. And, yes, four months in Japan would be a fantastic adventure. If Ken and I didn't have to mind the store, I'd love going along myself. Watch Brett move up another notch, start his film career. But I don't think I'd wish this job on you."

Carolyn made a brave attempt to save face. "You may be right. If I get buried in an office, I won't have time to keep going out after what I really want to do. But at least you wouldn't have had to worry about my falling in love with Brett."

Jennie's eyes met Carolyn's for a brief, half-knowing look. Then she said, "No, you'd be too sensible for that. Oh, Carolyn, I've had such a close-up view of the music business. And of women who fall in love with pop stars. They have to be fools or masochists. Every one of those guys is married already—to his music. Understand, if Brett was ever able to settle down, I'd hope it would be with someone like you. But he can't devote himself to one woman. He's become public property, in a sense. Not that I'm saying he's let success go to his head or that his values have changed all that much. But he's moved into another dimension."

Carolyn nodded. "He's a household name now."

"Exactly. Sometimes, watching him perform, I can see why romance-starved women go off the deep end. You ought to read some of the letters we process at the office! And the manic groupies that follow him everywhere he goes."

"I imagine he could even develop a contempt for some of them," Carolyn guessed.

"When they become genuine pests, yes," Jennie agreed. "Mostly, he's grateful for the attention. After all, fans are the reason for his success, and a star thrives on attention. But there's something unreal about Brett's new life. I never know, when he dates some gorgeous young starlet, if it's because he's interested in her or if Gavin arranged the date because it will be good for my brother's image. He's not serious about any one woman. Anyway, not that I know of."

How ridiculous it was for that statement to stir a flutter of hope! Starlets, stunning fashion models, other singers—Carolyn had read about Brett's appearances at chic supper clubs and Hollywood parties with beauties whose names were as well known to the public as his own. "I can assure you," Carolyn said with a conviction that belied the dismal feeling she felt inside, "that I'm neither a fool nor a masochist. I didn't fall head over heels with Brett when we were going to school together. And I certainly wouldn't do it now."

Jennie seemed to accept that declaration as fact.

"You always did have a good head on your shoulders. I think I'll worry less about you than I worry about Brett."

"I can't imagine what you'd have to worry about there," Carolyn said. "He seems to have it made."

Jennie's expression clouded. "Careerwise, yes. Financially, sure. He's had sold-out performances wherever he goes. His last three albums have gone platinum. And I know he'll be a smash in films. But on a personal level, I keep remembering the way he admired your folks, and ours. The way they had the stability, the security of always knowing there was someone who loved them, someone who was always *there,* no matter what happened. Family life was always terribly important to Brett."

"And it isn't now?"

"He hasn't stopped running long enough to think about it since his career took off," Jennie said. "And he's had so much thrown at him, how could he help but become blasé? I sometimes think there's nothing, nobody, he could want. Except something or someone he can't have."

Was Jennie just going on and on, the way she usually did? Or was she giving advice? *"Someone he can't have."* Was that the key to Brett Wells's heart—a seemingly impossible challenge? And after he had overcome the obstacles that stood in his way, what then? He would move on to the next challenge, tackling the next woman who said no to him, the way he was now taking on the challenge of becoming an actor in a film that would feature his already established talents as a songwriter and vocalist. Jennie was perceptive. And Jennie, who knew Brett Wells as perhaps no one else on earth knew him, was right; her brother had stepped into another world, one that didn't include a starry-eyed teenager he'd kissed good night after a silly high-school dance. Carolyn decided to say no more about applying for the job as assistant to Brett's manager.

They were trading small talk over coffees as Jennie said, "I love the Bistro. The food's great and the atmosphere's relaxed, at least on the surface. But like any other chic place in the Hollywood area, half the people come here to be seen, and the ones who haven't made it yet work so hard at seeing the names at the next table without appearing to be in the least bit interested, it's a wonder they don't all have stiff necks." She was explaining the protocol in seating and the attention to designer-label handbags that determined a female customer's importance, when Carolyn sensed an electricity in the air around her. There was a brief hush in the buzz of conversation, and she noticed that two couples at a nearby table were doing exactly what Jennie had described: they were trying to observe the entrance of someone without actually staring in the direction of the door. Carolyn had her back to the scene they were observing. Jennie's stare, over Carolyn's shoulder, was direct. Her round face broadened in a wide grin. "Well, guess who just came in out of the rain!"

Carolyn turned and saw Gavin Durham walking past the bar. In the next instant she felt her breath catch in her lungs. Towering behind his manager, radiant and more handsome than any man had a right to be, was the subject of all the excitement. Just the sight of Brett Wells, after all these years, brought a fluttering sensation to her heart. Dressed casually in denim, his perfectly chiseled features lighted by a bright smile, the once unruly waves of his mahogany hair now expertly styled, Brett made a commanding, self-assured entrance, probably aware of the sensation he was causing. In this sophisticated, celebrity-oriented company, he wouldn't be mobbed by autograph-hunting fans, but it was suddenly *his* room, and Brett knew that; he made everyone else around look dull by comparison.

His smile widened in recognition as he followed Durham toward the table occupied by his sister and Carolyn. There was an enthusiastic exchange of greetings, all four at the table talking at once. Then, moving toward the empty chair beside Carolyn, Brett leaned down to plant a kiss on her cheek. "I can't tell you how great it is to see you!" he said. "And how wonderful you look."

Carolyn's heart was now beating rapidly. Brett had taken her hand as soon as he had seated himself next to her, and he was saying to Gavin, "Understand, it's not as though I've just rediscovered the girl next door who had braces on her teeth and wore pigtails. Carolyn was *always* beautiful." Brett's dark, sexy gaze swept over Carolyn's face. "She had those dark-fringed, deep blue eyes all along, of course. And those luscious lips . . . that fantastic windblown blond hair."

"Which happens to be rain-flattened at the moment," Carolyn said. She felt nervous under Brett's appraising stare, wondering if such overt flattery was part of his new style. "And don't let him kid you, Mr. Durham. Brett used to splash mud on me. He'd ride across irrigation ditches on his bicycle and see how badly he could mess up my clothes."

"There was a yellow . . . sort of a . . . I guess you'd call it a pinafore," Brett remembered. Amazingly, he recalled the very dress Carolyn had made in hopes of impressing him. Should she remind him now that she had spent that whole afternoon sobbing?

Brett didn't wait for the reminder. "Is it too late for an apology?" he asked. "You'll admit I was more civilized when you wore that stunning white number, the night we went to your prom. You designed and made that, too, didn't you?"

"And *my* dress," Jennie pointed out. "But I don't

suppose you'd remember that, Brett. You never took your eyes off Carolyn that whole evening."

"Why would anyone want to?"

He was still smiling, still looking at her with that dark, intent gaze, leaving Carolyn too flustered for any bright repartee. She could only hope that her face hadn't turned a deep rose color. The very nearness of Brett, the subtle scent of his cologne, the virile maleness that exuded from him, had suddenly left her breathless and weak. She wanted to say witty things, to feel less like a country bumpkin in this sophisticated Hollywood company. But Brett's effect upon her was even more devastating than it had been the one night he had taken her into his arms and pressed his mouth hard against hers. She was grateful that witty repartee was evidently not expected of her. In fact, Brett launched into a series of nostalgic anecdotes about their years of growing up as neighbors. For Gavin Durham's benefit, Brett related incidents that Carolyn had forgotten herself, all the brief stories touching upon his admiration for her. "She had the figure of a fashion model when she was fifteen," Brett said, following that statement with a warm, deep laugh. "She'd come over to visit with Jennie, wearing shorts and a halter top. I was supposed to be practicing my piano lessons. It wasn't easy, Gavin, it wasn't easy."

There was laughter from everyone. Their waiter came to get cocktail orders from Brett and Gavin, and then the latter, who had been listening carefully to all of Brett's reminiscences, asked, "Is that what you do now, Carolyn? You're a fashion model?"

"Oh, heavens no!" Carolyn said. "I never thought of going into modeling. I—"

"She always wanted to design clothes," Jennie cut in.

Carolyn flushed as Brett's eyes, and those of his manager, cast admiring glances at the simple beige bouclé dress and jacket she had chosen for this occasion. "Not everyday clothes," she explained. "Fabulous costumes for plays and musicals and films and ballets. That's what I always wanted to design."

"And do you?" Gavin persisted.

Sometimes Jennie could be as amazingly unpredictable as her brother. "Carolyn *could* if she wanted to. It just happens that she's also talented in the public-relations field. *Publicity,* Gavin," she emphasized. "Carolyn's a sharp, experienced promoter."

Carolyn winced at the exaggerated buildup. Gavin's nonchalant, yet somehow all-seeing glance inspected her left hand.

The look was not wasted on Jennie. "No, she's not married, Gavin. But she may as well be. She was telling me about the very special man in her life when the two of you came in."

"Oh?" Brett's query hinted at disappointment more than surprise. "Anyone from back home?"

There was no doubt in Carolyn's mind now; her face must be glowing like a red neon sign. She wished Jennie hadn't told the lie, in spite of her good intentions. "No. No one from back home," Carolyn managed to say.

Jennie must have sensed her discomfiture. She took over quickly, talking about Carolyn's experience in public relations and concluding with "So, you see, Gavin, I've been trying to talk her into coming on board as your assistant during the Japanese tour."

"That'd be super!" Brett exclaimed.

Jennie shot him a look that was both reproachful and triumphant. "Gavin asked me to find someone who's as safe as Alice."

Brett frowned. "Well, you don't have to tell me that Carolyn isn't some hysterical groupie." His smile had vanished.

Gavin nodded, his pinkish face wearing a pleased expression. "You sound like an ideal candidate, Carolyn. Do you have work commitments now? Could you be ready to leave on such short notice?"

Carolyn opened her mouth, searching for the right words. None came to her, and she was grateful for Jennie's quick response. "If you and Brett approve, she's going to stay with Ken and me. We'll help her with her passport and visa, all the red tape. And she just finished an assignment, so she's free to go, aren't you, Carolyn?"

Free to *go?* To spend four months in an exciting faraway land she had always dreamed of visiting, to work at an interesting, good-paying job? To be with Brett Wells every day? He had let go of her hand when Jennie made that outrageous statement about her devotion to some nonexistent man, but she felt his presence even more strongly now, a presence that stirred old emotions. Bless Jennie and her big white lie. Why had she made it sound as though there were a romance in her life? Carolyn wondered. In the next split second she knew: Brett was interested only in someone beyond his reach. What was Jennie doing? Matchmaking in reverse?

They were all looking directly at her, waiting for a reply. Carolyn's eyes looked into Jennie's for a moment. She could almost hear her best friend's silent instructions: Go for it, Carolyn! And somehow, although a major earthquake was taking place inside her, she forced herself to sound as though miracles like this were everyday occurrences in her life. "It'll take a little doing," Carolyn said. "But, yes. Yes, if you think I'm right for the job, I'm sure I can get it together."

Chapter Two

$\mathscr{I}$t was during her stay with Ken and Jennie Macklin that Carolyn began to realize what Jennie had meant when she said that Brett had "moved into another dimension." Living in his sister's fabulous Tudor mansion, Carolyn had expected Brett to materialize at the poolside brunches, to drop in for dinner, to make at least a token appearance at a party given for Carolyn by her host and hostess. Until the day before their departure for Japan, however, Carolyn did not see Brett at all.

"He closed his week in Las Vegas last Saturday, didn't he?" Carolyn asked. She had just finished hours of filling in endless forms at the consulate, shopping, and learning the ropes from Gavin Durham at the agency office.

Gavin, who was going to be the most affable boss

imaginable, eyed Carolyn with a querulous expression. "Yes, but Brett's doing a benefit in San Francisco tomorrow night. And most of the time he's holed up in his cottage in Malibu, working on new songs. He doesn't have much time to socialize."

Had she been too obvious in asking about Brett? Carolyn assumed a more businesslike attitude. "And probably studying his lines in the film script. We've all been too busy for much socializing."

"Found time to say good-bye to your boyfriend yet?" Gavin asked.

"My . . . ? Oh. Oh, no. No, you see he . . . he's not here in California." Carolyn pretended a consuming interest in a review of Brett's last concert at the Greek Theater. "He . . ." She wasn't doing a very believable job. If Jennie was going to invent a romance for her, the least she could have done was to supply a plausible name, occupation and location to excuse his absence from the scene. Carolyn's mind hit on her cousin David, whom she hadn't seen in years. He was working as an oil-company pilot out of Anchorage. "Dave's in Alaska," she said. "I won't be seeing him before I leave."

"Unless we fly the northern route to Japan," Gavin said in a tone that would have suited a prosecuting attorney. "Though it's more likely we'll go via Honolulu."

Carolyn hoped that her sigh of relief wasn't audible. She must get that ridiculous story straight. And she must stop asking people about Brett. Even Jennie was beginning to give her worried looks.

Yet her mind and heart were possessed with him—his face, the sound of his voice, which filled the Bel Air mansion and the office almost continuously on records and tapes, the warm, possessive way in which he had held her hand during their reunion. He was busy now, preparing for a major concert tour and his first movie. But there would be days in Japan, maybe nights, when they would, inevitably, be together. Carolyn found herself living for those moments that lay ahead.

Her first major disappointment came on the morning when Ken and Jennie drove her to Los Angeles International Airport. Boarding was chaotic. Although she had known for several weeks that Brett traveled with an enormous entourage, it seemed unbelievable that so many of the passengers finding their seats aboard the giant 747 were "Brett's people."

The Macklins had appointments at the office and couldn't wait for the takeoff; Carolyn was relieved when they turned her over to Gavin Durham, who saw to her luggage and boarding pass.

"Everybody here and accounted for," Gavin said as he returned from checking Carolyn's carry-on luggage with the flight attendant. She had been assigned a window seat. Why was she surprised and disappointed when Gavin settled himself next to her? Had she really thought that she would be making this long trip with Brett Wells as her seatmate?

"Everybody?" Carolyn asked. She hadn't even seen Brett this morning.

Gavin scowled at the "No Smoking" sign and sighed. "Yep. Everybody." He extracted a notebook from his jacket pocket, showing Carolyn a list of checked-off names. "Tony Hanniman. You know him. Brett's pianist, conductor, arranger. Jerry Badler, our bassist. Rusty Johnson, drums. Carmen Battaglia, guitar. The younger guys partied all last night. I had to round them up personally this morning."

Gavin went on to explain that the rest of Brett's backup musicians would be hired in Japan. "Fortunately, I didn't have to worry about the technical gang. Steve Sherman has been doing our lighting since our first tour. His crew was at the airport before dawn, I think. And our sound man, Bill Gomez—you can set your clock by Bill. And every one of the roadies they're in charge of are accounted for and on board.''

While the motors rumbled their warm-up, Carolyn learned everything she could have wanted to know about the Brett Wells concert tour of Japan except the one question that was uppermost in her mind: where was *Brett?*

She didn't dare ask. Every time she mentioned Brett's name, Gavin gave her one of his querulous looks. She felt foolish in having supposed that Brett would occupy the seat next to hers—that he might hold her hand during this exciting trip, that he would, again, make her feel as though she were someone special in his life.

Minutes before the plane was to roar across the runway, Brett came up the aisle. Resplendent in an elegant beige suit and white shirt that contrasted with his darkly tanned throat, he paused next to Gavin, giving him a stare of mock disapproval. "And where were *you* when that mob of screaming females descended on me?" he asked accusingly. "I didn't think I'd get aboard." Brett pointed at a tear in his sleeve. "I thought I was going to get torn apart. I got away just in time, no thanks to my faithful manager."

Gavin grinned. "Your manager's job was to see that your fans knew where you'd be this morning. I figured you'd fight your way on board. And, needless to say, there were press photographers to record your ordeal."

Brett laughed. "Thanks a lot, buddy." He turned his smile toward Carolyn. "Hi, neighbor! Great to have you along!"

That brief encounter was the only time Carolyn saw Brett during the entire eighteen-hour flight between Los Angeles and Tokyo. Even during the brief layover in Honolulu, in which there was barely time for Carolyn to buy postcards to send to her parents and a few old friends, there was no indication Brett was on the plane or that he knew Carolyn existed.

"He's working with Tony Hanniman," Gavin explained. Brett's accompanist and arranger was also invisible during the long flight. Carolyn began to understand what it meant for a man to be married to his music.

She also began to understand what it meant to be working for a man who took a strong, seemingly paternal interest in her. Gavin was more than attentive. Though he was responsible for the entire crew, he devoted almost all of his time to Carolyn. In fact, it sometimes seemed to her that his interest was more personal than professional. Yet *her* thoughts were focused on her elusive employer. *Brett.* No longer the big brother of her best chum. An international superstar! Remembering him spending a Saturday afternoon with her father, the two of them puttering with an old bicycle purchased at a swap meet, Carolyn found it difficult to absorb the new reality. Brett was, as Jennie had pointed out, part of a glamorous world that his childhood associates could no longer enter. As thrilling as it was to be soaring over the Pacific, wined and dined in the most luxurious way imaginable, a dark, hurting melancholy fell over Carolyn. Brett had said it was great to have her along. It probably was great for him to have the presence of fourteen people who would see that his speakers were in the right place, and another dozen who would see that his spots blended from a dramatic blue to a flattering rose-pink while he was singing his heart out. Carolyn felt strangely out of place. The person she had loved as a boy seemed like a vision from some ridiculous childhood dream. He had become famous, important, unapproachable. Somehow, she felt more alienated from him now than in all the time when she had had nothing more than a Christmas card from him.

Brett was still secluded with Tony Hanniman when the plane finally made its swooping arc over Osaka. How much more exciting it would have been to look down upon the miniature storybook panorama of ships and gleaming buildings if Brett had been beside her. Here and there were the shimmering outlines of an ancient pagoda, and intriguing patches of green that must be the exquisite gardens for which the Japanese were famous. Along the coast was a lacework of islands and bays set in seas that ranged in color from pastel aquamarine to deepest cobalt blue.

They cleared customs in Osaka quickly, and were soon airborne again, making their approach to Tokyo. And then, wearied by the long flight, but still entranced by the newness of every sight and sound, Carolyn was experiencing a dream-come-true arrival at the glittering metropolis of more than eleven million people.

A fleet of limousines swept the Brett Wells entourage from the teeming, ultramodern Haneida Airport through a city of incredible contrasts. Seated beside Gavin in the luxurious limo, Carolyn marveled at the newness and cleanliness of the streets, sleek office buildings, cars and shops. Yet there were contrasts that dazzled the eye and the mind: a sixty-story skyscraper before which elderly women in traditional kimonos mingled with smartly dressed, hurrying businessmen; shops crammed with electronic gear which were decorated with artificial sprigs of paper blossoms; a wild kaleidoscope of neon lights and concrete expressways punctuated with quaint temples and tiny stalls selling colorful, unrecognizable craft items and foods. What fun it would be to explore the meandering little lantern-decorated alleyways that led away from the main streets lined with international restaurants, nightclubs and smart boutiques. She wanted to see and experience every aspect of this strangely dreamlike city, yet Carolyn could not imagine doing it alone. Embedded in her consciousness was Jennie's big brother from back home, to whom this unique mélange of old and new was also a bewildering experience. But where *was* he? Carolyn summoned the courage to ask: "Is Brett in the car ahead?"

Gavin's face creased with a weary half-smile. "He's still back at the airport, luv. I suppose I should have stayed, but some of the roadies will help him get away from the mob."

"The mob?"

"Fans," Gavin said in a matter-of-fact tone. "Should be at least five hundred, maybe more. He'll have a sore right arm before he signs all those autograph books."

Carolyn was shocked. "But he's got to be as tired as the rest of us. Maybe more so, because he spent the whole flight working. Couldn't you have arranged to protect him from . . . ?"

"From the people who make all this possible?" Gavin's pudgy, freckled hand made a waving motion, indicating the luxury of the chauffeured car in which they were riding. "Carolyn, my job, and your job, is to see that his concerts are sold out and his albums go platinum. That isn't going to happen if we protect him from fans and photographers. I personally saw to it that both would be waiting for Brett when our plane touched down."

Carolyn shook her head, visualizing Brett surrounded by the usual crush of squealing female fans. "Still, I feel sorry for him. People tearing at his clothes, reaching out to touch his face . . . kiss him. And never any privacy."

"My heart bleeds," Gavin said. He sounded hard and uncaring, and he must have realized that, because he added, "Brett would have been miserable if his arrival had been ignored. And he'd be looking for a new manager tomorrow morning. It's part of the price he has to pay, dear girl. Like a politician. Giving his public a touch of the Brett Wells mystique."

Carolyn's thoughts were still with Brett when his crew checked into the luxurious New Otani Hotel, which was to be their headquarters during their stay in Tokyo. Rising from a ten-acre seventeenth-century formal garden, it was the largest hotel in Asia, and its two thousand rooms were a study in opulence. It was more than a hotel, Carolyn realized amid the organized confusion of getting everyone settled in the suites that had been reserved for their entourage. It was a city within a city, boasting elegant shops, a sports-health salon complex called the New Otani Golden Spa, cocktail lounges of every possible description, and no fewer than thirty-two restaurants.

Thirty of the hotel's rooms on the twenty-first floor, Carolyn discovered, were reserved for women only. She was not relegated to this all-female area, however. She was the only woman on the Brett Wells staff, and she was quartered in a sumptuous, monochromatic beige suite located just across the corridor from the rooms that would serve as Gavin's office, reception center, and private bedroom. Conductor-arranger Tony Hanniman's rooms already boasted a baby-grand piano as well as a wet bar; he would be working with Brett next door to the "office."

"Usually the light-and-sound crew occupy less expensive quarters," Gavin said as they watched her luggage being carried into Carolyn's sitting room. "Sometimes, even the musicians wind up at another hotel. Not Brett's people. He insists that every member of his crew is equally important. He can afford to put them up in style, and he wants everybody close by for consultations."

Carolyn felt exhausted, but she managed an approving smile. "I heard the drummer—what's his name? Rusty? I heard Rusty all the way down the hall, yelling, 'Oh, wow! Can you believe this?'"

"He said that during our European tour about eighty-nine times a day," Gavin said. "Personally, I don't feel like 'wow.' If you're all set and there's nothing I can do for you, Carolyn, I'm going to get some sleep. Tomorrow's a big day. I don't want to be dragging around with jet lag."

"I'm too excited to sleep," Carolyn told him.

Gavin paused in the open doorway. "Call room service if there's anything you want. Tomorrow we have press appointments and a reception for TV reporters and music columnists. Meanwhile, having been here a dozen times before, I'll personally teach you how to convert dollars to yen. I can also fill you in on whatever you want to know about the postal system."

Carolyn was staring through the glass wall at a panorama of the sprawling city, golden in the late-afternoon sunshine. From this height, Tokyo appeared to be a toy town fashioned from gold. "What do I need to know about the postal system?" she asked.

"Well, you'll want to know how many stamps it takes to get a love letter from here to Anchorage," Gavin said. His tone was both wistful and edged with sarcasm. "I know the first thing you'll want to do is let your friend David know you've arrived."

Carolyn didn't turn from the window. She wasn't anxious to have Gavin see her face. "David . . ." she muttered absently. "Oh, yes. Of course. There's stationery on the desk, I'll . . . write to him after I've unpacked."

But she didn't write and she made only a half-hearted attempt at transferring her wardrobe to the dresser drawers and enormous walk-in closet. She dropped to the wide bed, sinking into the silky beige-on-beige embossed chrysanthemum covering, realizing that it was taking sheer effort to keep her eyes open. I should get out of these droopy clothes, she thought. I should take a hot bath. I should . . .

Her last conscious thought was of the huge metal plaque on the door next to her own. It was not inscribed with a name, but the gleaming gold star on the circular sign identified the man who would occupy the rooms next to her own. Carolyn brushed an old cliché out of her fading consciousness: "So near and yet so far." Before she could choose between being ecstatic over her fabulously good luck or depressed because Brett had moved out of her world, she was asleep.

How long did she sleep before she became aware of the insistent ringing of a telephone? Carolyn awoke to total darkness. It took several more rings before she oriented herself and groped for the receiver; looking for a bedside lamp switch seemed a hopeless effort. Her voice heavy with sleep, Carolyn said, "Hello?"

"You're supposed to say *'mushi-mushi,'*" a deeply resonant voice said. It was followed by a short, familiar laugh. "I hope I didn't wake you up, but I probably did."

"Brett!" As groggy as she was, Carolyn's mind raced with excitement. "I guess I did doze off. What time is it?"

"Five minutes to the witching hour," he said. "And I'm too wired up to sleep."

"I must have slept seven hours! If you hadn't called . . ."

"You'd have slept another seven," Brett said unapologetically. "You can do that later."

"Later?"

"From one until eight A.M. I'm hungry, thirsty, wide-awake and in need of company. And I'd like to show you something you won't see from the best hilltop in Escondido. I'm right next door, you know. Can I come by for you?"

"Now?"

"At the stroke of midnight. We'll have a few drinks together. Okay?"

Panic seized her. She had fallen asleep in the clothes she had worn to the Los Angeles airport; it seemed like a century ago. "I need a . . . a little time to get ready. Shower and change. . . ."

"You're not supposed to shower." Brett laughed. "You scrub up outside the tub and then you get into it to rinse off. When in Japan, do as the Emperor does." Maybe he was just silly from fatigue, or maybe he'd already had a drink or two. Carolyn had never heard him sound more lighthearted. "I'll set my chronometer. And I'll be very generous. You have ten whole minutes before you'll hear a knock on your door."

When Brett hung up, Carolyn made a concentrated effort to find the lamp next to her bed and to turn it on. The lavish beauty and the strangeness of her surroundings took a moment to register. So did the conversation with Brett. He wanted to see her, wanted to be with her! She was as tremulous as she had been on the one other occasion when she had, equally unexpectedly, had a date with Brett Wells. Except that the night of the prom, she had known what to wear; her choice had been hanging in her closet for more than a month. Now, years later and thousands of miles away, her entire wardrobe was still crammed into suitcases.

It was a relief to discover that the blue tiled bathroom boasted an American-style shower and that the seafoam-green suit she carried into the bathroom with her had been steamed free of wrinkles by the time she emerged. There was only time for a flick of a brush over her hair and a minimum of makeup. Her hands were too shaky to apply eyeliner, she decided. But she was as ready as she was going to get when, not ten but fifteen minutes later, there was a knock on her door.

Chapter Three

*N*othing in her most extravagant daydreams had prepared Carolyn for the thrill of sitting across the tiny table from Brett Wells and looking down at the magnificent sight below. They had been seated next to a ceiling-high pane of glass that gave an unobstructed view of the city, its streets delineated by rows of streetlights that, through the faint mist, looked like necklaces of sparkling gems. Moving headlights delineated the intertwined expressways, and multicolored splashes of neon lights turned the scene into a stunning palette of diffused reds and blues and greens. Carolyn sipped at her gin and tonic, shaking her head back and forth in awe. "I feel like your drummer, Brett. I can't believe this. I can't believe I'm here, seeing what I'm seeing."

Brett laughed. "You forgot to say, 'Oh, wow, man!' "

It was easy to laugh with him. "Oh, wow, man,"

Carolyn repeated. "That will have to do. There just aren't any words for a sight like this. And this whole room's *revolving!*"

She didn't tell Brett that there were also no words for the exhilaration of being this close to someone she had loved since her early teens. His handsome face, lighted by the soft glow of the candle on their table, was being eyed by the few other women in the Blue Sky Lounge, and she knew that they must be envying her. But looking at Brett, his dark eyes bright with pleasure at the sight they were enjoying, was almost too much. It was a face deeply etched in Carolyn's memory, yet it was that of a dazzling stranger, too—a man whose every wish was catered to. He had decided, like Carolyn, that he wasn't really hungry, after all. However, if he had wanted dinner, even though the hour was late and dinner was not usually served in this tower lounge, Carolyn was certain that he would have been indulged.

It was not merely his fame and importance that had her feeling like a star-struck adolescent. It was the almost overpowering physical presence of him that made her breathlessly aware of her own body. Her own body, and its need for his. Carolyn tried to concentrate on her drink, the magnificent view, Brett's beautifully tailored dark blue suit and the narrow silk tie he had chosen to dramatize it. Nothing worked. Her eyes were irresistibly drawn to his face, studying the strong chin, the classic line of his aquiline nose, the way his dark brows turned up only slightly at the ends to add a devilish touch to features already so perfect they were sinful.

And he was here not to view the sweeping vista of the city below; he had spent an hour here earlier, Carolyn had been told. He was here because he wanted *her* to share his exuberance, had chosen *her*, of all the people in his employ, to monopolize his attention.

He was smiling at her now with that bright white, always sincere smile, saying, "Not that there weren't some beautiful sights to see back home. Remember when we'd ride our bikes to that hilltop on Marion Lane? There was the stream below, with all those big sycamores turning color in the fall. And huge live oaks. Over to the left you could see the whole Pauma Valley. Orange and avocado groves, horse ranches all green with white rail fences." Brett had fixed her with that intent, meaningful stare that always sent a shiver through Carolyn. "I can get nostalgic about it now, but back then I wasn't usually looking at the scenery. Not when you were there."

Carolyn decided not to ask what he meant. She gestured instead toward the breathtaking sight that stretched for miles below them. "It's going to keep changing, too, isn't it? How long does it take for this room to make a complete turn?"

"An hour," Brett told her. "That's what I was told, and I timed it when I was up here earlier."

"Didn't you sleep at all?"

"No, I told you, I was too revved up. If the rest of the band hadn't conked out on me, I would have jammed all night. Use up this nervous energy."

Something about that statement struck a disquieting note in Carolyn. She was suddenly less delighted to be here. Brett didn't give her time to analyze the reason for her momentary change of mood. "I envy backup musicians. They can relax, party, do their thing and then go back to sleep without a care in the world."

Brett's eyes had clouded, and Carolyn noticed that his long, tapering fingers were drumming a nervous rhythm on the edge of their table. "To listen to you, a person would think you were apprehensive."

"Of course I'm apprehensive," Brett said irritably. "Three big concerts in a country I've never set foot in before. A big-budget musical film. What do I know about starring in a movie? I could fall on my face anywhere along the line."

"Elvis Presley was no Sir Laurence Olivier," Carolyn pointed out. "People flocked to his movies to hear him sing. And Gavin says your albums sell like . . ." Carolyn decided that "hotcakes" wouldn't be appropriate. "Sell like sushi in Japan. Right? And did you see the enormous posters with your picture on them as you came from the airport? There was a great big sign over one street that said, 'Welcome, Brett Wells!' I was astounded at the price of tickets for your Tokyo concert. The cheapest seats are twenty dollars, and yet Gavin says there's no doubt they'll be turning people away. How can you possibly be apprehensive?"

"Because," Brett said firmly, "a performer's only as good as his last performance. When you hit the top, there's only one way to go, and that's down. It's not an easy thought to live with."

"But you work so hard. Jennie told me you keep writing new songs and rehearsing for hours on end. And, Brett, I've never seen anyone walk into a room the way you do. As though you owned the place and everyone in it."

He seemed to have relaxed a little. Enough, at least, for a wry smile. "Keep talking," he said. "I need to be convinced."

Until this conversation, it had never occurred to Carolyn that Brett was less than one hundred percent sure of himself. Assurances and compliments came easily because Carolyn meant every word she was saying. And while they finished their first cocktails, Brett seemed to be drinking in her words like a stranded desert traveler who has been parched for days and then finds the cool waters of an oasis.

It was good to have Brett confiding in her, telling her of the night in London when members of the royal family attended one of his appearances. "It wasn't your usual pop-rock crowd of young people in jeans and T-shirts. This was a big charity affair Gavin had arranged—practically a command performance. Before I went on, I peeked out from the wings at all those VIP's, all the furs and the jewels, and . . ." Brett shuddered, remembering. "A few years ago I was playing in a second-rate crib in San Diego. Not long before that I was paying for my music lessons by spreading fertilizer under avocado trees. And I was going to step out on that stage and entertain *this* crowd? I broke out in a sweat. My stomach felt like it was tied up in knots, and I was convinced that when I opened my mouth, nothing was going to come out."

"But you were a smash," Carolyn reminded him. "I read about that concert in *Rolling Stone.*"

Brett edged forward in his chair. "You *did?*"

"Sure. Along with thousands of other people."

"But you cared enough to buy a magazine that I don't think you'd ordinarily read."

Brett was looking at her with an expression that implied astonishment and, yes, gratitude! She wasn't going to tell him that she had clipped that article and pasted it in a scrapbook, along with countless others. "Everybody in a star's hometown wants to read about him," Carolyn said lightly.

"But you never came to any of my concerts. Not in San Diego. Not in L.A."

"Maybe I was waiting for an invitation," Carolyn said.

Brett looked embarrassed. "I should have arranged to have complimentary tickets sent to you. But I didn't really know where you were." He looked uncomfortable with the excuse. He had known that she could be reached through her parents. The truth was that he had forgotten that she existed.

The revolving lounge had made a full turn, and they

were finishing their second round of drinks when the vague flutter of annoyance that had disturbed her earlier came back to plague Carolyn. She was in a land that places a high premium on good manners, and she should have said something that showed her understanding, some dismissing remark that would have eased Brett's discomfiture. Instead, Carolyn heard herself saying in a peevish tone, "You're like that British royalty you were so impressed with, Brett. They wouldn't have socialized with you. Really important people, when they have some use for you, order a command performance."

Brett's jaw fell open. Carolyn looked away from the bewilderment in his eyes. "What brought that on?"

She was breathing hard, staring fixedly at the rim of her cocktail glass. "Tonight, for instance. You needed someone to help you kill some time because you couldn't sleep."

"Maybe I needed some understanding from someone who really knows me. Knew me way back when, before everything became . . ." Brett released an audible breath. "Before my whole life became sort of . . . unreal."

She was sorry she had broached the subject. Even while she was speaking, Carolyn sensed she was being unjust. Maybe it was the combination of tiredness, of having two drinks when she was unaccustomed to having any at all—two drinks in fast succession without having eaten dinner. "But you wouldn't have called me tonight if there'd been someone else to talk with. You were in the mood to . . . what was it you said? To jam with your musicians. But you wouldn't have gotten *them* up out of a sound sleep." She was acting like an absolute witch. She knew that she was alienating Brett with these jabbing accusations, but she was unable to stop herself. Yet she wasn't really angry with Brett. She was furious with herself for having jumped when he summoned her as a last resort. "Gavin didn't tell me this was going to be part of my job."

In the next instant she wanted to apologize, blame the drinks. Exhaustion combined with the gin, which was making her head reel. But Brett wasn't waiting around for any apologies. He was on his feet, his face a grim mask. Carolyn got up from her chair, her legs wobbly under her, having to grab Brett's arm to steady herself.

In the elevator, Brett said, "I'm going to attribute that attack to jet lag and booze, Carolyn. I don't think you meant the things you said to me."

But he didn't deny that if an all-night jam session had been possible he wouldn't have called her. Quietly, her face turned away from Brett, Carolyn began to cry.

When the elevator doors slid open at their floor, Brett hesitated. "I wasn't thinking. You haven't had anything to eat since lunch on the plane. Trader Vic's would be great, but it's probably closed at this hour. There's an all-night coffee shop, though, and we could . . ."

"I think . . ." Carolyn struggled to keep her voice steady, unstrained by tears. "I think I'd rather go back to sleep."

"Fine." Brett took her arm, guiding her down the corridor. "I should have remembered that you're not a night person, as I am." At the door to her suite, Brett helped her fish her key from her handbag, then unlocked the door. Not until he opened it and stood back, waiting for her to enter, did Carolyn summon the courage to say, "I'm sorry, Brett. I can't explain it to you. I . . . can't explain it to myself, but I'm . . ."

She had been holding back her tears, but now they were like a torrent from a bursting dam. She stood in the open doorway, unable to say any more, her mind foggy with the knowledge that, somehow, stupidly and viciously she had spoiled whatever slim hope there was of winning Brett's love.

"Carolyn?" Brett's voice was husky, as though with pain. *"Carolyn?"*

She shook her head. "I don't know why I . . ."

Brett's arms reached out for her, pulling her close to his body. "Don't cry. I should have been more considerate. Carolyn, please don't cry. You *did* understand me tonight. You know I needed you. We're *friends.* My God, everybody in this whole damned hotel is a stranger, everybody in this whole country. But we're old friends. When I can find the time, we'll see some of this fantastic place together. Have something terrific to write to your folks and my Mom. . . . The two of us will see things we never dreamed of seeing. Come on! We'll chalk up tonight to bad judgment on my part."

While he spoke, Brett's hands had started caressing her back. The gesture was meant only to be comforting. How could she tell him that even the word "friends" was painful, that she wanted to be so much more to him, and knew, with bitter conviction, that this, too, was part of an impossible childish daydream? She was sobbing like a child, making a total fool of herself, her head pressed against the firmness of Brett's chest, so close to him that his heartbeat was a steady drumbeat in her ears.

Carolyn made an effort to control herself, moving back slightly and trying to disguise the emotions that raged inside her. "I'm . . . going to . . . get your shirt all smudged."

She darted a glance upward, her tearful eyes locking with Brett's. Dark with concern, probably reading her secret, Brett's eyes held Carolyn's for a breathless moment. Then he leaned down to cover her mouth with his with a swiftness that stifled the air in her lungs. It was no boy-next-door kiss. Brett's lips communicated an aching hunger, demanding and possessive, hurting her with an almost frenzied violence. She was locked in a fierce embrace, the stiffness of her body giving way beneath the expert roaming of his hands as they explored the small of her back, dropped to find more intimate curves, his tongue a darting flame that permitted no resistance.

There *was* no resistance inside her. Carried away by the sweep of Brett's unexpected ardor, Carolyn let herself melt in his arms, unable to stop herself from responding with a passion she didn't want to reveal. Somewhere in the dim recesses of her consciousness a warning voice told her that she must not let him know how much she loved him, how desperately she wanted him. But the desire his lips and hands had evoked in her, the virile press of his body against hers, left no room for pride or for reasoning. This was a moment she had yearned for. Carolyn gave herself to it with every fiber of her being, returning his kiss with a fire as consuming as his.

They were both gasping for breath when Brett finally released her. His fingers tilted her chin upward so that she was forced to look into his penetrating eyes. "Do you really want to go back to sleep?" he murmured.

Carolyn let the full significance of his question penetrate her mind. He was asking to be invited into her room. He was asking a question millions of women all over the world would have been thrilled to hear, a question that could have come straight out of her own most deeply ingrained desires. How could she tell him that it was not a concern for her virginity that filled her with trepidation? Until he had crushed her in his arms, she had not known that she was capable of this raging physical need for a man's body. No, it was someone else's voice that warned her now; someone who knew Brett all too well, telling Carolyn that he only wanted what he could not have. A night of intimacy with Brett would make an earth-shattering change in her life. To a man who was accustomed to getting whatever he wanted, it would be just one more casual encounter, a way to fill the early-morning hours when he was sleepless and the needs of his body were unfulfilled. If she invited him in, she would not be opening a door but sealing it shut.

She didn't have to tell Brett their evening together was now ended; Carolyn's hesitation, the way she looked away from his questioning gaze, was apparently all the rejection a sensitive man like Brett needed. Abruptly he said, "Yes, I guess that is what you want to do. Sleep. I'll say good night."

Carolyn started to offer an explanation, but anything short of the truth would have emerged muddled and embarrassing. She echoed Brett's good night and walked, still far from steady on her feet, into her room.

Brett waited outside her door, silent for a moment. Then, before he closed the door, probably enraged by the unbelievable rejection, he said in an incisive, mocking tone, "Don't worry about it, Carolyn. Going to bed with the boss isn't part of your contract, either."

Fury, anger, confusion, shame—a tempest of emotions swept through her. Carolyn heard the door close quietly behind her before she threw herself across the bed and waited for the scalding relief of fresh tears.

Chapter Four

If she could have dismissed from her thoughts the biting sarcasm with which Brett had ended their first night in Japan, Carolyn would have enjoyed, during the days that followed, the most exciting time of her life.

There was constant turmoil in Gavin's office suite. Gavin's preliminary work had guaranteed that everyone who wrote a column, hosted a talk show or variety hour or was an important figure in the Japanese media was apprised of the arrival of Brett Wells. The telephones on Carolyn's desk rang constantly. In between calls, members of the entourage ran in and out of the office, each with production problems that could only be solved by Brett's manager. It was hectic, but it was also fun.

Fun, except for a series of telephone calls from London. "A woman named Lisa Westerbrook," Carolyn told Gavin after the first call. "She says it's urgent that she speak with Brett."

Gavin, who presided over the chaos in his office with an incongruously placid manner, waved a warning finger at Carolyn. "The switchboard downstairs has instructions not to put any long-distance calls through to Brett. None, that is, that aren't cleared through this office. Sorry I forgot to tell you, Carolyn. We don't give out Brett's room number and we don't bother him with any messages from Lisa Westerbrook."

Carolyn frowned. "He can't be worried about creditors. And he's usually very friendly with fans."

"But not *this* fan," Gavin said. "She's a British socialite. Money to burn. I suspect that a good part of it goes to finding out where Brett's working and driving him up the wall with emotional phone calls. The lady is convinced that Brett's going to return her affections if she persists, and she's prone to hysterics."

"Does Brett know her?" Carolyn wondered aloud.

"They went out together in London. Met at a very exclusive party, if I remember correctly. And she's been making a pest of herself ever since."

Carolyn visualized a frumpy, dissipated dowager insanely in love with a glamorous younger man. Gavin corrected that impression when the next call came through later that day. "I *know* she sounded as though she was crying," he said. "She always does. Hard to believe that a gorgeous creature like that could have so little pride or be so damned neurotic."

Shortly afterward, Gavin announced that he would be going to the post office in about an hour. "If you have anything you want mailed, any *personal* mail, I'll take it along," he said. His quizzical tone reminded Carolyn that she was here precisely because there was no danger that she would fall in love with Brett and create a nuisance of herself like Lisa Westerbrook.

"Oh, thank you," she said. "If I get a minute, I'll dash off a letter to David."

Her letter to her cousin David was a brief, flippant note. Her mother had insisted that Carolyn drop cards to all the family's friends and relatives, so David's name had been included in her address book. She had not seen David in years, and they had never been particularly fond of each other. He would be astounded to hear from her, Carolyn knew. Along with the "love letter," she stuffed in a New Otani hotel circular to fill out the envelope, feeling like a hypocrite when she handed the letter to Gavin before he left the office.

"Sensible lady," Gavin said approvingly as he took the letter from Carolyn. He didn't have to explain that he thought women who fell in love with the star he managed were fools.

Carolyn worked hard at covering up her emotions. At their first press party, she had stayed a room-length distance from Brett, busying herself with handing out the releases she had helped Gavin prepare. Promotion for his concert in Tokyo was unnecessary by then; tickets were being scalped at staggering prices and there was a news story in the English edition of *The Japan Times* about crowds of disappointed fans being turned away from the ticket windows.

She couldn't fault Brett for ignoring her during that cocktail reception or the next. Brett was never seen without a wall of people around him. He didn't even dare venture into one of the hotel's many restaurants; his meals were taken in the suite where he and his conductor, arranger and accompanist worked endless hours at the baby-grand piano. Never had Carolyn felt that Brett was more distant.

Fortunately, Gavin did not let up on the publicity blitz because of the sold-out concert. And Carolyn was kept more than occupied writing publicity releases that would be sent back to America, human-interest stories about Brett's taking Japan by storm, buildups for the forthcoming movie in which he would be costarring with Sadi Hayashi, Japan's most glamorous female actress. Filming would begin shortly after the concert. Meanwhile, there were chauffeured trips to television stations, usually with Gavin but sometimes alone, setting up Brett's appearances. On two occasions during their first week in Japan, Brett sang numbers with which the audience was familiar through his best-selling albums. Other guest shots were confined to interviews, through interpreters.

Her activities confined to the hotel and to offices in broadcasting studios, Carolyn might almost have been in Los Angeles. Except for the nationality of the people with whom she was dealing, and occasional glimpses of the city from a limousine window, she was not experiencing the excitement of being in an exotic, faraway country. Brett had talked about wanting to see this intriguing land of contrasts with her, but that prospect had been shattered by two gin and tonics and her unfortunate remarks their first night in Tokyo.

To stop herself from thinking about Brett, Carolyn worked at a feverish pace. But alone in her suite when the days came to an end, she was torn between wistfulness and anger. How gentle and thoughtful and attentive he had been during that first hour in the sky-high cocktail lounge! Brett had sounded totally sincere when he talked about their sightseeing together. The sweet recollections would be tempered, in the next minute, by a furious resentment. How did he dare to assume that she would leap into bed with him just because he found himself bereft of more interesting company? How many other Lisa Westerbrooks had he left behind him—women he had used and discarded? One thing was certain: there would never be a time when his manager would have to protect Brett Wells from irritating telephone calls from her!

Carolyn found herself making excuses for Brett's indifference. When he came into the office for brief conferences with Gavin, he was invariably pleasant to her, but he was always in too big a hurry to do more than exchange a few words of small talk. Certainly he was not aware of Carolyn's breathlessness when he walked into the suite, the heart-pounding excitement that she disguised with a casual "How's it going, Brett? Keeping busy?"

He *was* busy. Completing a new song that would be introduced at his concert, rehearsing with the band, darting to one interview or television appearance after another. It was, ironically, a part of Carolyn's job to keep Brett busy. And she found herself wishing there was more she could do to relieve his tiredness. Idealizing him, the way women always overlook the faults of men they love, Carolyn yearned for a second chance. Yet she did not know how she would react if he once again deigned to invite her to bed with him. Besides, he had made it clear that she was only his friend. Her confused reactions to Brett made Carolyn's hours alone a mental and emotional torture.

But hadn't she been warned that Brett was married to his work? Eager to hear him sing, to see him for more than a few harried moments, Carolyn accepted Gavin Durham's invitation to watch the dress rehearsal for Brett's concert. Seated in the drafty, sparsely filled arena, from which the press as well as the public had been barred, Carolyn let the sound of Brett's beautifully modulated baritone carry her out of herself. His poise, his shading, the conviction with which he used his own lyrics to convey his emotions, were the ingredients of his astounding success. When Brett sang about love, even facing an almost empty rehearsal hall, there was a personal quality, a wrenchingly complete giving of himself that reached out and touched everyone who was present. Enraptured by his voice and by the emotional story he was telling in song, Carolyn closed her eyes and heard him singing only to her. Yet all the while she knew that every woman who listened to him felt the same way; it was this ability to personalize his music that transformed a talented vocalist into a consummate artist.

But how nerve-racking it was, each time Carolyn let herself become immersed in the romantic aura, to have Brett wave his arms in the air and shout, "Hold it, hold it . . . hold it right there! This isn't the circus coming to town!"

He criticized musicians, found fault with the lighting, repeatedly stopped to question the sound. Katsumi Funabashi, noted as the country's outstanding trumpet player, along with three other Japanese brass players, had been added to the core group to fill out the backup band. Carolyn marveled at Katsumi's patience; during a jazz interpretation of an old American standard, Brett insisted upon going over a single phrase repeatedly until he was satisfied with the effect.

On a few occasions, tempers flared. It was well past midnight when Brett reluctantly agreed that they should all "take ten" and restore their energy with coffee and hamburgers brought to the concert hall from a popular American fast-food restaurant. Brett used the time to confer with his chief sound technician, Bill Gomez. Carolyn found herself sitting in the front row of the auditorium with some of the band members and the technical crew. To establish her sympathy for them, she said, "Brett's going to have all of you worn out before tomorrow night."

It was apparently the wrong thing to say. Carmen Battaglia, the band's self-appointed comedian, was untypically serious as he said, "We'll stay here all night if we have to. And he'll have us perfect by tomorrow night, you can count on that."

Covering up her gaffe, Carolyn said, "But you sound so great now. All that going over and over—"

"It's not nit-picking," Rusty Johnson said firmly. Between handfuls of french fries, the dapper little percussionist added, "He knows what he wants, and what he wants is the best we can give. Sure, it's a lot of work. When Brett gets on my case about the beat in his new number, I wanna throw my sticks in the air and walk out."

"Yeah, but you don't," one of the light crew said. "I get mad sometimes when he harps on Steve and the rest of us. But the man's usually right. And where would any of us be without him?"

In a modest, unassuming voice, Eiji Takayama, one of the two newly added trombone players, summed up their discussion: "Excuse me, please. I work with Mr. Wells very hard because he make me proud."

Respect for Brett's musical knowledge and his insistence upon a flawless production was what kept the uncomplaining crew hard at work long after Gavin and Carolyn had returned to the hotel. Carolyn's last recollection of the evening, before she fell into a tired sleep, was a remark made by Rusty Johnson as she was leaving the hall. "You just started working with Brett, honey. Wait'll you know him awhile. You'll find out that he drives himself ten times harder than he drives the people who back him up. He's not a prima donna, kid. He's a perfectionist."

Thousands of people reaped the benefits of that perfectionism the next night. Carolyn had never seen Brett in concert before. Neither had the thousands of enthusiastic fans who crowded the largest auditorium in Tokyo. There was a scattering of American and European tourists, but most of the audience was Japanese, and although the study of English is compulsory in Japanese schools, Carolyn knew that many, if not most, of those in attendance did not understand the lyrics of Brett's songs. But he was communicating—oh, how he was communicating—through the one medium that breaks all national barriers, music.

"This is all he needs," Gavin said quietly between the first and second sets. "An audience that responds. Look at their faces, Carolyn. These people *love* the man."

"And he's loving them back," Carolyn said. She exchanged smiles with a row of bubbling schoolgirls. Their adoration shone in their coal-black eyes, delight lighting their exquisite doll-like features. One, turning shyly toward the conspicuous blonde in the audience, practiced her high-school English by saying to Carolyn, "He is very well, yes?"

Carolyn nodded. *"Very* well." She didn't explain that "well" and "good" were not quite interchangeable. It was enough that her admiration for Brett Wells was shared by youngsters to whom the nearly five-thousand-yen admission might have meant months of scrimping.

Poised and elegant in the white suit that was his hallmark, Brett sang his love ballads as though each woman in the audience was the only one for whom they were intended. His rock numbers brought a wild response from the predominantly male audience. And even Gavin, who was no stranger to Brett's performances, was touched by what was apparently a supreme effort on Brett's part. He kept shaking his head back and forth through every screaming, hand-clapping response, muttering, "Dynamite. Our boy is sheer dynamite! You see all the TV cameras? We'll want videotapes."

There were five encores before his audience let him

go. And when Brett turned the full impact of his personality on his audience, throwing out a kiss and saying, *"Domo arigato! Domo arigato*—Thank you. I love you all!" the standing ovation threatened to shake down the ceiling and walls.

Tokyo traffic, Carolyn had learned, was a study in madness, especially during the morning and late-afternoon rush hours. The night of the concert, cars and human beings jammed the streets surrounding the auditorium. Foreseeing the crush, and knowing that Brett would be wrung out after throwing himself so completely into a lengthy performance, Gavin had coordinated policemen, security guards, members of the staff and a cordon of limousines calculated to confuse the fans who waited for Brett outside the auditorium. It was an operation worthy of an international spy ring, but Brett, as well as his musicians, was somehow whisked back to the hotel within half an hour of the concert's tumultuous finale.

Brett would be exhausted, Carolyn guessed. He would probably head straight for his suite, down a relaxing drink, and collapse.

But as Rusty Johnson had said, she didn't know him very well, after all. Enjoying cocktails and what Gavin referred to as "a delirious postmortem" with a small group of well-wishers, hangers-on and members of the press, Carolyn was astounded to see Brett and Tony Hanniman come bounding into the office suite. Tony, a tall, thin, bespectacled man, was usually quiet and reticent. Tonight he announced his presence with a loud whoop. "Was that a smash or was that a smash?" Everyone present cheered, and Brett, grinning, said, "Have you ever heard the guys play better? I could have gone for a walk around the block. Somebody pour me a drink . . . I want to listen to the tapes."

Gavin and Brett congratulated one another. Carolyn

walked to the bar and mixed Brett's favorite Canadian and soda. He was bouncing around the room, listening to compliments, laughing, giving credit to everyone in his company for the fantastically successful evening. As Carolyn approached him, glass in hand, Brett cried out, "Carolyn! I'm so blind from spotlights, I didn't see you. I'd have been miserable if you weren't here to share this with me." The highball glass nearly fell from her hand as Brett threw his arms around her in an impulsive hug. "Isn't this terrific? So many wonderful people!"

Carolyn managed to extricate herself without spilling Brett's drink. "It was a beautiful concert, Brett. You couldn't have been better."

He thanked her for the drink, then said quietly, "Almost as good as the night of your senior prom?" Brett laughed. Energy and joy seemed to be pouring from him.

Carolyn faked a thoughtful expression. "Well, let's say the lighting effects were a little better. You sounded pretty good to me that night, too."

"Carolyn . . ." Brett reached out his free hand to touch her face, his fingers resting tenderly on her cheek, his eyes locking with hers. It was as though there were no other people in the room. "We're a long way from home," he said softly. "But with you here, I never feel lost."

"You've hardly seen me since we got here," Carolyn reminded him.

"But you understand why."

Carolyn nodded. "I know what it took out of you to do what you did tonight. And I know you've done it many times before."

"Every time is the first time," Brett reminded her.

"You must be worn out."

"If I am, I'm too tired to know it. To hell with hearing the tapes. We're going out to celebrate."

Gavin had been sidling closer to them; apparently he had heard most of their conversation. "You'll get ripped to shreds out there, Brett. You know that once the concert sold out, we arranged for live TV coverage. Everybody in this city will recognize you."

"*Not* in my ingenious disguise," Brett told him. "Everybody's invited. You're going to fall down when you see me in my new red wig and walrus mustache."

He was being facetious about the disguise, of course, and during the late-dinner tour of the Ginza district's nightclubs, Brett *was* recognized. Perhaps it was the size of his party, or innate Japanese courtesy, but he wasn't mobbed.

For Carolyn, it was not a date with Brett; he included everyone in the group in his laughing byplay. But it was her hand he held as they left the hotel, her shoulders over which his arm rested intimately as their limousine whisked them from the gaudy lights of the downtown entertainment center to a plush club in the Akasaka district, ten minutes west of the Ginza. It was a night to remember, a whirl of blaring music and fabulous decor, of showgirl hostesses fawning over the star and his retinue, of elaborately presented Kobe steak and succulent lobster, of premium French champagne. And, always, Brett laughing, playing the host, unmindful of the expense.

Thrilled with the excitement of the frenetic tour and with Brett's attention, however divided, Carolyn kept reminding herself that drink had been her undoing on her first date in Tokyo. She sipped cautiously at her champagne, declined stronger drinks, and gloried in the warmth of Brett's hand whenever he reached out for hers.

It was Gavin who finally said in a weary voice, "Brett, I know you deserve to let off a little steam, but there are fifteen thousand clubs and cabarets and bars in this city. Could we hold this junket down to only fifteen hundred?"

Everyone in the party laughed and applauded. The newsmen and a young couple from one of the television stations remembered that they had to be up early in the morning and that it already *was* early in the morning. And Brett, pretending that his heart was broken, sighed, "If I had known you were a bunch of tired party-poopers, I would have suggested a quiet game of checkers."

Gavin had ridden in the same limousine with Brett and Carolyn and he was still with them when they took the elevator to their floor at the hotel. "I'm ready to fall on my face," he admitted when they reached his room. "You young folks can go on partying if you want to. I'm saying good night."

Was he making a discreet disappearance, assuming that Brett had further plans for the evening? Maybe it was only tiredness that made Gavin look somewhat churlish, Carolyn decided. She didn't dare entertain the idea that there was a jealous edge to the way he spoke. Yet, during the past week, there had been times when she had seen Gavin looking at her with more than a fatherly interest. Was that what made Brett's sandy-haired manager add a postscript to his good night? "Terrific show, Brett. Great evening. Carolyn, you'll have something exciting to write to David about now, won't you?"

Gavin made a swift entrance into the office suite, which included his bedroom, leaving Brett and Carolyn in the corridor. She tensed, hoping Brett would not want the night to end just yet—hoping that she would not regret it later if this was only the beginning.

"Got your key?" he asked, nodding at Carolyn's handbag.

"Hope so." Her hands were unsteady as she fumbled for her key. Their eyes met as she handed it to Brett.

"Any orange juice in your refrigerator?" he asked.

"The maids keep it well stocked." Carolyn turned her face from the penetrating stare and Brett unlocked her door. He didn't ask to be invited in. As though it was the most natural thing in the world to do, he followed her into the suite. And, surprisingly, he opened the small refrigerator in her sitting room, found orange juice and ice cubes, and then said, "It's okay for you to have a drink now if you want it, Carolyn. You're in safe hands."

"I . . . think I'd like . . . just soda water."

"Still being cautious," Brett said.

"Cautious?" Carolyn kicked off her high-heeled sandals and sank into a comfortable chair. "What makes you say that?"

"I noticed you were being a teetotaler all this evening." Brett poured the soda, then his orange juice, into two ice-filled glasses. "Afraid to let yourself go?"

"I had a wonderful time," Carolyn protested. "And I have a better time if I'm not drinking myself insensible. You'll note that you didn't have to guide me up the corridor just now."

"Sensible," Brett said. He seemed, suddenly, to be curt and almost formal. He handed Carolyn her glass, then crossed the room to drop into the sumptuous brocade sofa. "Cheers," he said, raising his glass.

"Cheers," Carolyn responded. They drank down the toast and for a few seconds there was an uncomfortable silence in the room.

After a while Brett said, "I thought maybe you were making sure that when you write to . . . what's his name . . . David . . . you won't have to tell him you were nearly seduced by a lecher who plied you with spirits and . . . what's the old phrase? Took advantage of you."

"Now *you're* being nasty," Carolyn told him. "Please

don't be, Brett. This was such a glorious night, let's not spoil it with sarcastic little innuendos."

Brett nodded. "You're right. I'd like this to be a memorable night." He was quiet again for a few moments, swirling the ice in his glass, his handsome face looking as though he might be savoring the perfection of his concert. Then he looked across the room and asked, "Tell me something about the light of your life. This David. What does he do, what's he like?"

Nervously Carolyn made a stab at describing the cousin she had not seen since a backyard family barbecue at her parents' home years ago. She had still been in college then. "Oh, he . . . flies a plane. He's with the government, actually. Something to do with the Alaska pipeline." She was doing badly. "He's a rather quiet person." That much, at least, was true. She decided not to add "self-centered, boorish and dull."

"Loves you very much, I imagine?"

She could feel Brett's eyes boring through her. "I imagine," Carolyn said weakly.

"And you're in love with him?" Mercifully, Brett didn't wait for an answer. "Is he the reason you gave up following your career as a designer?"

"I've never had a career as a designer. I just took an art school course and knocked on a few closed doors. And they stayed closed."

"You've got to keep knocking until one opens," Brett advised. "If you have the talent, and you do, you *pound* on doors until you get inside."

Carolyn released a sigh. She was on more comfortable ground now. "The way you did. Oh, Brett, you were so great tonight. I felt so proud just thinking that I know you. That we're . . . friends."

"Friends don't have to be afraid to sit on a comfortable sofa next to each other," Brett said. "Instead of perching on the end of a silly damned chair." He patted the space next to him. "Come on over. I have a proposition for you."

Carolyn hesitated. "What kind of proposition?"

"A kind even your boyfriend might approve," Brett said. Before embarrassment could rise in Carolyn, he added, "I want to talk to you about your assignments for the next week."

Carolyn got up and carried her soda to the soft-pillowed couch. Sitting down, with only a few inches of space between Brett and herself, she wished that her heart would stop beating like a jackhammer. I love him so much, she thought, that I'll be devastated by whatever he decides to do.

What Brett decided to do had nothing to do with making love. "I have a whole week. No, nine days, to be precise. A whole nine days before I report to the Akasaka film studios. We'll be shooting most of our interior shots there. About eight or nine weeks' filming here in Tokyo, then I have to do another concert. I can't even remember the name of the city, and after that we go south to Matsuyama for the outdoor shots. It's going to be one hell of a grind. And I've told Gavin that the next week and two days I'm on vacation. No interviews, no TV, no publicity parties. I mean *nothing!*"

"That explains it," Carolyn said.

"Explains what?"

"I thought I'd scored a terrific coup. Got a television interview scheduled for you next week with this woman who's one of the top personalities on the tube in Japan. The Nipponese Barbara Walters, you might say. I made that arrangement all by myself and I was so excited. I couldn't believe it when Gavin said you wouldn't be available. It just about did me in."

"Then you can imagine what it did to Gavin," Brett said, his grin tired but triumphant. "But he was very understanding when I told him I needed a break. He didn't even rebel when I told him about my assignments for you."

Carolyn's hopes rose despite all common sense. "What am I going to be doing while you're off on vacation?"

"You're going to be helping me see as much of this city and environs as we can cram into nine days," Brett announced. "We're going to do it all, Carolyn. Everything in the guidebooks and a lot that isn't. You haven't seen much more than the inside of this hotel and a few broadcasting studios. I don't think David would begrudge you a little sightseeing?"

"No, of course not. But Gavin . . ."

"Gavin manages my career," Brett stated flatly. "Not my life."

"Oh, Brett, that sounds so fantastic! Are you sure? Are you sure you want to spend that much time with me? I mean, so many people want to be with you—glamorous, interesting people. People in your . . ."

"People in my what?" Brett demanded.

"Well, in your own sphere. Professional people." Carolyn mentioned an American rock star who had shared a television appearance with Brett. "You have so much more in common with her."

"Are you serious?" Brett sounded genuinely incredulous. "Oh, you and Gavin saw to it that we were photographed in a very friendly pose. That'll give the supermarket scandal sheets a chance to headline our sizzling romance. But, Carolyn, the woman's so wrapped up in herself, she'd bore me to death." Brett gave Carolyn a searching, melancholy look. "Why do you keep selling yourself short? You're beautiful, you're talented, you're the most understanding person I've ever known." He gave her a mischievous smile. "Except when you've had two gin and tonics, that is. I have very little time for myself. Do you think I'm not very, very particular about who I want to spend it with?"

She was actually going to have Brett to herself for nine days! She was going to see undreamed-of sights with Brett as her companion! Carolyn couldn't contain her excitement. She did an imitation of at least one of the band musicians, crying out, "Oh, wow, man!"

Brett laughed. "Oh, there's so much to see," Carolyn exulted. "You'd have to stay in this city alone for months, years, before you could see a fraction of it. And there are day trips I read about, so different and so beautiful, I . . . Oh, Brett, I can't tell you how thrilled I am."

"Try." He grinned.

Carolyn's next move was wholly unconscious. She leaned over and threw her arms around Brett's neck to hug him.

It was to have been one of those quick bear hugs. But the instant her body made contact with Brett's, Carolyn knew she should have controlled her impulse. His arms folded her in, holding her tightly. For a breathless time that might have been only a few seconds, but might have been a lifetime of closeness and sharing and love, they remained locked in the fusing embrace. Would he kiss her again? Should she obey the overwhelming need to kiss Brett, tell him that she loved him, had always loved him, didn't know how to stop loving him?

Brett relieved her of the tormenting decision. Gently but firmly he extricated himself from the clasp of Carolyn's arms. Before she could feel the humiliation of being rejected, the same pain that she had inflicted upon him once before, Brett said quietly, "I'd better get out of here." He placed his hands on her shoulders, holding her so that she could not avoid looking into the smoldering, dark, desire-filled depths of his eyes. "Otherwise it's going to get dangerously hot in this room."

She could think of nothing to say. Tell him that her need for him was less dangerous than the agony of being separated from him? A woman in love could drown in those eyes!

Brett got to his feet abruptly and crossed the room. "We don't want to generate enough heat to melt the snow up in Anchorage."

It was a perfect time to tell him that she had somehow, with help from his sister, been caught in a web of stupid lies. All she had to do was to tell Brett that she had wanted this job so badly she had fallen into a shoddy trap. But she couldn't bring herself to destroy this newly rekindled rapport with Brett. Carolyn said nothing.

Then he was at the door, turning to melt her with his devastating smile. "I'll be your big brother for nine days, Carolyn. Jennie won't mind the loan. That's a promise."

He was gone then, with the full implication of his promise casting a dark cloud over the dream-come-true days that lay ahead. He must think of her as a fool, turning him away one night, throwing her arms around him with total abandon just a few minutes ago. Yes, Brett must be thinking of her as a total idiot or, worse, a tease. She knew that he was drained by the effort he had exerted onstage this evening. But she knew also that he was probably too wired up for sleep. He would be in the room next to her, wide-awake, thinking, maybe pacing the floor. It would take only a phone call to bring him the company of a woman who knew what he wanted and needed. Carolyn wished that she was a woman of the world with the nerve and self-assurance to call Brett's number and to tell him that she didn't want to borrow Jennie's big brother. She wanted to spend what was left of this night in the arms of the man she loved.

Nine days of seeing Japan was a prospect that was almost too wonderful to comprehend. But nine days of being close to Brett, yet never close enough, would be unbearable torture.

Chapter Five

It was shortly after nine when Brett phoned the next morning, sounding amazingly rested, eager and impatient to start their tour. "I didn't wake you up?"

"No, no, no, I've been up and ready for an hour. Will a pantsuit be all right?"

"Anything's all right if you're in it," he assured Carolyn.

She was relieved. The butter-yellow linen suit had waist-flattering lines and could be worn with comfortable sandals; she was sure that much of the day would be spent walking. "Just give me a few minutes to check with Gavin, okay?"

"Gavin?" Brett sounded disapproving. "You don't need a permission slip from Gavin. I told him he wouldn't see much of you for more than a week."

Carolyn crossed the hall, nevertheless, to make sure that nothing Gavin had wanted her to do was left undone. He was in a cold, quiet mood, though he assured Carolyn that he could easily manage without her help for nine days.

"You make me feel superfluous," Carolyn protested. "I feel so guilty, drawing a salary for going sightseeing."

"Our incomes," Gavin said tersely, "generous as they may be, are dependent on the vocal cords of one Brett Wells. Our duties are to keep him successful and, only incidentally, happy. You'll be more than earning your keep, in the latter category, at least. Go have fun."

There was just enough of a hint of sarcasm, maybe even resentment, in the way Gavin spoke the words to throw a damper on Carolyn's anticipation. But the feeling of guilt disappeared almost instantly when she encountered Brett in the corridor outside Gavin's office suite. Resplendent, as always, in a fine white cotton shirt and casual slacks, he was like a race horse at the starting line. "Big day ahead," he said, taking Carolyn's arm and guiding her toward the elevators. "I can't wait, can you?"

His affectionate squeeze of her forearm was enough to erase Gavin's jealous-sounding remarks from Carolyn's mind. When she was with Brett, she was conscious of no one else. And suddenly it was their world alone, their city to explore, their carefree conversation and laughter the only important sounds in the universe.

Brett had engaged a driver, a polite but taciturn English-speaking guide named Hiro, to chauffeur them to points of interest. But most of their morning was spent on foot. "We're starting at the hub around which old Edo was built," Brett pointed out.

Back when the capital was known as Edo, the Imperial Palace had been the heart of this now sprawling, crowded city, the center from which streets radiated in all directions. It was still the center of modern

Tokyo, yet Carolyn felt transported back to ancient times as she strolled through the estate's garden park. She was carried back in time to the days when *shogun* and *samurai* warriors held sway. The immaculate 250-acre grounds surrounded a two-story palace that covered a full acre, its clean Japanese lines imposing in their very simplicity.

"We won't be able to visit the interior," Brett explained. "The Emperor only opens the immediate palace grounds on New Year's Day and his birthday later this month. But if Gavin had really been doing his job, we'd have had an invitation for tea."

"An inexcusable oversight," Carolyn agreed. "I'm not thinking about having tea with the Emperor. I'm thinking about what my folks would say if they saw all these lovely trees. A bit more impressive than a five-acre nursery in North San Diego County, wouldn't you say?"

They were holding hands by the time they reached the famous old gates that lined the rock-faced moat, and the press of Brett's fingers reminded Carolyn that this was really happening, that she had not been whisked to some beautiful dream world in her imagination. At the famed Niju-bashi double bridge, where groups of tourists were having their pictures taken, Carolyn was quickly ushered away from the graceful landmark. It was her first realization of how little freedom Brett enjoyed. He didn't say that he wanted to avoid being crowded by autograph hunters, but his haste in getting away from the scene was self-explanatory. How little privacy there was for a man whose face was recognizable to most of the world!

If the Imperial Palace was impressive, it paled in size beside the monstrous Grecian building that was the seat of Japanese government. The National Diet Building, with its soaring tower, covered a full thirteen acres. From its perch on a knoll overlooking the palace grounds, the quarters of the prime minister and parliament were the very essence of the contrasts that characterized Japan. The Imperial Palace housed the traditional head of state, the Emperor. Yet the two-house body, called the Diet, ran the country in a democratic fashion, modeled upon that of the United States.

"It's amazing, isn't it?" Brett commented. "Here you have a city of over eleven million people, crowded onto something like eight hundred square miles. And a lot of that land was reclaimed from the sea. We have seven million people in Los Angeles County, but we have more than four thousand square miles to stretch out in. My point is that as crowded as these people are, they've given over a good part of their real estate to beautiful parks."

It was true. Elevated trains and expressways criss-crossed the city, but there seemed to be room everywhere for trees and flowers. Holding hands tightly, Brett and Carolyn strolled through the gardens bordering the picturesque Sengakuji Temple, where a grave-yard held the remains of a seventeenth-century feudal leader named Lord Asano. "His forty-seven retainers avenged his murder," Brett informed Carolyn. "And then they committed ritual suicide. We'll see their armor and swords in the museum before we leave. The temple is dedicated to their memory."

"You sound like a walking guidebook," Carolyn said. "Are you sure this is all as new to you as it is to me?"

She couldn't help feeling a flutter of excitement when Brett replied, "I started planning this tour the day I found out you were coming to Japan with me. Read everything I could get my hands on. You see, I knew it would be twice as enjoyable if I knew something about the country, even just the difference between Buddhist temples and Shinto shrines." Brett's smile was as simple and honest as the lovely temple they were visiting. He was an international celebrity, yet he had lost none of the unpretentious charm that had won Carolyn's heart long ago and far from the exotic scene in which she found herself now. How would it be possible not to love him? Carolyn wondered.

"The reason I brought you here today," Brett went on, "is that this whole story is the basis of a classic Kabuki play called *Chushingura.*" He threw Carolyn a playful grin. "If you're a good girl and clean up your plate at lunch, you just might get to see it some night."

Carolyn did more than clean up her plate. At a charming garden restaurant, bustling with smartly attired people, they lunched from tiny plates of *sushi* and other Japanese delicacies that were sheer works of art in their presentation. Even the lowliest vegetables had been transformed into exquisite little flowers by gifted chefs whose many years of apprenticeship and schooling had made their culinary efforts worthy of being called an art.

Enjoying the unique flavors of the unfamiliar foods, Carolyn found herself laughing at Brett's eagerness to experiment. "I'm not *quite* ready for eel and octopus just yet," she admitted.

"Unsophisticated palate," Brett said, assuming a critical attitude. "What can I expect from a small-town nurseryman's daughter?" He showed off his newly found skill with chopsticks by transferring a huge pink shrimp from his plate to Carolyn's. "This isn't too radical."

They were reluctant to leave the delightful garden, with its huge parasol-shaded tables, but there was so much yet to see. "Ready for Phase Two?" Brett asked. His energy was as boundless as his enthusiasm, curiosity about every sight and sound and experience propelling him at a pace that would have tired someone less thrilled to be with him than Carolyn.

"I'm ready," she assured him.

"More walking," he warned.

"Remember when we used to walk along the creek back home? You were the one who always wanted to sit down for a while under an oak tree."

"Only when Jennie wasn't with us," Brett reminded. "I always had some sort of illusion that if you sat still long enough, I'd get to kiss you."

"You never tried!"

"I was bashful." Brett laughed, dropping the subject. Did he know that such remarks stirred unreasonable longings and hopes inside her? Apparently not.

They were being driven by Hiro once again when Carolyn remarked that there were no old or dented cars on the fast-paced expressways or on the jammed streets. "Even in Beverly Hills, along Wilshire, you see a few junkers here and there," she said. "Every car I've seen here looks polished and new."

Hiro was asked for an explanation, and he provided it: a dented car was a form of disgrace here. After even a minor mishap, it was not driven until it was back in pristine condition. And, yes, many people could afford new cars because salaries were now comparable with those in American and European cities, but with the scarcity of land and housing, few people could afford to buy homes. Hence, they *did* have money for new automobiles and the last word in electronic gadgets.

"Maybe that explains why everyone I've seen is smartly dressed," Carolyn guessed. That, too, was obvious. The working people might live in cramped houses and apartments, but pride in their appearance typified the Japanese. And Hiro's theory may have also explained the popularity of Tokyo's night life, which ranged from raucous, tawdry cabarets never visited by tourists, to jumping discos and elegant nightclubs. "I suppose if you're crammed into a tiny apartment with all your relatives, you're anxious to get out where you can dance. I couldn't believe the Ginza last night. It was wall-to-wall people. And they all looked as though they'd just stepped off the pages of a fashion magazine."

Brett said it then—the first of a series of comments that reminded Carolyn that he moved in a glamorous sphere that could not possibly include her: "A lot of the women take their cues from Sadi Hayashi. I've only seen stills of her, but she appears to be stunningly elegant. I can't wait to meet her."

It was ridiculous to feel a surge of jealousy toward the Japanese film star. Brett had an eye for beauty and he was lavish with compliments. Still, Carolyn was reminded that he was graciously escorting an old friend from back home during this short vacation. Nine days from now he would return to the glittering world in which he now moved so easily. She suddenly felt less than adequately dressed in the simple yellow pantsuit that had looked so good this morning when she checked herself in the mirror. She was certain that her makeup left something to be desired. She was melancholy and silent during the rest of the drive to Ueno Park, site of the museum in which countless national treasures were on display.

"Almost," Hiro pointed out as they got out of the limousine near a walkway lined with trees. "Not many more days, yes?"

He was calling their attention to the rows and rows of cherry trees, covered with buds swollen from recent rains, thousands of them on the verge of bursting into bloom. "I will bring you to the Hanami Sakura Festival, if you please," Hiro added. His small-boned, delicate face lighted with a smile that was soft with sentiment.

With typical understatement, he said, "You will very much enjoy." It was clear that Hiro shared his country's reverence for the *sakura*, the cherry blossoms that symbolized this lovely land. Carolyn looked out at the acres of cherry trees, visualizing the incredible bouquet they would form. "We're so lucky to be here at this time of the year," she said. She had forgotten the twinge of jealousy over the mention of Sadi Hayashi. I'm here with Brett now, Carolyn thought. I'm not going to worry about the times when I'm not with him.

Hiro guided them through the vast museum, only one of many in Tokyo that attracted tourists and residents alike. There was no time to see all the exhibits of art and science and history with which the city was dotted. Here, at the National Museum, Hiro softly but proudly acquainted them with Japanese history and its distinctive art. *"Kochira,"* he would say, *"Koko,* please. This way . . . here." And they would be standing before a glass case of priceless picture scrolls from the Heian period, a time when beauty in dress and art conformed to a rigid standard and the slightest show of bad taste was considered a moral offense. Hiro led them to displays of delicate ceramic vases and figurines dating back to the two centuries when the shogunate cut Japan off from the rest of the world, when warriors occupied the upper ranks, followed by the farmer, the artisan and the lowly merchant. Today, the enterprising business people of Japan had reversed the order of status, but the works of Tokugawa artisans remained, still looked upon with awe by modern Japanese visitors to the museum.

It was impossible to see even a fraction of this treasurehouse of arts and artifacts. Brett checked his watch. "I hope we can come back before we leave Tokyo," he said. "Right now, we're on a tight schedule."

Carolyn experienced a momentary disappointment when Brett asked that they be driven to their hotel. The return, she learned, was to allow them to freshen up and change clothes for a somewhat more formal evening. It was fun to have Brett allay her concern about what to wear by following her into her suite and personally selecting a simply cut silk suit dress of her own design. "Blue," he said with authority. "With your eyes, you can never go wrong with blue."

He could never go wrong with any color, Carolyn decided when they met again, after showering and changing. He was wearing a black silk suit, white silk shirt and a narrow tie that might have been chosen to match her dress. With his tall, lean frame, broad shoulders and overwhelmingly handsome face, he could have stepped out for a gala evening in denim overalls and he would have been an imposing figure. Yet it was *he* whose eyes swept over Carolyn appreciatively, making her feel terribly self-conscious. And it was Brett who gave her the self-confidence she needed in his impressive company. "You look like ten billion yen," he said. "It bothers me to have you sitting at a typewriter, writing all that flowery nonsense about me. With your flair for designing . . ." He shook his head back and forth. "There's got to be a place for you in the fashion world, Carolyn."

How could she tell him that she wanted to be a part of *his* world, even if it meant forgetting about a career in a field that excited her? Even if it meant working as Gavin's glorified secretary? Succeeding in the field for which she had studied would mean being apart from Brett, not even catching the glimpses she had caught of him during the time when he was preparing for his concert.

Brett was secretive and funny, insisting that their next few destinations were surprises. "You'll see," he said when Carolyn asked where Hiro was driving them next. "Learn patience."

They both laughed, knowing that patience was the least of Brett's virtues. Whatever he wanted to do had to be done immediately.

Carolyn was patient. And she was rewarded, first, with a ride to the observation platform of the Tokyo Tower, a structure resembling the Eiffel Tower that she had seen only on postcards. It rose a full thousand feet into the air to offer a commanding sight not only of the twinkling neon lights of the city, just being turned on as the sun began to set, but also of the snowcapped volcano that symbolized Japan. Its white cone glinting rose and gold, catching the last rays of the dying sun, Mt. Fuji was a sight Carolyn knew would be engraved forever in her memory. It was almost superfluous to say, "It's beautiful. So beautiful!" Carolyn turned to Brett, her eyes misting over. "How am I ever going to thank you for bringing me here?"

Brett was touched by the scene, too, but he brushed off Carolyn's thank-you with another of his wicked smiles. "If you insist upon thanking me, I can think of a few ways to show your appreciation."

Always hinting at being more than her brother, always reminding her that the one time he had wanted her body she had turned him away. Maybe he was just being funny, but maybe he was being snide, too. It was as though he were teasing her, reminding her that she had had her chance, and now the thought of making love to her was a subject for joking and nothing more.

For a long while they circled the tower's viewing platform, their eyes drinking in the sight of giant ships outlined in diamond-sparkling lights in the bays far below. The darkening stretches of tiny farms and forests and rice paddies could be seen in the distance. They returned for a final glimpse of Mt. Fuji, but it had been swallowed up by the fast-falling night. They were silent, then, while Brett's arm closed around Carolyn's shoulders, his fingers stroking her upper arm through the soft silk fabric. Did he expect her to make the next move? Last night, when she had thrown her arms around him, Brett had removed them. Yet, at the same time, he had hinted that he was having to control his desire for her. *David!* What a barbarous mistake she had made! But what a greater mistake it would be to become one of the lovesick groupies that neither Brett nor Gavin would tolerate on a foreign tour. It was a no-win situation, Carolyn decided miserably. To have Brett was to lose him; it was that complicated and that simple.

And in any case, Brett had removed his arm from her shoulders, letting her know that it had been just a casual, friendly gesture dictated by the romantic surroundings. He was looking at his gold watch again, like a tour director. "We have a dinner reservation," he said.

"Here in the tower?" The structure was more than just a viewing spot. It housed television studios and a complex of exhibition halls, entertainment centers, smart shops and restaurants.

"No, not here in the tower," Brett said. Faking a bad imitation of a French accent, he added, "No, *ma chérie*, tonight we weel dine *à la cordon bleu.*"

They were maneuvered through the mad snarl of traffic, through narrow streets that had been intended for rickshas and could not be widened because each square centimeter of land was priceless, to the Sony Building, which encompassed a branch of the famous Parisian restaurant Maxim's. Even here, in this elegant French restaurant filled with the subdued conversations of appropriately chic patrons, there was a polite stir of recognition as the maître d' led them to their reserved table. Brett, accustomed by now to creating excitement whenever he walked into a public room, carried it off nonchalantly. Carolyn lifted her chin, hoping bravely that she did not look too out-of-place among these wealthy diners.

In this posh atmosphere, an interruption would have been unthinkable. They were not disturbed by autograph seekers, although one of their waiters made it a point to say, "Oui, Monsieur *Wells*" repeatedly while he was taking their orders, and the overly obsequious *sommelier,* recommending Chateau d' Yquem to accompany their first course of oysters, also confided in a glorious mixture of French, Japanese and fractured English that his three young daughters had every record made by their singing idol and would be thrilled beyond measure if only Monsieur Wells would perhaps write his name on three separate order pads?

It was a leisurely, luxurious meal, beautifully complemented by the dry yet mellow white wine. Carolyn, complaining that she had eaten a huge lunch, refused to be goaded into anything heavier than the *gateau de crêpes à la florentine,* light-as-air French pancakes filled with a delectable combination of spinach, cheese and tiny mushrooms. Somehow, a puffy asparagus soufflé materialized before her, too beautiful to resist. Brett shrugged his shoulders. "Okay, starve yourself if you want to. I'm going to do this place justice."

"Maybe I'd better do the same if we're going to get our money's worth," Carolyn relented. "I looked at the prices on that menu and nearly died of shock."

"You still haven't gotten accustomed to figuring in yen," Brett argued. "When you see all those thousands . . ."

"Yes, I know they aren't thousands of dollars. But thousands of *anything* still give me the willies."

He patted her hand and then withdrew his from the

warm contact. "Carolyn, Carolyn, it's taken me a while to get used to it. Took me all of about three days, actually. You're just not aware of what happens when an album goes gold, let alone platinum. And royalties come in because some D.J. decides he likes a song you wrote two years ago. Or someone else decides to record it. Or when you have two sharp managers who insist upon a piece of the action when you sign a film contract. It's a long way from mowing lawns so that we could go to the roller rink on Saturday afternoons."

"You're telling me you're a very wealthy man," Carolyn said. "No, I guess I . . . I guess it hasn't really dawned on me yet. You've put a lot of space between us since the days you're talking about."

"I don't want a lot of space between us," Brett said. He had taken on, suddenly, a sober air, his dark eyes clouded by a kind of sadness Carolyn had never seen there before. "I don't want to leave those days behind, Carolyn. I don't want to live in a world that doesn't include you." He had picked up his fork again, waving it slightly to indicate their plush surroundings. "That would be too high a price to pay for all this."

But Brett was not inclined to remain somber for long. They were sharing a nonsensical private joke when they left Maxim's, and laughing even more as Brett tried to explain their next destination to an uncomprehending cabdriver. Hiro had been dismissed for the evening, and it took five minutes of hilarious pantomime before Brett got his message across. Even then, Carolyn was still mystified. "I don't know where we're going, but I know it's got to be a funny place. Couldn't you just have had the desk clerk at the hotel write out the address?"

"That's not sporting," Brett told her. "The challenge here is that most of the streets don't even have names. You tell the cabbies the number of a block or a neighborhood and then the two of you go on a wild search. However, the place we're headed for is very well known. I just had to give the man my version of what goes on there."

What went on there was related to their earlier visit to the Sengakuji Temple, for Brett's miming had told their driver that he wanted to go to the imposing National Theater for a traditional Kabuki performance. From her third-row-center seat, Carolyn watched a dazzling, stylized reenactment of that tragic tale of vendetta and vengeance to which Brett had introduced her earlier that day. Samisen music accompanied dramatic dance-mime that transcended language as the artists unfolded the great epic of Japan's Tokugawa period. But even more entrancing than the danced portrayal was the wildly imaginative setting and the lavish costumes. There was subtle, expressive artistry in the painted faces of the actor-dancers; their hands moved with incredible grace in which every motion was rife with meaning; but it was their stunning garb that held Carolyn transfixed. She kept wishing for a sketch pad; surely her memory would not hold every line of those flowing sleeves, the meticulous draping of sumptuous fabrics, the play of brilliant contrasting colors.

During the applause that followed the performance of the *Chushingura* play, Brett's enthusiasm exceeded that of the Japanese people seated around them. A great performer himself, he was also an appreciative observer. "Super!" he repeated several times. "And wouldn't I love to have that lighting crew!"

"The costumes," Carolyn said. "Wouldn't I love to get my hands on some of those brocades!"

Brett patted her hand, his expression thoughtful. "You've got to do that, Carolyn. I can see you designing fabulous theatrical costumes. Making a name for yourself, maybe on Broadway or in Hollywood. You don't belong behind a desk, one step up from being a gofer.''

It was flattering to have Brett think of her as a successful career woman, but it was depressing, too. He visualized her behind a drawing board, not beside him, not a part of his life. Yet he seemed reluctant to part company with her tonight. A variety of short dance and pantomime selections, one a solo by an elderly man who depicted his encounters in returning home from a visit to a shrine, another a stomping, mane-tossing lion dance extravaganza that brought cheers from the onlookers, concluded the colorful performance. Anything beyond what they had seen would have been an anticlimax, but Brett was not yet ready to quit. "Going from the sublime to the sensational," he said. "What about hitting a few nightspots?"

Miraculously, though neither of them had gotten much sleep the night before, they held out through an elaborate cabaret show at Tokyo's fabulous Copacabana, where the dancers were outfitted less traditionally, but with even more extravagance than the Kabuki performers. Once again Carolyn felt her creative impulses whetted by billowing yards of multicolored chiffon, elaborate jeweled headdresses and intricately patterned swirls of sequin embroidery. Seminude, the showgirls were like visions of perfection whose bodies were both revealed and enhanced by the genius of a theatrical designer. Someday I'm going to make gowns like that, Carolyn thought.

One thing she had learned about Brett during this nonstop day and night: when he worked, he let the work consume him; but when he played, it was as though he had to savor every moment, every experience. They capped the night off at a disco, where the flashing colored lights, the deafening, insistent beat, the gyrating bodies pressed onto a clear plastic dance

floor under which whorls of violet melted into blue and
erupted in orange-red flames of color, revealed another
Japan in which tradition had been replaced by the last
word in modern apparel, the newest craze in sound and
movement.

As intriguing and stimulating as it was, the disco-
theque did not hold them long. After two dances, Brett
said, "I don't really like dancing this way. Maybe I'm
dating myself, but I liked it better the night of your
prom when there were at least a few ballads and we
could dance *together.*"

Carolyn agreed, although it was fun to give herself to
the intoxicating rhythms and to exchange happy, word-
less smiles with the young people who jostled them and
each other on the ever-changing dance floor. The night
of the prom Brett had held her in his arms, bending to
press his lips against her ear as he sang along with the
band—romantic songs that thrilled her to the core, the
way the nearness of Brett, pressing her warmly against
his body, thrilled and excited her. They were dancing
apart now, each locked into a private rhythmic response. Somehow, it struck Carolyn as symbolic; she
had been much closer to Brett on that long-ago night
than she was now. When Brett said, "Don't know
about you, but I think I'm ready to go," Carolyn was
more than ready.

During the cab ride to the New Otani, she thanked
Brett for a fabulous day. She hoped he might say
something about its not being over yet, that the best
was yet to come. His reply was hardly promising: "I
had fun too. We always did have a good time together."
The words were spoken so casually that Carolyn knew
that this was not a memorable day in his life, as it would
always be in hers. And any illusions she had about
ending the night in Brett's arms were dispelled when he
congratulated her on having stamina that equaled his
own. "I didn't think you'd hold out beyond the theater.

I was sure you'd conk out on me and I'd end up going to hear Dorie Lang's last set at the Okura.''

Visiting other stars on his nights off was a normal pattern for Brett. Gavin had said that it was a form of kindness; appearing with lesser luminaries was a great boost for their careers. But his mention, now, of the sexy rock star whose picture Carolyn had seen in the Tokyo tourist weekly was like a slap in the face. Did Brett have to remind her that he could have spent the past hour, and maybe the rest of this night, with a beautiful rising star in his own field? She couldn't help sounding snippy as she responded, "I'm sorry I held you up. If I had known you had other plans . . ."

"It wasn't a plan," Brett said carelessly. "It would have been a way to use up some leftover energy if you had deserted me at ten-thirty."

It was an acceptable explanation, yet the thought still rankled. When they reached her door, Brett kissed her lightly on the forehead and said, "Thanks for the good company. Tomorrow's Sunday. I won't call you before ten."

Carolyn hid her disappointment by saying, "Better make that eleven. I've had a lovely time, but I can hardly keep my eyes open."

Brett had unlocked the door for her, when a door on the opposite side of the corridor opened. Brett turned at the sound of familiar male voices and Carolyn looked back too, to see Tony Hanniman, Carmen Battaglia and Sumitashi Kawabe, one of the Japanese trumpet players.

There was an exchange of greetings, and then Brett asked, "What's happening?"

"We're going over to catch Dorie's twelve-thirty show," Tony said. "Maybe jam a little."

Carmen winked at Carolyn. "I suppose you have better things to do."

"Be super if you could come along," Tony invited.

"All right," Brett said. "Carolyn's had enough, but I've still got the energy to sit in with Dorie."

His band members whooped their enthusiasm, Brett repeated his assurance that he wouldn't call Carolyn too early, and the quartet took off.

Carolyn closed her door on one of the happiest days of her life and faced the loneliest night imaginable.

Chapter Six

It was closer to noon, rather than just past eleven, when Carolyn joined Brett for what he said was going to be a shopping day.

"On Sunday?" Carolyn asked.

"That's apparently the big shopping day here," Brett told her. "All the big department stores will be crowded, so we'll head for a section Gavin tells me is called 'The Paris of Japan.' I have people back home I want to send gifts to. You probably do, too."

Carolyn had gotten over her jealousy and disappointment of the previous night. Brett dismissed his late-night session with Dorie Lang, making it sound as though it had been just another pleasant episode in a life devoted to music and to having a good time. Besides, he was here with her again, Carolyn reminded herself. If she enjoyed his company when he was around, if she trained herself not to expect too much of

him, she would add another wonderful day to her page
of memories, a day to remember when Brett was again
too busy to remember her.

Hiro drove them to a district called Harajuku, one of
the many interesting neighborhoods within the sprawling city of Tokyo, each with its own distinctive ambi-
ence and flavor. But while they were in the area, the
driver insisted they see the famous Shinto shrine dedicated to the Emperor Meiji and his consort. "The
stores will not close until nine at night," he assured
them. "Plenty time, yes?"

Once again, it seemed natural for Brett's hand to
close over Carolyn's as they passed through the massive
torii gateway fashioned from seventeen-hundred-year-
old cypress trees. Walking along the crowded, yet
tranquil pathway to the elaborate shrine, they paused
to buy packets of colorful postcards that would save
them the impossible task of describing to relatives and
friends the wonder of sweeping rooftops, elaborately
carved frescoes and layers of what Brett called "Japanese gingerbread." It was amazing enough to find
themselves viewing this jewel of Shinto architecture in
a wooded park that covered seventeen hundred acres of
this city where every square meter was priceless.

"You come back in June," Hiro told them. "In that
time, everywhere you will see the iris blooming. One
hundred different kind . . . many, many, many."

Yes, they would try to come back, Brett assured their
driver. But he was anxious to begin the shopping tour
now, and Carolyn was reminded of yet another aspect
of Brett's character: when he wanted to do something,
he wanted to do it immediately. And if the moment
passed, he was equally capable of erasing it from his
mind, moving on to something else that piqued his
interest. Maybe there would be no second chance for
her. Although he sat close to her in the backseat of the
limousine, their legs pressed close together as Hiro

maneuvered the sleek black car through thick traffic, Brett seemed indifferent to the intimacy that sometimes left Carolyn breathless. At times, it even seemed to her that his hand-holding and touching were deliberately intended to tease her, evoke a physical response in her, as though he were punishing her for that night when she had rejected him.

All that was forgotten as they roamed the endless little shops and elegant boutiques of Harajuku. It was here that Carolyn learned what it meant for a shopper to have limitless funds. Most of the shops were youth-oriented, displaying unique designer fashions, and they were uniformly expensive. Brett bought as though he were attending the Escondido Swap Meet. Silk shirts and ties for himself, as well as for the members of his band, an exquisite antique embroidered kimono for his mother, and yards of silk in Jennie's favorite color, mauve. "She's been wanting new draperies for her bedroom," Brett said lightly. "Ken will have a fit." He laughed as the smiling young clerk counted out his change. "I can just hear him saying this stuff is suitable for a casket lining. But Jennie's been so good to me, she ought to have a little fun."

Carolyn, in spite of her generous salary, still found herself outpriced in these elegant shops. And when she finally decided on an Italian silk scarf for her mother, Brett insisted on paying for it.

"It's not right," she argued. "It's not really a gift from me if you pay for it, Brett."

"It's not right if you don't let me enjoy the fruits of my success," Brett countered. "And what about you? Haven't you seen *anything* you like?"

She was hesitant, as a result, to admire anything out loud. Oh, there *was* a stunning ensemble that delighted her sense of fashion. It was a black silk jumpsuit affair topped with a multicolored silk coat that resembled batik or tie-die artistry. "Very fine *boumake*," the clerk said admiringly. Carolyn checked the size and the astronomical price tag, using the former as her excuse. "I know Japanese sizes run smaller than ours," she told Brett. "I'd never get into it."

"Try it on," Brett urged. "There's another, almost like it." He was examining a similar, even more exciting garment that he had taken from its rack. "Here you go. This is a size larger."

"Brett, it's so . . . so eye-catching and dressy. Where would I wear anything like this?"

Carolyn gave her attention to a line of less elaborate blouses from Greece, hoping that Brett's quick conversation with the saleswoman was an apology for her lack of interest and not a hurried purchase.

The limo was piled with bags and boxes when Brett decided it was time for lunch. They were walking, almost pushing their way through the jam-packed narrow streets, when they paused before an interesting-looking restaurant. "You see?" Brett said. "You don't have to know a word of Japanese." He indicated the wax replicas of colorful foods in the window. "You just point at what you want."

"It's a good system," Carolyn conceded. "But it would be nicer to learn a little Japanese. Think how much more fun we'd be having if we knew what people around us are saying."

"It's a next-to-impossible language," Brett said. "Apart from 'thank you,' I don't think I'm ready to tackle it. I have absolutely no aptitude for foreign languages. And who knows if I'll ever get back here again?"

"But don't you remember how your audience reacted when you said that one word in Japanese?" Carolyn reminded him. "It probably wouldn't hurt you to learn a few phrases. Maybe even a Japanese song."

Brett made an irritable, dismissing motion with his hand. "I'm a singer, not a linguist. These people love learning English. They're a lot more patient than I am. And, face it, the albums I've sold here weren't sung in Japanese."

Carolyn decided not to interfere in his way of selling himself. Her job was to help publicize his appearances, not to dictate how he was to conduct a career that was already a proven success. As the day wore on, there were numerous indications of just how successful a man Brett was.

He was recognized and fawned over at the Jisaku restaurant on the banks of the picturesque Sumada River, and again by the elaborately gowned and coiffed "mama-san" who reigned over a spectacular Ginza club they visited that night. Carolyn felt a pride in being seen with him, yet there was resentment inside her, too. She was extraneous, a nobody. Loving Brett was a horrendous mistake. For as much as Carolyn glowed when he spoke to her intimately, as hopeful as she felt when he held her hand, she could not help being aware that hand-holding and light kisses and affectionate terms were part of his charisma. They were all charming gestures calculated to impress every woman who admired him.

At the end of the evening, when Brett hesitated at her door and leaned down as though he might kiss her good night, Carolyn quickly put out her hand. A handshake between friends at least had some significance. His kisses came too cheap.

"Sometimes I'm damned if I can understand you," Brett said. But he didn't take offense. "Tomorrow," he said, "let's have a low-key day, away from the crowds. Are you game?"

She was game. She would always be there, she knew, when Brett wanted her at his side. Yet she carried her pride into her sumptuous suite with a heavy heart. She meant no more to him than the thousands of other people who all but worshiped him, and she could only be grateful that she had not given herself to him in that brief, casual moment when he had wanted her.

Brett was unpredictable in many ways, but it came as no surprise to Carolyn to find a beautifully gift-wrapped dress box on her dresser. Running her fingers over the silk ensemble she had admired in the Harajuku boutique, even trying it on and discovering that the most expensive costume she had ever owned fit her perfectly, Carolyn could not help remembering that she was only one of many people Brett had bought elaborate gifts for today. Should she phone him and express her thanks? No, she decided. No, he might have other plans for the rest of the night, and the call might sound like an invitation. She would thank him tomorrow, when there would be no possibility of his misconstruing her gratitude.

Chapter Seven

It was a week that she would never forget. Brett and the wonderland that was Tokyo filled every day, and the hours disappeared in a continuous round of sight-seeing. Their "low-key" day was more tranquil, fortunately, than the Sunday that preceded it. They witnessed the lovely tradition of the tea ceremony, demonstrated by a fragile young woman whose appearance and every movement were grace and beauty personified. They marveled over the skill and dedication that had produced a miniature forest of gnarled cypress trees in a bonsai dish, and regretted that living sculptures like this could not be sent to California. "My parents would love this juniper," Carolyn exulted as they toured the bonsai gardens. "Can you believe this tree would have grown to seventy feet? And it's only inches high, perfectly formed and twenty years old!"

Since there was no bucking their home state's agricultural laws, they settled on the purchase of two handmade figures representing Japanese farmers. They came across the figurines during a tour of a doll shop and museum. The displays, they were told by a gracious, elderly museum director, were of the type that were shown proudly by little girls on their special day. The gray-haired, birdlike woman shook her finger playfully. "Not to play. To show friend, one time in year."

Ceramics studios and a shop where cultivated pearls were sold added to their purchases and their enjoyment, and when they reached the imposing twin gates that opened onto a colorful avenue lined with vendors' stalls, they heaped fans and folk-art objects into two brightly embroidered carrying bags they had bought from a street entrepreneur earlier.

Seeing the crowds around the five-story pagoda they had come to see, Carolyn had visions of another autograph-hunters' crush. It was a joy to discover that a different kind of celebration was taking place today at the Asakusa Kannon Temple. "We've really lucked out," Brett said. "This probably happens only once a year."

They had arrived in time for a children's festival, in which four- and five-year-olds, dressed in traditional finery, paraded before their proud parents, their black eyes darting to catch the approval of onlookers, their round faces solemn but shining with pleasure. A dark-suited businessman and his wife, typical of the Japanese who were eager to make foreign visitors enjoy and understand their culture, explained that these were the little *"chigo,"* celestial children whose good behavior had earned them the honor of participating in a ceremony that was almost as old as the elaborately carved temple. The building dated back to the seventh century, when local fishermen had found in their nets a miniature statue of the Buddhist deity Kannon.

When the parade of gorgeously dressed "little angels" ended, it was fun to see their unangelic scramble for mundane goodies. It had been a lovely surprise bonus in their visit to the famed pagoda, and they talked about the parade of children during the drive to a surprise lunch spot that Brett refused to describe. "They were *so* adorable," Carolyn heard herself repeating. "And those beautiful kimonos and obis! They were like the dolls in that museum, except that you wanted to hug them."

Brett was suddenly plunged into one of his rare quiet moods. "You love kids." It wasn't a question; it was a sober, approving statement.

"Of course I do. I know you do, too. You were always so great with the little ones in our neighborhood." Carolyn paused. "Why do you look so . . . ?"

"So what?"

"I don't know. Sort of . . . well, not sad, but . . . wistful."

"I was just thinking. About how much I might miss if I never have any of my own. Imagine the thrill of having a child who's part you and part somebody you love. Must be the greatest miracle in the world."

"Why do you say that's something you 'might miss'?" Carolyn asked. "You're still young. You could afford to do so much for a family . . . your own family."

"In absentia," Brett said, his tone edging on bitterness. "It wouldn't be much fun for children to have a few minutes with me between flights or concerts or rehearsals. Not much in it for a woman, either—a wife."

"You'd think there wasn't a star living who had a happy home life, from the way you're talking," Carolyn chided. She was beginning to sound dangerously close to promoting marriage. "Someday you'll have the time you feel you want to devote to children."

"Someday," Brett repeated. He brightened, casting off the subject as though it was too far off in the future to waste time discussing now. He made another of his radical mood changes, teasing Carolyn with a guessing game about where they were to have lunch. "No raw tuna, no pickled squid, no exotic vegetables cut to resemble lotus blossoms. But I know you'll love it."

Carolyn not only loved it but also joined Brett's infectious laughter as Hiro deposited them at the curb in front of Shakey's Pizza, where their laughter continued through most of the familiar meal, and where, except for the crowd of Japanese patrons, they might almost have been at the restaurant's counterpart in Escondido. "Like touching home base," Brett said.

There was time to shower and change at the hotel before they had to choose between the traditional Noh theater and a celebrated Japanese puppet show. They compromised, going to neither and deciding, instead, to attend the all-female spectacular presented by one of four such troupes meticulously trained in the city of Takarazuka. Obviously adored by their audience of two thousand, the women danced and acted and sang a revue of opulently costumed fantasies. It was a frothy, dream-evoking show, ranging from ancient folk tales to the latest Broadway hits, and once again Carolyn was entranced by the imaginative use of satins and chiffons, glittering gold lamé and brocade.

"No wonder they're so popular here," Brett said over a nightcap in one of the New Otani's cocktail lounges. "They spin pure fantasy. I hope the last scene in my film is produced half as well."

Carolyn sipped at her daiquiri. "What sort of scene is it, Brett?"

"Oh, it's a romantic-dream-type number. Instead of ending with Cho-Cho-San's tragic death, the movie will conclude with Pinkerton returning to our heroine. It's a dream sequence, set in a garden—we'll be shooting that on Shikoku Island, down south, at some famous spa. There's a ballet—a big-production number in which the beautiful lady, who thinks I've deserted her, dreams that I come back. And of course I do." Brett smiled. "Otherwise who'd sing 'When I Dream About Love,' which I wrote especially for this shot? Anyway, it's a fantasy number, big reunion and clinch. Having seen pictures of Sadi Hayashi, I don't think that should put too much of a strain on my acting ability."

Brett had spoken facetiously, but he had shattered Carolyn's own dreamy mood. She had been picturing herself meeting the designers of the costumes that would be worn in that closing scene, getting her first close-up look at the inside world of costume design. Mention of the actress came like a splash of water in the face of a happy dreamer. She finished her drink quickly. "I'm sure you'll be very convincing," she said. Minutes later, Brett escorted her to her door, apologizing for having tired her out.

She couldn't blame him, Carolyn decided in the long time during which she waited for sleep. How could he know that he was hurting her when he couldn't possibly know how much she loved and needed him, how out-of-place she felt in the circles to which he belonged? Her arms ached to hold him and her body hungered to be possessed by him. Yet she herself had instituted the casual handshake that had ended another glorious day in Brett's company. She could not be angry with Brett; he was being more than friendly, and when had he promised to be any more than that? Carolyn's anger was directed at herself. She was a fool. A naive, blind fool. Somehow, in some way, even if it meant leaving the Brett Wells touring company, she would have to stop being another of the lovesick females Jennie and Gavin deplored.

When she stopped in to talk with Gavin Durham in the office the next morning, he was businesslike and pleasant, displaying none of the sardonic glances or insinuating remarks that had characterized several other brief conversations with him recently. "You're having the grand tour," he said. "Good. I remember how excited I was the first time I came here. That was back when Ken and I had a booking agency. We were just getting started handling talent for overseas gigs. Not that I've gotten blasé after all my visits to Japan, but that first time . . ." He made a soft whistling sound.

Carolyn sat on the edge of her desk, pleased that Gavin wasn't worrying about her emotional state. "It's all so different and . . . You know how welcome you're made to feel . . . you can get lost on some little narrow side street and there'll be half a dozen people going out of their way to lead you where you want to go. Every shopkeeper has given a courteous little bow when we come in and say . . . Oh, I forget the exact words, but they mean 'Welcome to my shop.'"

"'*Ira shai mase*,'" Gavin said. "'Welcome,' and 'may I help you,' all rolled into one. At least you're trying to pick up the language. I had to actually pressure Brett into learning to say one simple phrase, 'Thank you.' But remember how the audience responded? Talk to him about that, Carolyn. He's big here, but there's a lot of competition. Lots of American and European stars making appearances. It wouldn't hurt him one bit to learn a few Japanese songs, for that matter. Maybe just one popular love ballad would do it. His film's going to be distributed here, too, as you know. A few words, one song, would make a tremendous difference at the box office."

"I don't try to direct his career," Carolyn said simply. "That's your job. But I did have a promotional idea the other day. You may not think much of it, but . . ."

"But I'd like to know what it is," Gavin said. He was standing close to her desk, the fond half-smile on his always pleasant face inviting Carolyn's confidence.

"Well, Brett was deploring the fact that tipping is frowned upon here. There's a charge added to your bill usually, but the business of handing somebody money is considered demeaning, right?"

Gavin nodded. "Right. And?"

"And I thought, since gift-giving is a big thing here, Brett could show his appreciation to waiters and cabbies and whoever by giving them a personal sort of gift. Maybe one of those forty-five records with his picture on the jacket—something he could autograph. He's mobbed by fans wherever he goes anyway."

Gavin pondered the idea for a moment. "Good idea, but how many could he distribute? Assuming he eats three meals a day, that's only . . ."

"Oh, but the records could be sent to everyone who writes to him. We could do a real promotion, advertise on television, if that's not too expensive. Or have a contest of some kind, where everyone who enters gets one of the little packages and the winner gets . . ." She thought about the kind of first prize one of Brett's fans would treasure. From her own experience, she came up with the perfect winning award. "Dinner and a night on the town with Brett Wells!"

"Terrific idea," Gavin cried.

"Really? Do you honestly think . . . ?"

"We'll get it in the works right away. Well, *I* will, anyway. You're going to be busy for a few more days. The record label will argue, but they'll have to see the value of a free promo like this. Mr. Y. will like it, too."

"Mr. Y.?"

"He's one of the investors in Brett's film. Owns a

variety of businesses, hotels and clubs. You'll meet him when we get to Matsuyama. I got my start booking talent through Mr. Yoshinaga, and he's very conscious of smart promotion. I'll call him right away. And then we'll get Brett to decide what he wants to record for the giveaway."

"Shouldn't you ask Brett if he approves first?"

"Brett has sense enough to know that he's not a businessman or a promoter. That's why he has me." Gavin leaned forward to pat Carolyn's shoulder, his chubby hand lingering there as he spoke. "And why he has *you*. You were a perfect choice, honey. You're good for Brett, and you're not spoiling things by getting hung up on him."

Carolyn hoped that her sudden uneasiness did not give her away. "I'm glad you know that," she said with a firmness that would have won her an Academy Award.

"I also know you've been sleeping alone," Gavin said.

"You know . . . what?"

"I'm Brett's manager, remember?" Gavin removed his hand from Carolyn's shoulder, but the sense of intimacy remained. "I make it my business to know what he's up to, what could be bad for him. I learned that lesson when he got involved with Lisa Westerbrook."

Carolyn had forgotten about that. "Has she called again?"

"She subsidizes the international telephone network. Has she called again!" Gavin made a derisive sound. "She makes me glad I made the right choice in you, Carolyn. Sometimes I'm sorry there's already a man in your life, but sometimes, speaking as a manager, I'm grateful."

He was referring to David, of course. David. She would have to remember to talk about him once in a while, not only to secure her job but also to make Gavin stop looking at her the way he was looking at her now. She was reminding him that she and Brett were old childhood friends and nothing more, when the phone rang. Carolyn turned to reach for it.

"I'll get it," Gavin said. "I'm expecting a call from Matsuyama."

A few moments later it was clear that it was not the call Gavin was waiting for. "I'll get the travel service downstairs to arrange it," he was saying. "Sure, I've done it. It's a great trip. What about hotel reservations?" He listened for a second or two and then said, "Okay, play it by ear if you want to, but remember these places are usually booked far in advance. . . . Right. . . . Yes, she's right here with me now. . . . I'll tell her. . . . Fine, Brett, I'll tell her."

Gavin dropped the receiver. His affable manner had altered perceptibly. "Brett said he's been trying to call you in your suite. Said he thought he might catch you here."

"We're going to do some more sightseeing today," Carolyn said carelessly. "And sitting around at . . . what do they call them? The little tea shops that mostly serve coffee and make you think you're in Paris."

"Kitsa-ten," Gavin said. "Means 'sipping tea shop,' but you're more likely to see everyone sipping coffee." He was looking at Carolyn warily now. "Brett said to pack an overnight case."

Startled, Carolyn could only gape at him.

"He wants to take the Kamakura-Hakone drive and take the bullet train back." Gavin's pinkish face had taken on a strangely gray appearance. It seemed that he was working at sounding casual. "Some beautiful sights along the way, and the train is an experience you'll enjoy."

"It can't be done in one day?" Carolyn was more than annoyed; she was embarrassed.

"It can." Gavin paused significantly. "But you'd be rushed. There are some nice mountain resorts in the area."

"If you're making the arrangements," Carolyn said, "book two rooms."

"Brett said he'd rather make the overnight arrangements himself. Play it by ear, in case you run across an interesting spot you don't want to leave. He knows I'm familiar with the route, so he asked if I'd check out the train schedule." Gavin's voice stopped. His back was turned to Carolyn as he said, "You don't sound too pleased, Carolyn."

"Doesn't it sound sort of . . . sort of imperious to you? Being told to plan on spending the night?"

"Depends on who gives the order," Gavin said. "If it's just an old friend, one you've made it abundantly clear *is* just an old friend, I shouldn't think you'd be too upset about it. You know how much Brett likes to surprise people. And if he was planning a—what shall I call it?—a romantic getaway or an assignation, I don't think he would have asked for my help. He assumes that I know his feelings for you are strictly platonic."

That spinning confusion of emotions again! A shiver of excitement at the thought of Brett wanting to spend the night with her away from the hotel where he was under constant scrutiny; resentment that he thought he could snap his fingers and have her agree to the overnight trip he'd planned; then the sinking sensation of knowing that Brett had let Gavin know that he had no interest in her beyond their compatibility and childhood friendship. He had probably discussed her with Gavin: "Oh, she's just a nice kid from back home. Want to show her a good time. Her folks will expect it of me." Carolyn felt as though she were being patronized. She was so out of Brett's sphere that it could be assumed he would not want to make love to her. Yet he had wanted to, one night. Her pride almost made her want to say this to Gavin, but she didn't. "It sounds like an interesting trip," she said with a ho-hum tone that was reasonably convincing to her own ears.

She crossed the hall a few minutes later to begin the process of selecting clothes for what Gavin told her would be an informal lake-and-mountain trip. "Might be chilly in the evening," he had said before Carolyn left the office suite. "Take a sweater." His last words before Carolyn closed the door behind her were, "Your David's a very lucky man."

Oh, wonderful! She was being congratulated on her loyalty to a lover who didn't exist. And by taking the overnight trip with Brett, wasn't she all but admitting that she was available? Carolyn's thoughts and feelings continued to jumble together as she packed her overnight case. Should she take the lovely new black silk jumpsuit and the elegant *boumake* coat? No. It was much too dressy for a mountain resort. She hesitated for a long time over a choice between sensible cool-weather pajamas and a slinky peach-colored nightgown-negligee ensemble with a plunging lace-trimmed neckline. She visualized wearing the latter in a secluded mountain hideaway with Brett's eyes drinking in the sight of her in the clinging gown. Perversely she folded the flower-printed unglamorous flannel pajamas and placed them in her small satchel. Carolyn had finished packing when she had second thoughts about the lacy gown; it was added to her overnight case. Just to be safe.

The image of the flimsy night apparel remained in the back of Carolyn's consciousness throughout the chauffeured motor trip. They drove along winding roads gazing out at pastoral scenes, and as they climbed higher, towering evergreen trees. Brett was as enthusiastic as ever, asking questions of Hiro, telling Carolyn how much he enjoyed sharing this experience with her. "Sights like this should never be seen alone," he said when the sparkling Pacific coastline was behind them and the spectacularly beautiful highway through the Hakone Mountains brought them to a placid lake from whose shores they looked up to the majestic heights of Mt. Fuji.

Was Brett also thinking about how this day might end? He had made no apologies for proposing an overnight trip, nor did he offer any explanations. En route to Lake Hakone, which was the epitome of peaceful scenic beauty, they had stopped to view one of the most celebrated landmarks in the entire country. And Carolyn had gazed at the awesome, perfectly preserved statue of the Giant Buddha, aware that she was looking at one of the most impressive wonders of the world.

"Unbelievable, isn't it?" Brett said. "Seven hundred and twenty years old and still intact. Did you have any idea it was so huge? The face alone is nearly seven feet high!" But Carolyn saw the serene face of the Buddha with only half of her mind. The other half had projected itself forward to the evening, to the time when Brett might possibly reach out for her, when they would be truly alone together.

Carolyn's acute awareness of Brett stayed with her through their crabmeat luncheon on the viewing terrace of a lakeside hotel, through a boat excursion on the mountain-ringed lake. Not knowing where or how their night together would be spent kept her tingling with anticipation. There was no more argument inside her; whatever the consequences, she wanted to sleep in Brett's arms. He *must* be having the same thoughts! For all the loveliness of the sights that unfolded before them, Carolyn was impatient with the sightseeing. It seemed that the moment when Hiro departed and drove back to Tokyo alone would never come.

Hiro left them, at last, at the rustic Hotel Kowaki-En. The cool, crisp mountain air was at once invigorating and tiring. Carolyn's nervousness built through an elaborate dinner which she could barely swallow, then through cocktails in a lounge crowded with a mixture of Japanese, American and European tourists.

Brett, however, showed no signs of nervousness whatsoever. He reminisced about funny incidents from the past, laughed over the day's attempts to communicate with people they had met, sighed and said it was wonderful to be relaxing at last. "I'm not even letting myself *think* about the hell that's going to break loose on Monday." He nodded at Carolyn's empty glass. "Ready for another?"

Under other circumstances, Carolyn would have said no. She had consumed two of the strong drinks and her thoughts were becoming dulled. But tonight she needed the soporific effect of more alcohol. She wanted to go up to their room feeling at ease, as uninhibited as one of the women of the world Brett had made love to in his previous travels. "I'm ready for another," she said.

Brett gave her a warning smile. "Two's usually your limit."

"It's the mountain air," she said. "It works up your appetite."

Brett shrugged and signaled for the waiter. "If you wake up with a hangover, don't blame me, little neighbor."

She was wound up like a tightly coiled spring by the time Brett decided it was time to retire for the night. Carolyn's walk was steady enough as they left the lounge. There were surreptitious stares and whispers from the tourists at other tables, and Carolyn realized there were women present who envied her.

She had a fleeting impression of a long walk through a corridor lined with shoji screens outlined from behind with soft amber lights. They came to a door. Brett checked the number and stopped. "Here we are.

Two-oh-four." How remarkably unselfconscious he was! This was no new experience for him, of course, but surely he felt some of Carolyn's tremulousness! She watched him reach into the pocket of his off-white sports jacket. He extracted a long plastic rectangle with a key dangling from it. No. No, not one white key holder. There were two. And he was unlocking the door and saying, "Doesn't matter which one's yours or which one's mine. Both rooms, I was assured, have the same terrific view."

She wanted to die, to scream, to do anything but stand out in that hall and know that the lacy gown was a humiliating joke. She knew that her face was burning scarlet. It was as though someone had filled her insides with molten lead—heavy, painfully burning lead.

Carolyn paused only for a moment in the open doorway, seeing the charming simplicity of a room decorated in subdued earth tones, a lighted lantern on the rustic table separating the twin beds. Brett was peering over her shoulder. "Looks comfortable. It's been quite a day. Why don't you sleep as long as you like tomorrow."

Was it up to *her* now to change the course of the evening? Should she, with a word or a gesture, let him know that she didn't want to spend this night alone? She felt too insecure. If she turned to Brett now and asked him to come in, and if he rejected her, she would not be able to face the rest of this night or the morning. Carolyn forced out a polite thank-you for the beautiful day.

"I enjoyed it, too," Brett told her. "Gavin was right. It's a great side trip." Why was he still lingering in the open doorway? Why didn't he leave her alone? "I took all his suggestions, you know . . . as well as some he said that you made."

"Oh." Carolyn turned, though she was barely able to

face Brett. "You mean the separate rooms." Inside, a voice was crying: I didn't really want this, Brett. Please make it easy for me. Please take the initiative, because I'm too scared, and because you know what to do if you want me tonight.

Brett looked deeply into her eyes for a moment, just long enough to let her know that he was not beyond desire. Carolyn turned away quickly. "Good night, Brett."

He echoed her words. Then, as if to show that Gavin was wrong, that he *did* have some interest in the Japanese language, he added, *"Oyasumi nasai."*

They were words Carolyn remembered from the tourist dictionary at the back of her guidebook. "Good night, sweet dreams!" The door closed and she was left with the irony and the fury and the burning, inexpressible hurt. Brett *knew* she wanted his lovemaking tonight. He was too experienced, too perceptive not to know that she didn't want to sleep alone in this place that had been built for romantic escape!

Her overnight case had been brought to the room by a bellhop earlier. It sat on a folding wooden luggage rack at the foot of one of the beds. Trembling with frustration, Carolyn snapped the case open and pulled out the flowered flannel pajamas. A sensible, practical decision, because the room was uncomfortably cold. The peach-colored night ensemble fell to the floor as she yanked the pajamas from under it. The satin folds lay crumbled on the *tatami* floor mat, piled there like some symbol of shame. He had known what she wanted and he'd turned her away!

A hot bath did nothing for her keyed-up nerves. She shivered in the sensible pajamas, and felt chilled even under the thick down quilt that covered her lonely bed, yet her body was burning with desire. The intensity of this insane love she felt for the unattainable Brett Wells had left her body as well as her heart aching for his touch, his kiss, the joy of complete union with him.

Far into the still, pine-scented, piercingly cold mountain night, Carolyn cursed Brett, cursed herself for wanting him, and swore to herself over and over that she would forget he even existed.

Chapter Eight

There wasn't much to do in that mountain resort except to enjoy the scenery. And neither of them, it seemed, was in a mood to admire the view or go tramping through the dark evergreen forests surrounding their hotel.

Breakfast-table conversation was polite but strained. Was Brett thinking, as she was, how different it all might have been? It was a relief when Brett announced that it was time to catch a bus to Odawara, where they would board the bullet train for Tokyo.

It was on the silver bullet-shaped train, racing toward Tokyo, that Brett finally broke the long silence between them. "I've always wanted to do this," he began. "Almost like flying, isn't it?"

"Yes." She felt flat and deflated. "Yes, it's almost like flying."

"Look out the window. Everything zips past you so fast, you can't really know what you're seeing."

"No, you can't. You really can't."

There was a sullen silence for a while, and then Brett said, "But we had a good time. I'll never forget all those sulfur fumes and all that steam rising up out of the ground. What was the name of that valley?"

"Mmm . . . Owakudani," Carolyn told him. "Yes. The Owakudani Valley. It was beautiful, but it was sort of frightening, too, wasn't it? Like my idea of Dante's Inferno."

"No. No, that was last night," Brett said.

"Last night?"

"Oh, dammit, stop pretending you don't know what I'm talking about!" Brett exploded. He turned in his seat to fix Carolyn with his eyes, his look both regretful and accusing. "You're too honest for game-playing, Carolyn. You know we should have been together last night. Who was going to get hurt? You? Me? Some guy in Alaska? Come off it. We've had some fabulous days together. We're both edgy as hell today, and why? Because we were too stupid to admit that we wanted each other last night. You ordered separate rooms, and I, like an idiot, went along with the idea. Tell me, please, who would have gotten hurt if we had been together last night? It would have made this a *perfect* week."

Carolyn fumbled in her purse for a tissue. She knew who would have been hurt. She tried hard to keep the tears from coming, but they came in spite of her efforts. She blotted her eyes with the crumpled tissue. "Jennie told me," she said, sniffing, "that you've moved into another dimension, Brett. I don't belong there. I don't want to get hurt trying to . . . trying to be there."

Maybe Brett understood that statement. Maybe he agreed with it. He reached out to take Carolyn's hand

and press it warmly with his fingers. "It's not quite like that, honey. Everything's happened so fast, I'm not really sure what it's like. I know I can't offer you emotional stability, the little house surrounded by the picket fence and living happily ever after. It's not like that and I don't want to lie to you and make you think that it is. But I like to think we're close, Carolyn. I need to know that we're close. I saw the damned sun come up over the mountains this morning. All I could think about was that I needed you. Can you understand that it wasn't just sex I wanted?"

Carolyn swiped at her eyes with the tissue again and nodded.

Before their forty-minute race to the city had ended, Brett had stopped looking backward and was, typically, looking forward again. "We'll get some rest tonight," he said. "Dinner at the hotel. I don't know about you, but I'll be ready for some sleep. Are you with me?"

Carolyn managed a smile. "I'm with you. I'm going to need most of today to recoup."

"And we'll take it easy Saturday, too, because we have a big night scheduled."

"Not another surprise?" Carolyn teased. "Not that I don't like surprises, but . . ."

"No, it's not another surprise. Cherry-blossom festival. Or ceremony or celebration, whatever you want to call it. Remember the trees about to bloom in Ueno Park? There's been no rain, so they'll be at their height tomorrow night. And we have an invitation."

"Oh, yes. Hiro said we had to go back to see them."

"That's not what I'm talking about," Brett said. "No. You've met Katsumi Funabashi? My lead trumpet?"

"Of course I have."

"He's asked us to join him and his family for the festival. That's tomorrow night. It's a sort of potluck.

Remember the potluck suppers we used to go to back home? I used to gorge myself. We'll be doing that tomorrow night, except that instead of avocado and oak trees, we'll be sitting under the cherry trees. Nice?"

"Nice" was a mild word to describe the loveliness of the evening that followed. Ueno Park was a seemingly endless sea of delicate cherry blossoms. There was such a profusion of petals that it seemed the entire world was wrapped in a mist of pinkish-white flowers and a subtle, heavenly scent.

They had left the hotel dressed in Japanese garb, a result of Brett's afternoon excursion to one of the city's huge department stores. "Nothing like getting into the spirit of the occasion," he had said as he helped Carolyn tie the eleborate sash that bound her new chrysanthemum-flowered kimono. Brett's was black, decorated with turquoise and aqua and gold dragons. He had ordered some gourmet contributions to the potluck dinner from the hotel's best chef: a brandied beef pâté, an herbed lobster dish the chef had invented especially for the occasion, and an artistically arranged tray of succulent pastries. Carolyn suspected the cost of these extravagances would have kept her solvent for a month during her art-school training in San Francisco. Brett had arranged to have three bottles of *sake* added to the straw basket, along with a bottle of imported Scotch, and other gifts for Katsumi's family.

They carried this epicurean bonanza into a milling crowd of happy, smiling Japanese who had come to celebrate the cherry-blossom festival. Making their way through the throng, they finally spotted their group at the prearranged meeting place.

Jazz trumpeter Katsumi gave them a warm welcome. "I did not dare to hope you would come!" he cried, shaking their hands alternately and letting his pride and delight show in a smile that seemingly could not be erased from his face. "Welcome . . . welcome to our Ha-na-mi!"

There were more smiles and bows as Brett and Carolyn were introduced to Katsumi's mother and father, grandmother and two aunts, a shyly smiling, lovely wife and three playful, excited children, all in their traditional best.

Communication was sparse in words, but not in the looks and smiles that bind all humanity together. Seated under the mist of cherry blossoms, their faces lighted by exquisitely formed and painted lanterns that had been strung between the blossoming trees, they shared food and drink, poured *sake* with abandon, laughed and sang strangely touching Japanese folk songs that dated back to time immemorial. Brett and Carolyn could only hum along with their hospitable new friends, but they were so touched by the beauty of the scene that they sang in their hearts.

Gavin and Carmen and Tony arrived to join them. There were fresh toasts to greet the newcomers. All around them, other family groups feasted and drank and sang, and the doll-like children ran from group to group to be welcomed with treats and tiny, colorful gifts. This was the *ha-na-mi,* the cherry-blossom festival that they had waited for all year. And this year, rains had not destroyed the brief, inspiringly beautiful explosion of the cherry blossoms. They were everywhere— fragile, softly scented, a dearly loved representation of the Japanese spirit, the very core of their culture.

It was late at night when Katsumi's friends and family broke into the old, sentimental song that had thrilled Japanese hearts for more than one thousand years. How Carolyn wished that Brett's resoundingly deep voice could rise above the others! He could only hum along as the group seated on the grass around them sang:

Sakura, sakura
Yayoi no sara wa
Miwatasu kagiri,
Kasumi ka kumo ka.

Brett's trumpet player, his hair cut in the latest Western fashion, his California-style shirt and slacks a far cry from the traditional clothing of his wizened old grandmother and even his conservatively American-dressed parents, sidled over to where Brett and Carolyn were seated. "I try to play my horn like your Miles Davis," he said between verses of the song. "But I only visit jazz. This music is my *home.*"

Carolyn's eyes misted over. How loving and caring this family was, how sincerely they had welcomed strangers from far across the sea! They sang:

Nioi zo izaru
Izaya, izaya
Mini yukan!

Everyone in the lantern-lighted park had taken up the chorus. Quavering young voices, powerful voices, the feeble voices of the old, had all joined in the haunting melody that sang of the beautiful blossoms under which they sat tonight—blossoms whose loveliness was somehow enhanced by their brevity. "One week," Tony Hanniman said when the last note shimmered in the air for a moment and then was silenced. "Isn't it sad? The blossoms last only one week."

"I'd say something trite," Brett said, "like, nothing beautiful lasts. Except that we saw that gigantic sculpture of Buddha this week. It's been around for centuries."

"Oh, that was massive and impressive," Carolyn

countered, "but it wasn't like this. Millions and millions of flowers. And this loving company, this music! Tony, you've got to do an arrangement of that song for Brett."

"'Sakura, sakura'?" Tony called over to Katsumi, who was affectionately known to the band as "Kat." "What do the lyrics mean, Kat? Is that a popular new song here?"

The trumpet man finished filling a *sake* cup for one of the guests. "New? Ho! Older than the Giant Buddha. Maybe a thousand years old." He moved over to their part of the circle and explained that "sakura" was the word for cherry trees, but the word did not refer to the tree's fruit but to the blossoms. They were hearing the best-loved song in Japan echoing through the park. And the words? Katsumi enlisted the help of one of his sisters, who taught English in an adult night school.

"A literal definition is difficult," the young woman said in a rather clipped Oxford manner. "It is like a *haiku* poem. The form is as disciplined as the meaning is subtle. It does not translate with ease. 'Cherry blossoms, cherry blossoms! As a cloud in the morning mist they perfume the air. Shall we sit beneath the cherry trees and enjoy the tea ceremony?'"

Her brother laughed and waved his bottle of rice wine in the air. "Tea? Tea? Who wants tea?"

There was laughter while he went on filling small, traditional stoneware cups and even plastic picnic glasses. It was rude to fill your own glass here, but equally rude for your host to allow it to sit empty for a moment. Kat's father, who had set everyone an example of serious wine-drinking, was leaning against a cherry tree, smiling blissfully. There were happy shouts and peals of laughter from every acre of the huge park. And when it was time to go, when the musician's family and friends had bowed and thanked them for coming, and had been sincerely thanked in return, the small party of Americans walked along the beautiful lantern-lighted path, still hearing the tender melody that extolled the cherry blossoms under which they strolled:

> *Sakura, sakura,*
> *Noyama mo sato mo . . .*

Streets and walks were always crowded, but on this Saturday night it seemed that the entire population of Japan was gathered here, and that each of them wanted a taxi. It was close to midnight before Brett and Carolyn said good night to Gavin and the two American musicians, who had decided to cap off the night in one of the hotel's lounges. Brett didn't suggest joining them. In the elevator, with the "Sakura" song still floating through her mind, Carolyn hummed a few bars and then said, "I'd love to hear you sing that, Brett. It's such a lovely song."

"Not my style," Brett said. "Look, I've already got enough people managing my career. And all the wrong ones wanting to take over my personal life."

"What does that mean?"

Brett scowled, then shook his head as though he were being bothered by an annoying gnat. "Nothing. Forget it."

Carolyn shrugged. "You looked a little disturbed when you had that brief talk with Gavin at the park tonight. But if it's none of my business . . ."

Carolyn left the sentence hanging in midair, and Brett must have agreed it *was* none of her business, for he changed the subject as they walked up the long corridor. "I can't remember a more beautiful night. The people, the lanterns, the singing, the cherry blossoms. It was fun, but it was, somehow, very touching."

"Sad," Carolyn said.

"Oh, I wouldn't go that far."

"Sad and symbolic," Carolyn went on. She hoped it wasn't the rice wine that had created her melancholy mood. "Katsumi told me that rain is predicted for tomorrow. By the next morning, it'll all be over."

At her door, Brett went through the now customary routine of waiting until Carolyn had found her key. As he unlocked the door, he said, "You're not thinking about Monday? About the two of us being too busy to see each other?"

They were inside the room. Brett had followed her in without waiting for an invitation. "Maybe I am," Carolyn admitted.

As she crossed the sitting room to turn on a second lamp, Carolyn heard the bolt clicking, locking the door behind them. She was standing at the wide plate-glass window wall, looking down at the blurred lights of the city. Fog was creeping in; tomorrow would probably be a wet day. One rainy Sunday and this fabulous adventure would, like the *sakura,* be only a memory. But there was more than sadness in her heart. There was a tension, a tautness of every nerve in her body. Brett had followed her into the room!

"Carolyn?"

He was standing behind her. The heat was only in her mind, but she felt as though she were standing before a column of steel that had just been removed from a blast furnace. His nearness left her trembling and speechless.

"Carolyn, the other day, when we were on the train and I talked about our having missed a beautiful opportunity, do you remember what you said?"

"No, I . . . I don't recall."

"You implied that you were afraid of me. Afraid of getting hurt."

She wanted to deny that, but she was still afraid. Carolyn felt as though she were burning up with fever, yet she was now shivering, not knowing what to say, not knowing what was expected of her. The wrong word would send Brett away again, and she didn't want him to go. She couldn't bear the thought that he would leave her alone again tonight.

"Carolyn, turn around." Brett's hands fell firmly on her shoulders, and he turned her so that she could not avoid facing him. "Look at me."

Carolyn looked up into the depths of his dark, intense gaze. She felt as though every secret desire in her heart was being explored. "Brett, I . . ."

"You wanted me that night up in the mountains." Brett's arms slipped from Carolyn's shoulders and wrapped themselves around her in a sudden fierce embrace. "You've known me too long to be afraid. You want me *now.*"

His lips possessed hers, warm and ardent, yet tender, too. Brett's kiss lasted for a long time, as strong and irresistible as the uncompromising pressure of his body against hers. Then he lifted his mouth from Carolyn's, breathing rapidly, still pinning her with his demanding stare. "You do, don't you? You want me as much as I want you!"

There were no words inside her, no denial. Brett's kiss had kindled a flame that swept through her body like wildfire. Carolyn lifted her lips toward his, letting him know, silently, that he was right. Her arms were held close to her sides, and Brett released them, taking her hands, pulling upward until her arms circled his neck. "I wasn't going to ask to be invited in tonight," he murmured huskily. "Tonight I couldn't have taken no for an answer." He kissed her again, lightly. Then, as though a volcano of passion had erupted inside him, he tightened his fervid hold and kissed her again. This time Carolyn's response was a match for the fevered desire that she sensed in him. Brett's hands caressed her body, slowly at first, and with a gentle touch, as though he were outlining the contours of some fragile, treasured object. Then his fingers found one breast and the caresses became more impassioned.

For a moment Brett lifted his lips from hers. "Carolyn . . . darling," he whispered. "Why did we waste so much time?"

Their kisses became eager then, as though all the need they felt for each other was being compressed into one microinstant, as though this throbbing urgency had to be fulfilled at once. There was no thought of resistance in Carolyn. Brett's darting tongue was a flame that swept away thoughts and fears.

She did not remember the exact moment when Brett led her into the darkened bedroom. In the dim light that came from the open door, she saw Brett's face, still stirringly handsome, but other-worldly, somehow, as though his aroused passion had turned him into a stranger. Yet a provocative stranger, a man whose exploring hands as he eased her down on the bed were expertly dedicated to awakening in her a stirring, undeniable need to become one with his body.

He had said that too much time had been wasted. But now it seemed that Brett had at his command all the time in the world. Locked in his arms, her lips pressing now against his hard chest, now kissing his throat and, again, his hungry mouth, Carolyn trembled with an impatient desire that she had never known existed inside her. For a fleeting moment she remembered that Brett was a man of experience; he knew exactly where to touch her. There was even a momentary fear that she would disappoint him, that she would not be good enough for a man who had made love to sophisticated women whose techniques were as sure as his. She had long heard the phrase "good in bed." What did she know about arousing and satisfying a man? It didn't matter. She only knew that she ached to give herself to Brett. And a long time later, when he moved his body so that he could remove her clothes, it seemed that he undressed her too slowly.

"You'll have to help a *little*," Brett said softly when he had untied the bright kimono top, now dampened and pressed against her breasts. His smile was soft and tender, as though he knew that she was shy about letting him see her nakedness. Carolyn lifted herself so that Brett's hands could find the back of her bra and undo the hooks. There was no awkward or tremulous groping; Brett was knowledgeable and natural. His calm self-assurance would have raised doubts in Carolyn, except that by the time he had run his hand over her stomach, stopping to massage its softness with slow, sensual strokes, sliding her loose-fitting trousers and beige lace panties to her knees in one deliberate motion, she was too inflamed to entertain regrets that this was not the first time for him, as it was for her.

The rectangle of pale golden light from the doorway fell across her nude body when the last of her clothing had been eased to the floor at the foot of the bed. Carolyn closed her eyes, knowing that Brett's gaze was upon her as he said, "You're so beautiful, Carolyn. I used to visualize you this way, but I didn't do you justice. You're exquisite!"

He had gotten off the bed, and Carolyn dared a look at the shadowy form of his body standing nearby. His movements were swift now, and although he was usually meticulous about his clothing, the Japanese-style robe and trousers were tossed carelessly across a chair. Then, without really having seen him as intimately as he had seen her, Carolyn felt his arms, his practiced kisses and the warm, naked weight of his chest against her breasts. The now-familiar spicy cologne blended with the male scent of him, intoxicating her senses. She heard herself moan, as if from some far-off place, "Brett . . . Brett, what are you doing to me?"

"What are you doing to *me?*" He was breathing unevenly as his hand took Carolyn's and guided it down to touch him. "What are you doing to *me?*" Brett repeated.

They were like unthinking jungle animals then, lost in obedience to primal instincts, consumed by an ardor that grew with every shifting contact of their bodies. She could not kiss him deeply enough. He could not run his hands over every curve, every hidden crevice of her quivering body often enough. And the knowledge of how to please him came naturally enough to Carolyn; when one loved a man the way she loved Brett, the body not only knew what it should do—there was no stopping it from expressing its passion.

She was consumed in a raging impatience, his caresses finally rousing her to a cry of, "Don't wait any longer, Brett. Please. Please take me!"

"Carolyn . . . Carolyn! I want you so much!" Brett's knees parted her legs with a slowness that was not reflected in his panting breath. Her eyes pressed shut, her arms clinging to him, Carolyn suppressed a cry of pain as Brett entered her, a cry that was stifled by the clamp of his mouth over hers and the hot weight of his body. There was a fusion of flesh with flesh, and a rapture that engulfed her entire being. Brett's sure motions sent her soaring until it seemed that the whole universe was in flames.

When Brett's sharp outcry came, it was mingled with her own, and her own was a cry of ecstasy. Did she moan the words aloud, or only in the bursting adoration of her fulfilled heart? "I love you, Brett. I love you, I love you, I love you!" She thought she heard

Brett echo her declaration, but she could not be certain; her senses blacked out in a faint that was like truly being alive for the first time in her life, and dying, all at once.

They clung to each other for a long time before Brett withdrew to fold her in a sweetly serene embrace. Her head cradled against Brett's warm chest, Carolyn heard him say in a quiet, regretful tone, "I hurt you. Believe me, I didn't know . . . I didn't want to hurt you."

Carolyn shook her head. "No. No, you didn't hurt me."

"I had no idea. And by the time I realized . . . I couldn't have stopped myself if my life depended on it. Carolyn, why didn't you tell me there's never been anyone else? This . . . this David of yours comes home from Alaska once in a while, doesn't he? He's not a eunuch. This *is* the twentieth century."

Carolyn began to cry. The whole world seemed strange to her suddenly.

"You're not unhappy? You're not angry with me?" Brett kissed her wet cheek. "Are you all right? Are you sure you're all right, Carolyn?"

"I'm fine," she finally managed to assure him. "And I'm such a . . . such a ninny. Such an anachronism in this day and age."

Brett squeezed her warmly. "Yes, but tonight you were *my* anachronism. Would you believe me, little ninny, if I told you I've never experienced anything like that before? Never. And if I live to be a hundred, probably never will again."

Maybe she only dreamed that for a long time afterward, stroking her forehead gently, brushing her damp and rumpled hair away from her face, Brett hummed to her in his throaty baritone a song made popular by another star not too many years before. He didn't have to sing the lyrics; she knew them well. It was a dream, perhaps, but Carolyn drifted off into a heavenly sleep with her head resting against Brett's chest, hearing, or only imagining, a familiar melody . . . and words that promised he would sing her to sleep after the loving.

Chapter Nine

Carolyn awoke to a hushed, steady sound. She did not have to get up and draw open her bedroom draperies to know that it was raining outside. It took her only a few moments to remember the momentous event that had taken place in this bed the night before. She was a whole woman this morning. She had been loved by the man to whom she'd long ago given her heart.

Sometime before dawn Brett must have left her room. Of course. The soul of discretion, always under surveillance, he would not have stayed with her until morning. Would she see him today? Had he only been polite when he lay beside her, cradling her in his arms, when his need for her had been satisfied? And had he been disappointed? Would he now treat her with condescending courtesy, but be grateful if she did not claim more of his time? Carolyn lay on her bed, reliving the soul-stirring event that had changed her life, alter-

nately remembering that Brett lost interest when a
challenge had been met, and recalling his words: "I've
never experienced anything like that before."

Her mind was still crowded with questions after she
had showered and dressed in a mauve angora sweater
and slacks in a darker, complementary shade. Mauve.
Jennie's favorite color. Should she write to tell Jennie
what had happened? Of course not. Ludicrous thought.
But she wanted the world to know that Brett had held
her in his arms and made love to her last night.

Carolyn was hanging her kimono costume in the
walk-in closet, stopping to run her fingers over the
silken fabric sentimentally, when she was summoned to
her door. A young bellhop smiled, bowed, and presented her with a long florist's box. How typical of
Brett! He could have afforded a roomful of roses, but
the waxed green paper was folded back to reveal a few
sprays of cherry blossoms, somewhat wilted already,
for they did not survive long after being cut. The
accompanying note card read, "Good morning, love.
Your turn to visit me. I'm right next door in case you've
forgotten my address. Waiting. Brett."

She let out an audible whoop of joy. Then, taking
time out to make sure that she had done all she could to
bring some order to hair that had been hopelessly
rearranged the night before, adding a touch of lipstick
and a quick spray of floral cologne behind her ears,
Carolyn made the quick trip to Brett's door.

"Good morning!" He greeted her with an enthusiastic smile. Dressed in tan pajamas and an embossed
maroon silk smoking jacket, he looked every inch the
successful pop music star. He was overwhelmingly
attractive, Carolyn thought. It was almost impossible to
believe that he had lain naked beside her only a few
hours ago and called her beautiful.

As he took her arm and led her into his sitting room,
Brett said, "The *sakura* arrived, I gather. With my

message. I couldn't wait for the knock on my door. If it had been Gavin or anyone else, I'd have kicked him down the hall."

They both laughed, and Brett stopped to give Carolyn a kiss of welcome. "You look great. Like you're ready to go places and see things." He motioned at the sumptuous arrangement of overstuffed love seats. "Make yourself comfortable. I haven't had coffee yet, let alone thought about getting into some clothes."

"But you had time to order cherry blossoms for me," Carolyn said, sinking into the cushioned depths of a mammoth hassock. "I was very touched, Brett. I'm going to press them in a big book and keep them forever."

He was pleased with her reaction to his thoughtfulness. "Might be the last you see of the cherry blossoms. Look at what's going on out there." The window wall in his sitting room was a moving mural of gray. "I'd hoped we could go back to the park today, but it looks like the sky's coming down. So I have a bright idea instead."

"We go for a walk in the rain?"

"No, we have Sunday picnic right here, and stay *dry*," Brett said. He dropped down to the floor at Carolyn's feet, looking relaxed and comfortable as he kicked off his wine-colored leather bedroom slippers and leaned his head back against Carolyn's knees. How could anyone look so unbelievably handsome this early in the morning? Carolyn had to restrain herself from leaning down and slipping her arms around him. "Yep, I've decided," Brett went on. "We'll call room service and order a really spectacular brunch. We'll let the switchboard know that my phone is not to ring unless a national emergency has been declared. We'll put one of those funny-lettered 'Do Not Disturb' signs on the doorknob outside, and we'll tell anybody who manages to get through to us that we are not, repeat *not* interested in seeing one more temple, shrine, museum, gourmet restaurant or snowcapped volcano. Right? And then we'll spend this last day of my vacation eating and drinking and talking and doing whatever else may occur to our fertile imaginations. Sound like a good plan to you?"

"It sounds like a fabulous plan," Carolyn said, catching his whimsical mood. "And I'm ready for coffee right now. I've been ready for a good hour."

"Slave-driver!" Brett got up from the floor with seeming reluctance and made his way to the telephone. He was laughing a few seconds later, obviously having difficulty in making the clerk understand his complicated breakfast order. "For *two*," Carolyn heard him emphasizing. "Yes, two people, two orders toast, two everything. *Two*." He gave a cry of triumph. "Aha! Now you've got it! I have a guest for breakfast!" Dropping the receiver a moment later, Brett said, "I *think* he's got it. But don't be too surprised if we get salami sandwiches for forty and a keg of Japanese beer. These people are so polite, they can't say no to anything. Even when you ask them if they really understood you."

They shared laughter that verged on the hysterical when a smiling, bowing room-service man arrived with a rolling table heaped with enough eggs, raw fish, rice and other unidentifiable foods to feed the Emperor's army. Plus exactly two slices of toast. And two carafes filled with strong, steaming coffee.

There were intermittent bursts of laughter while they shared this bountiful "picnic," so different from the many they had enjoyed along the oak-leaf-strewn banks of Keys Creek years ago. Seated on the floor Japanese style, they discovered that they were both ravenous. It was an unusual day, a fun day, a day filled with the happy promise of being together now that they had really discovered each other.

How did it all change? Exactly what was said, what

was done, what turned all the joy of being in an undreamed-of place, doing a childishly funny thing, into a hurt-filled exchange of accusations and recriminations?

It was Carolyn's mention of the rain-destroyed blossoms in Ueno Park that must have triggered it all. She had placed Brett's flowers in a water-filled glass from her bathroom, but she had known they would soon be dead—dead and colorless. How sad it must be to see the thousands of blossoms in the park being pelted by rain this morning, knocked to the ground and left to be trampled underfoot on the walkways. "Sort of like real life," Carolyn said.

Carolyn had not reckoned with Brett's sensitivity or his keen ability to read between the lines of her every expression. "You're making it sound like you're the fragile blossom and I'm the relentless downpour."

"I didn't say that, Brett," Carolyn replied.

"Not in so many words, but I get your drift," he countered irritably. "You're reminding me that starting tomorrow morning I'm going to be up to my ears in work and that I won't have time to squire you around. Well, that's true! We've had a hell of a week and now it's time for me to go back to work. To doing what I know best how to do. And to what means a great deal to me, Carolyn. Can you comprehend that? Does that mean that we can't still be good friends? Get together whenever time permits?"

She knew that what Brett was saying was true, but an unreasoning jealousy had swept over her. "Is that what it was, Brett? Just an interlude before you go back to doing what really matters to you?"

He was on his feet, agitated, looking down at Carolyn as though he couldn't understand her lack of comprehension. "It was beautiful. We'll probably have other times together just as good or better. What are you trying to make of it, Carolyn? They went to bed and got married and lived happily ever after? You know what my life's all about. I'm glad you fit into it. You do. Last night—my God, last night was incredible. But you know I have work to do. You know every minute can't be sightseeing and laughing and holding hands. I have a career to think about. A future. And so do you!"

He could not have hurt her more with the repeated stabs of a knife. And the irony was that she knew he had never promised her anything, that she had given herself to him of her own volition. She understood the demands of his career. What were they arguing about? Her sentimental reference to the short-lived cherry blossoms! Yet Brett had been flatly warning her that these past days were no more than a pleasurable hiatus in a life far different from her own. Her mind understood all that Brett was saying, but her heart burned with jealous resentment. Of what? Not another woman —a whole *world* full of women. Of his time? She knew that his stardom was maintained at the price of endless hours at the piano, writing songs, rehearsing with his band. She loved him insanely and wanted desperately to understand his way of life, but Carolyn's own insecurities, her own possessiveness, came first. "I know I can't ever make you understand," she said. "Listening to you makes me feel . . ." She stopped, reluctant to go too far.

"Makes you feel what?" Brett demanded. He was pacing the floor now, his face stern. "Used? *Used,* Carolyn? Like you've been taken advantage of and discarded?" He crossed to the window wall, spreading his arms and exclaiming, "It's raining! Oh, dear God, it's raining and the damned cherry blossoms are falling to the ground!" Brett whirled to face Carolyn. "Does that mean we didn't have a great time together when we had the chance? Does that make me some kind of insensitive monster?"

"You wouldn't understand," Carolyn told him. She had gotten to her feet, wanting only to escape, to be alone where it would not be humiliating to let her tears flow freely.

Brett's voice was cutting with sarcasm. "Oh! Now I don't understand! You make it sound as though I made you all kinds of romantic promises! Well, I didn't, Carolyn! Last night, all this past week, I thought the way we felt about each other was a two-way street. I thought that what we had between us was beautiful."

"So did I!" Carolyn cried. "I honestly thought I meant something more to you than . . . What was the term you used? Than 'having a great time together.'" An agonized confession was wrenched from her. "You've had all the worshipful fans you've ever wanted. All the lovesick Lisas you could make love to and dump like garbage! I thought I'd mean more to you than that! Damn you, I'm not some stupid groupie. *I love you!*"

Brett released a vicious curse. "And that's all you've got to say about me? You 'love me' and you think I'm a user?"

"Isn't that enough?" Carolyn started toward the door.

"No!" Brett had intercepted her walk, leaping before her and blocking her way. "No, it's not enough! Do you think last night could have been replaced with a call to room service? Send up two orders of toast and a woman I can spend the night with?"

"Easily!" Carolyn shouted. "Easily! She could have been young and gorgeous and accommodating. And a lot better at making you feel good than I was!" A biting, bitter sarcasm crept into her voice. "One of your hysterical fans would have made last night a lot more interesting!"

"More interesting than the innocent little girl next door?" Brett's voice was full of contempt. "Tell me some more, virtuous virgin! Tell me you weren't prepared for an encounter like last night and that I'll have to explain to your folks that I wasn't planning on being a daddy. Maybe you're not as naive as I thought you were. Maybe you've caught me with my guard down and I'm going to be held responsible for your delicate condition!"

It was a stupefying thought, and one that had not occurred to her. But the cruelty of the accusation was sharper than any concern she might have. "What a despicable thing to say! What a . . . a revoltingly detestable . . ."

"We seem to be trading insults," Brett said. He had turned to face the window again and the torrent of rain that was inundating the city. "I'll apologize for that, Carolyn. That was dirty pool. It's just that I can't handle your implying that I'm some kind of scalp collector. Don't you know the difference?" He whirled around to face her. "Don't you know how much it's meant to me to be with someone who knows me for what I am?"

"I'm not sure I do know you anymore," Carolyn said. "Maybe I never did." Words. They were just foolish, meaningless words. Carolyn would have given anything to erase everything she had said, but her insecurity, her knowledge that tomorrow Brett would have no time for her, filled her with a need to strike out at him. "How much can it mean to you? You're a big celebrity now, Brett. How many times can we talk about the good old days when we were kids? Eventually you'll get bored with looking back. And I've got to start looking ahead, too."

"With a man you don't have to share with anyone else?" Brett's challenge had a bitter sound. "You're right. You'd have to be above possessiveness, above petty jealousy to be a part of my life. Because I can't change. I've worked hard to get where I am, and I can't stop being public property. I had hoped you, of all people, would understand that."

"And settle for a few days of fun . . . and going to bed with you when you're in the mood?" Carolyn crossed the room and opened the door. "It was fun, Brett. And I thank you. I'll try to remember that it wasn't any more than that. Fun."

"Write to your damned David and give him my apologies," Brett shouted after her. Carolyn turned away from the fury that was written on his face and closed the door behind herself.

Her rage would have found some outlet if the cherry twigs had snapped with a loud crackling sound when she attacked them a few minutes later. They didn't. The branches were flexible, bending to her fury and righting themselves again. But the carpet at her feet was covered with fallen blossoms when she jammed the bouquet into a wastebasket. Outside, a howling wind slammed the rain against the broad window. In the park, a short distance away, the grass and the pathways must have been ankle-deep in pale pink blossoms.

Chapter Ten

Work had piled up during her absence, and Carolyn buried her misery in catching up. She wrote press releases for Brett's upcoming concert in Hiroshima. She submitted liner notes for the free record that would be used to promote his personal appearances in Japan. Strange. Brett hadn't even mentioned her idea for the giveaway record. She felt ignored, and appreciated it when Gavin talked to her about the promotion.

"Only trouble is, Brett's being stubborn about his choice of a selection," Gavin said while they were having lunch in the hotel coffee shop on Monday. "It's a new song he's written and he has Tony and all the guys in the band sold on it."

"But you're not?"

"Oh, it's a good song, but it's about a subject people here won't relate to. In California, maybe. Not here.

Try to talk him into a simple love ballad, will you, Carolyn?"

She didn't tell Gavin that it was unlikely she would be talking with Brett about anything. "What's it about?"

"The chorus goes, 'And music is my mistress, only one I ever had.' It goes on about lonely nights in hotel rooms, being away from home on Christmas, killing lonely hours reading magazines and doing cross-word puzzles. And the weariness of one-night stands. The musicians identify with it and the song's got a great beat, but Brett's fans here don't want to hear all that. They want to think of him as a great lover."

"His biggest hit was about unrequited love," Carolyn reminded him.

"Sure. 'How Little You Remember.' Great song. It made every female who heard it want to step in and take over from where his lover had dropped him. Okay, maybe Brett will sell this one on the beat alone, but I doubt it." Gavin speared a forkful of salad. "The last line is like a slap in the face to all his adoring fans. 'And music's still my mistress, only one I'll ever know.' You see why he needs a manager?"

"But he's ignoring you?"

"He's in a position to do so," Gavin said. "He needs me a lot less than our agency needs him. And Brett wouldn't be human if success hadn't gone to his head just a little."

"And I suppose he'll get his way, right or wrong?"

"He'll get his way," Gavin conceded.

Carolyn looked away from a questioning stare. Did Gavin know how far things had gone between her and Brett?

Apparently not. "I'll say one thing for you, Carolyn. I was worried about you for a while there, but you've kept your feet solidly on the ground." His admiring expression made Carolyn uneasy. "I wouldn't have thought of going into competition with Brett, but I might try to turn your head now, if it weren't for what's-his-name in Anchorage."

Gavin had spoken lightly, pretending to make a joke of it, but Carolyn sensed that his interest in her ran deeper than a careless quip. She turned the conversation back to their work. "I'll be talking to publicists from the film studio tomorrow. And there's that notice from the P.R. office at the distributing company in Hollywood. They're promoting a prerelease romance with the female star. You know, sort of a story within a story."

"American pop star meets and falls in love with glamorous Japanese actress. Big torrid romance, pictures of the two of them dancing cheek to cheek in posh Tokyo nightclubs." Gavin rattled off the angle, then waved a dismissing hand. "That's out, kiddo."

"Too trite?" Carolyn asked.

"That gimmick is never going to get too trite."

"Then why . . . ?"

"Orders from Miss Hayashi's manager, her agent, and Mr. Yoshinaga, who's a personal friend of Sadi's. Sadi's contract specifies no publicity about invented romances."

It seemed odd to Carolyn, but she devoted her efforts to other angles that would guarantee press coverage. Brett occupied her thoughts, inescapable. The very work in which she tried to bury herself revolved around him. She promised herself that she would start meeting other people, stop letting Brett consume her consciousness. Yet her need for him was not tempered by her anger over the way she had let herself fall in love with him. Oh, she had always loved him, but now his kisses burned on her lips, her body yearned ceaselessly for his touch. And her mind refused to stop thinking about him. How was he faring at the film studio today? Surrounded by glamorous people, how could he possibly be giving one thought to her, or to the night they had spent in each other's arms?

There were two tearful telephone calls from London that afternoon, reminders that being in love with Brett Wells was a painful, unrewarding experience. Carolyn was as kind and as tactful as she could be. "Mr. Wells is at the film studio," she said truthfully. "He's going to be very busy for several months." That, too, was true. Carolyn added a sentence that was less honest. "He's not staying here at the hotel just now and I don't know where he can be reached." She dropped the receiver on a tormented voice that was saying, "I only want to *talk* with him! Just for a moment or two!"

The second call from Lisa Westerbrook strengthened Carolyn's resolve to stop living in a dream world. Brett himself had let her know that he had no intention of becoming seriously involved with any woman, certainly not one outside his profession who didn't understand what it meant to be married to a career. His new song might not appeal to audiences who didn't understand the lyrics, but Carolyn knew it had come from his heart; music was his mistress, the only one he'd ever know.

Gavin flew to Hiroshima that evening to lay the groundwork for Brett's reception in that city. If Brett had returned from the studio in Akasaka, there was no sign of him. Carolyn stayed at her desk until past seven. Then, running into Rusty Johnson in the corridor, she was grateful for his offhand invitation to join him for dinner. "I know Brett's working with Tony tonight," the affable young drummer said. "So he won't mind. Or will he?"

"He won't mind," Carolyn assured the drummer, who was responsible for the driving tempo that had helped to popularize Brett's records.

At one of the swank hotel's more informal, American-style restaurants, over messy barbecued ribs, they discussed the separate adventures they'd had since their arrival in Japan. "Brett won't need us at the studio until later this week," Rusty said. "But we'll be rehearsing nights, starting Wednesday. The guys are having a ball."

"Doing what?" Carolyn asked. She was only mildly interested. She had hoped the conversation about Brett would continue. Brett, Brett, Brett! She had to get away from him. And chatting with Rusty was better than pacing her lonely room and trying to fall asleep in her empty bed.

Rusty was telling her about the girl Carmen had fallen in love with and how Jerry Badler, having discovered a gourmand's paradise, was eating himself out of his clothes.

"And you?"

"I've discovered pachinko!" Rusty said ecstatically. "You've seen all those places—you can't miss the pachinko parlors. There's one on every block. You can get mesmerized. There's a lighted board up in front of you, see, and you buy these little steel balls, and . . . wow . . . I'm so good at it, couple of nights ago I had an audience standing around me. The trick is to establish a rhythm. No skill. Just a rhythm. And you *know* I've got that. So I win all these dumb prizes, like packs of cigarettes and stuff. It's even better than the video games back home."

Rusty was going on like an excited ten-year-old when Carolyn looked over his shoulder to see Tony Hanniman entering the restaurant. A few seconds later, Brett followed him in, both of them looking tired and unsmiling. They were close enough so that when the hostess nodded toward the table at which Rusty and Carolyn were seated, Brett's voice could be heard saying, "Thank you, but we want to sit alone and discuss work."

There had been one terrible moment in which Brett looked directly at her, then at Rusty, and back again to Carolyn. Then, with a casual wave, he followed Tony and the hostess to a booth at the opposite side of the room. Rusty was not even aware that his fellow musicians had come into the restaurant. For Carolyn, the incident was another twist of the knife that seemed to be embedded in her heart.

She hoped, while she was trying to find her way around the vast film studio the next day, that she might see Brett on one of the sound stages she passed. She might as well have been hoping to find one specific grain of sand on a ten-mile-long beach. She learned, when she finally found the publicity office, that there were twice as many films produced here as in Hollywood. She felt lost in the sprawling, ultramodern complex and only half-satisfied with the results of her meeting with two reserved middle-aged men who seemed to have their own ideas about popularizing the still-untitled musical. Carolyn returned to the hotel feeling depressed by the meeting and unnerved by the *kamikaze* cabdriver who drove her there.

She fared only slightly better the next day, when she had an appointment at the film studio in Akasaka with an Italian correspondent who was covering Japanese entertainment. The man arrived nearly an hour late, breathlessly apologizing for having gotten lost in the traffic. He was disappointed to learn that Brett was too busy to see him and that Sadi Hayashi, who would not be needed for another few days, had not yet arrived in Tokyo from her home in Matsuyama. Giovanni Costello acted as though Carolyn had inflicted a personal trauma upon him and was further annoyed because he was told point-blank that there was no romance going on between the two stars. They hadn't even met each other yet. Carolyn had a typewritten press release for him and she promised to do what she could to set up a personal interview with Mr. Wells and the film's director, Verne Damian. Mr. Costello left the publicity offices in a huff.

Carolyn used the interview as an excuse to find the set on which Brett was working. He was not there, and Mr. Damian, a dour, fortyish man dressed incongruously in a navy-blue velour running suit and sneakers, explained that he was in a hurry to get to the airport. He was shooting the hero's arrival in Japan today and his camera crew and Brett were probably there already. "But while you're here," Verne said, "you're invited to the party Thursday. You and Gavin." The director looked at his watch impatiently.

"A press party? Gavin didn't tell me—"

"No, the studio just cooked this up. Welcome cocktail bash for Sadi Hayashi. Cast and crew on the set." He was racing toward the mammoth open doorways when he threw back the dictum, "Be here. Four o'clock. If Gavin's back in town, let him know."

It was something to look forward to, Carolyn thought disconsolately. She would see Brett. She would let him see her looking her best. There would be interesting people to meet, and she might feel less like an outcast.

Carolyn cleared her desk by noon on Thursday, had a sandwich and tea in her suite, and spent the rest of the time getting ready for the party. From one of the photographers she had met through her contact with *The Japan Times,* she had learned that everybody who was anybody in show business had been invited, but the set was to be closed to the press. "Very swanky *private* party," the American-born photographer had said ruefully. It would take hours to get ready for the scintillating affair.

Surveying herself in the mirror, Carolyn wondered if the black silk jumpsuit would be dressy enough for the occasion. With the brilliant full-sleeved coat added to her ensemble, and with the addition of a pair of long leaf-shaped gold earrings, Carolyn decided that she looked elegant enough to mingle with the cast and visiting stars. She wasn't supposed to stand out; she was only a minor member of Brett's staff. But she had learned, discreetly, that the band members had not been invited; they were probably not even known yet to the studio moguls who were hosting this affair. And if Brett had not personally invited her, it was probably because he was only one of the guests himself. At least, that was what Carolyn chose to believe. When he saw her in this stunning suit, he would remember the day he had bought it for her. He might remember all the days they had spent together. He might even remember the other silken coat that he had slipped away from her body on a night that she would never forget.

Minutes later, Carolyn summoned one of the limousines that was available to her. She arrived at the studio fashionably, and deliberately, late. But as soon as she entered, she realized just how unfashionable she was going to be this afternoon.

There were perhaps three hundred people milling around the elegantly set snack tables, obscuring the long portable bar, balancing cocktail glasses, cigarettes and hors d'oeuvres plates as they stood around filling the huge, high-ceilinged area with the buzz of conversation. *Almost without exception, they were wearing T-shirts and jeans!*

Carolyn drew in a deep breath, wondering if she could slip away from the party unnoticed. Feeling that all eyes were focused upon her, she realized that this was a workday on the set and that cast and crew were wearing what they usually wore to rehearsals. Oh, they looked smart enough, their tight-fitting denims boasting expensive designer labels, their shirts a background for the ubiquitous solid gold chains. Nor had she ever seen more beautiful women or more striking men gathered under one roof. But the stunning cocktail dresses with which she had hoped to compete, the dark silk suits that were the hallmark of Japanese businessmen, were nowhere to be seen. She wished that she, and her eye-catching silk ensemble, could step into another dimension and disappear.

There was no escaping. Verne Damian, the director, spotted her immediately, and apologizing for his haste on her last visit to his set, insisted upon introducing her to a set designer and his wife. There were several dancers from the chorus, both male and female, who joined the circle, and Carolyn felt that although her clothing was eyed appreciatively, she might as well have arrived in the nude.

Her face burning with embarrassment, Carolyn looked around the cavernous hangarlike space for Brett. She saw him near the bar, towering over the casually clad group that surrounded him. He was smiling, of course, charm radiating from him, as always. And when some of the people moved aside to make room for a waiter carrying a cocktail tray, Carolyn saw that he was not the only object of attention. He was posing for a snapshot with his arm around an exquisite creature whose perfection of face and figure evoked visions of temple bells and lotus blossoms. Yet, she, too, was wearing a T-shirt and jeans that revealed her slim yet rounded figure.

That was the last straw. Carolyn had edged toward the door to make good her escape when she saw the director walking toward her, accompanied by none other than the svelte female star of his musical. A sudden panic came over her. Where was Brett? She looked beyond the approaching couple and saw that he was still the center of attraction far across the sound stage, still turned away from her. And in the next second Verne Damian was saying, "Sadi, dear, I want you to know Carolyn Chandler. Carolyn's a very important part of Brett's success. Carolyn, I know you've already recognized Sadi Hayashi."

The star, who in spite of her lithe figure conveyed the impression of voluptuousness, beamed a totally sincere smile. She held out her hand to shake Carolyn's with a warm squeeze. In barely accented English she said, "I have been anxious to meet you and compliment you on your beautiful taste."

Carolyn felt herself blushing. She wanted to say something to cover her embarrassment, but no words came.

Sadi was perfectly at ease, her black eyes twinkling for a moment and then turning serious. She leaned closer to Carolyn and said, "I must apologize for the way I look. I was late catching my plane from Matsuyama and there was no time, when I arrived here, to change into something more proper for the occasion." She made a disparaging motion. Her tiny hand tugged at a pale blue T-shirt on which, oddly, were imprinted the words "California City." Laughing a bell-like laugh, the actress added, "This advertises a disco owned by friends in my home city. Imagine that I am so rude as to wear it to a party given in my honor. These other people, they are working here today, so they can be excused. I cannot. And you . . ." She flashed a smile that had won the hearts of millions of Japanese fans. "You, Miss Chandler, are to be complimented. For your good taste. And for the honor you pay me."

It was impossible to dislike this vivacious, gracious woman. No bowing and scraping; she was direct and self-assured. Complimenting Sadi on her excellent English, Carolyn learned from the director that the star spoke five languages fluently. "That is because my parents were fond of seeing the world. When you travel, you must learn," Sadi said modestly.

Then, with her porcelain-doll face still reflecting her delight, her black bangs glistening under the harsh overhead lights, Sadi Hayashi touched Carolyn's coat lightly and said, "I must go, if you will excuse me. But please be so kind as to tell my wardrobe mistress where you found this lovely coat."

Brett was posing for amateur photographs now. It seemed that the entire grip crew and film-company staff of secretaries had arrived with garlands of cameras strung around their necks. He flashed his bright smile obligingly, posed with the tittering females, every inch the American celebrity.

It was unbearable. If Carolyn had needed an object lesson in feeling cut off from Brett's new life, it could not have been pounded home more convincingly than in these circumstances. She swallowed back her misery and headed for the door again.

Sadi Hayashi was posing beside Brett when Carolyn slipped out of the room.

She hated them all, Carolyn told herself during the endless cab ride to the hotel. *I hate all of them!* Sadi, for being so undeniably lovely; the adorable starlets and enthusiastic secretaries, for pressing their heads against Brett's chest as they posed with him; Brett, for having been too busy basking in flattery to even notice that she had come to the party. In the back of her consciousness, a voice accused Carolyn of only hating herself because she had made a stupid *faux pas,* because she was a nobody who had tried to mingle with the somebodies who peopled Brett's world, because against all good advice and her own common sense she had aspired to the love of a dazzlingly handsome superstar. But Carolyn's fury was sidetracked, directed at all the people who consumed Brett's time and interest. And now her unreasoning jealousy had a specific focus. Lovely, personable, unassuming, considerate! Sadi Hayashi was all of those things, but Carolyn hated her nonetheless.

Chapter Eleven

At her desk early the next morning, Carolyn was mapping out a schedule for preconcert television appearances in Hiroshima when the first telephone call came. It was from a woman who introduced herself as Billie Watanabe. The unusual combination of her first and last names led Carolyn to assume that she was probably an American married to a Japanese, but she soon found her guess was wrong.

"I'm Miss Hayashi's assistant," the voice said. "I was so anxious to meet you yesterday, but you must have left about the time Sadi asked me to talk with you. You see, I was told by Mr. Wells that you studied fashion designing in San Francisco. That's where I grew up."

It became a friendly chat, in which Carolyn also learned the origin of Billie's unique name. "I was born in Fresno, actually, where my uncle had a farm. I was named after an American neighbor who taught my parents English in a night school. My parents have since returned to Tokyo—they own a fabric store here now."

They talked about California for a few minutes before Billie remembered the reason for her call. "I am in charge of Sadi Hayashi's wardrobe. And she was so taken by that beautiful jumpsuit and coat you wore yesterday. Would it be rude to ask where you bought it? There wouldn't be two exactly alike, since each *boumake* is individually dyed."

Carolyn felt a small measure of pride in telling Billie that the purchase had been made by Brett Wells. "It was a gift. And I can't remember the name of the shop, but it's on the box and I still have it in my room. Could I call you back?"

Calling back was not necessary. From Carolyn's description, Billie recognized the smart little boutique. "It's only a block from my parent's store." In the next breath Billie was inviting Carolyn to drop by the fabric shop the next time she was in Harajuku. "I'm usually there helping my parents on Sundays. Is that your day off, too? I'm sure it is. Please come. We'll have tea in the back room and you can tell me all about San Francisco."

It had been good to talk to Billie Watanabe, Carolyn thought when she dropped the receiver into its cradle. Making new friends would ease her heartache and sudden homesickness. She would have to savor the memories of her time with Brett as the once-in-a-lifetime dream-come-true that it was. And forget him, forget him, forget that he had held her in his arms and made her a woman.

It was jarring to be thinking about Brett just as he came bounding into the office. Carolyn's breath caught in her lungs. Her hands shook as she pretended to be busy with the calendar before her. Their good-mornings were exaggeratedly polite and unnatural.

"Came to check my mail," Brett said hurriedly. "The desk clerk said everything was here in the office."

"There's a stack of fan letters," Carolyn said. "And something from Ken Macklin addressed to you, but I think it's some copies of contracts Gavin's been expecting."

Brett placed a brown-paper-wrapped package on the end of the desk and started thumbing through a pile of mail. Barely glancing at the return addresses, he tossed the letters back on the desk. "Not what I'm looking for," he said. Carolyn had the distinct impression that he wasn't looking for anything in particular at all, though she might have been wrong.

"I'm late," he said tersely. "Verne put out a six-A.M. call for this morning and then changed his mind. Some problem with Sadi's wardrobe. But we're supposed to start shooting at eleven."

"Are you enjoying it?" Carolyn asked, still looking at the schedule she had been scribbling. Looking up at Brett would have been devastating, considering her mood.

"It's a living," he said noncommittally. There was a brief silence. "I hear you were at the studio yesterday. You didn't even swing by to say hello."

"You were busy," Carolyn said. "And since you hadn't invited me, I didn't see any reason to take up your time."

"I didn't invite you," Brett replied exasperatedly, "because it wasn't my party. You ought to know that. I thought it was going to be a ten-minute break to welcome Sadi and then back to work." Brett's tone softened, but he sounded guarded. "Did you enjoy yourself?"

"I managed to . . ." Carolyn cut herself short. He didn't have to be told that she had managed to make a fool of herself. "I managed to meet a few people," she said.

"Good. You're getting around on your own." Another pause and then Brett said in a testy voice, "Dates with musicians, invitations to jet-set parties . . . you're really getting into the swing of things while I work my tail off."

He remembered seeing her in the coffee shop with Rusty Johnson! Did she dare hope that there was a hint of jealousy in Brett's tone? No. A second later he was saying, "I'm glad you've realized I have work to do."

"And that you're not a tour guide?" Carolyn threw the words at him with a sarcastic intonation. "I'm not sitting around and waiting for you to come down to my level."

"What kind of snide talk is that?" Brett leaned over her shoulder to pick up the calendar-schedule and shake it vigorously before he slammed it back to the desk. For an instant their bodies touched, and the scent of a cologne she remembered all too well made Carolyn want to turn and throw her arms around him. She restrained herself, of course. Groupies responded to Brett's nearness that way. She still had a shred of pride left in her.

"You, of all people, should know," he ranted. "I can't see to your social life. You're the one who piles more and more appointments on me. Why can't you—?"

"It's my job to make appointments for you," Carolyn snapped. "And don't worry about my social life again, please."

"No, you seem to be doing fine without my help," Brett countered.

The ringing of the phone prevented any reply. A few moments later, having recognized the voice on the long-distance line, Carolyn perversely handed the instrument to Brett. "It's for you," she said.

He was standing next to the desk and glaring at her,

his handsome features ravaged by fury as he said into the mouthpiece, "I'm sorry. I've asked you to please stop calling. . . . Lisa, I'm a busy man and I don't want to hear any more damned hysterics. . . . No. . . . No, I don't Get hold of yourself and recognize it for what it was. . . . No. No, I *don't!* I'm going to hang up now. And I hope you get some help, Lisa. I think you have a serious problem."

Brett slammed the receiver down. "Why did you do that? You were told I didn't want any calls from her!"

"It just seemed the humane thing to do," Carolyn said, avoiding the dark blaze of Brett's eyes. "I feel sorry for Miss Westerbrook. And I didn't want to lie to her with you standing right here."

"She's a neurotic pest," Brett shouted. He had started a systematic pacing of the office. "I have enough pressure on me now without having to play shrink to her! Doesn't the woman have any pride?"

Carolyn fought back the urge to tell him that she understood why the British socialite had lost control of her pride. There had undoubtedly been a night when Brett had undressed her, caressed her body, called her beautiful and demonstrated his skill as a lover. *I can sympathize,* Carolyn thought.

Brett perched on the edge of the desk, his leg brushing Carolyn's for an electric half-second. "Trouble with women like that," he said, "is that they get all hung up on a man because they don't have anything of their own going for them. That isn't love. They could replace these make-believe romances with a new puppy, anything that would wag its tail and show them some attention. They create an illusion around a man they barely know and then they want to *own* him. I try to be kind, but that woman's been nothing but a thorn in my side."

Carolyn kept her lips pressed tightly together. It

would only make matters worse to tell him she felt used and discarded. He was right—she didn't have anything of her own going for her.

Worse than his tirade about the foolish women who fell in love with him was his respect for the new female in his life. He was talking about Sadi Hayashi. "She has so many interests. She's been just about everywhere in the world . . . a linguist . . . fascinating hobbies. All that, and she's a real pro, intensely devoted to studying and rehearsing her scenes. A perfectionist. I can respect that. Besides, she's unbelievably beautiful."

Carolyn wondered how much more she could listen to without bursting into tears and running out of the room. She forced herself to tell Brett, in what she hoped was a calm, businesslike manner, some of the promotional ideas that would publicize his concert in Hiroshima the following week. He didn't seem interested. "That's your department and Gavin's," he said. "Hiroshima's going to be a costly interruption in the shooting. Verne's having to make up time, and he's got us on a back-breaking schedule."

Brett remembered that he was due for costume fittings before the day's filming began at eleven. He was on his way out of the office when Carolyn called to remind him, "You forgot your package."

Brett turned. "Oh, that's a little something for your folks. After dinner last night we stopped in a bookstore to pick up some language books we need. Among other things, Sadi's an expert gardener. When I told her your mom and dad own a nursery, she said they'd probably like this book."

Brett waved, said, "See you later," and was gone, leaving Carolyn with only the flimsy comfort of knowing that he had talked about her to his highly praised co-star, not once, but twice. Billie Watanabe had revealed that much. Carolyn unwrapped the package to find a beautifully illustrated coffee-table book titled

The Flowering Trees of Japan. The text, printed in both English and Japanese, was filled with beautiful color plates of blossoming trees. It was an expensive gift that would be treasured by her parents.

At least, for a little while, between dinner and whatever other pleasures he had shared with Sadi Hayashi, Brett had remembered the people who used to live next door. He seemed, however, to have forgotten their daughter.

Chapter Twelve

Carolyn arrived in Hiroshima alone; Gavin had gone on ahead more than a week before, leaving her in charge of the Tokyo operations. But once she'd rejoined him in Hiroshima, it appeared there was little work to do. The mammoth baseball stadium where Brett was to perform had been sold out almost from the day tickets became available. "Of course, a little extra promotion would be good for record sales," Gavin said soon after her arrival, "but I don't want to put any more pressure on him. He's driving himself hard enough as it is."

Later that day, over cocktails and dinner at the Hiroshima Grand Hotel, he repeated his concern for Brett. "Have you talked with him much lately?" He waited for Carolyn to shake her head and admit that she had barely seen Brett in days. "He's edgy as hell. I tried to talk him out of using that new 'mistress' number in the concert here and he just about bit my head off."

Gavin had not been exaggerating when he said Brett was driving himself. Carolyn was shocked by the lines of exhaustion around Brett's eyes when he and the entire concert crew arrived. He seemed distracted, as though his mind were elsewhere when people talked to him, and his customary demands for perfection put a strain on everyone during the preconcert rehearsal. He didn't indulge in any temperamental explosions, but he was quick to snap at his musicians and technicians, offering apologies later that revealed a tired nervousness untypical of him.

But on the night of the concert, Brett was the poised, confident star once again when he stepped into the spotlight and acknowledged the cheers and applause of his audience. Carolyn responded, as she always did when she heard him sing, as though she were just another of his adoring fans. Yet she knew that there was a difference between her and every other young woman attending that gala concert under the stars. They all loved him. But one night he had loved *her*. One night, he had belonged only to her, and she had been a physical part of him.

Did Gavin notice when she closed her eyes, transported into her own romantic dream world while Brett sang:

> Do you think, now the night is dark
> That a star never shone?
> Must I dream, now you're gone,
> That the light will return
> And again you'll be mine alone? . . .

Rusty emphasized the question with a pounding beat. The screaming response was overwhelming.

"He's got them in the palm of his hand," Gavin said,

professionally unromantic. "Every woman in the audience *knows* he's singing to her. And every man seems to identify with him—thinking he's up on that stage. He doesn't hold anything back. Puts his heart into every number!"

As the evening wore on, Gavin's face was creased by an almost constant grin. "They're hot tonight! I'd love to own a percentage of every record store in town tomorrow morning."

By the time he began his new rock number, Brett had the audience in his pocket. He held the microphone as though it were a scepter as he launched into his new song, lamenting the exhausting nights in strange towns, the meaningless encounters with unknown women, the need for one solid human relationship, the sameness of planes and trains and sterile hotel rooms. And then came the final renunciation of human love. It was a rejection of Carolyn, his fans, *all* women.

Brett sang with a passion and sincerity that topped any of his previous efforts. His band could not have backed him with more conviction. And when the last words were sung, half-whispered, and then driven home with a thundering beat from Rusty, when Brett had told his audience that "Music is my mistress, only one I'll ever know," he lowered the microphone and then his head, waiting for the wild applause.

There was applause. Brett at his worst was always a polished performer. But there was no tumultuous ovation. The fans had rocked along with the beat, but the words had not communicated themselves. The rapport he established when he sang of familiar themes, of love, of rejection, of heartbreak, was missing. It was a song comprehensible in its full meaning only to artists who had shared the experience of "paying dues." And although the young people in the stadium applauded dutifully, the wildly enthusiastic reception Brett had counted on did not materialize.

Something was missing. It was as if his audience was telling Brett: "All right, that was a good number to dance to, but we can't dance here, so sing us something we can *understand.*"

Gavin, more attuned to audience reaction than Carolyn, was shaking his head. "I was afraid of this, I was afraid of this. I just hope he isn't too demoralized."

It must have taken great courage to go on to his next number. Brett finished the concert to rousing applause but he was obviously not himself. "It was downhill from that big disappointment," Gavin moaned afterward. "He'll be a wreck for days."

The band, light crew, soundmen, as well as Gavin and Carolyn, felt Brett's hurt almost as keenly as he did. And when they congregated in the hotel cocktail lounge, chief lighting engineer Steve Herman said, "Hey, Brett, I've been around a long time and you were never better."

Brett faced him squarely and said, "I've never been worse." He seemed to be working hard at covering up his great disappointment, even making jokes to keep up the company's morale, but anyone who knew Brett at all realized that he was crushed. They took turns analyzing the concert, its high and low points. All except Carolyn. She sipped a glass of Chablis silently while it was decided that no one felt up to the usual after-concert celebration. Gradually they all drifted out of the lounge until only she and Brett remained.

Then he came to where she was sitting and whispered in her ear, "Let's get out of here."

She should have resented his sudden turnabout, the command performance following a long period of neglect. Maybe she *did* resent it just a little. But wasn't this what she had been praying for? An opportunity to be with Brett, to have him need her company?

Everyone else had blamed the audience, the acoustics, the sound system, everything but the fact that

Brett had made a mistake and had let it throw off the last portion of his concert. Carolyn took another, more realistic tack. In the taxi, on their way to what had been recommended as the liveliest nightclub in town, she decided to confront Brett with the truth. "Why can't you accept the fact that you're not infallible, Brett?"

"Infallible? I've admitted I was lousy tonight."

"But you weren't! You're good and you know you're good. But you're not a god, Brett. You misjudged your audience with one damned number, and I think your ego's strong enough to survive it." Carolyn paused to catch her breath. The last thing Brett needed now was a long lecture. Still, she added, "You don't have to bring down the house *every* time you open your mouth."

She expected either a blowup or another reminder that when a star was at the top there was only one way to go and that was down. Brett might have repeated the old show-business cliché that a star was only as good as his or her last performance. But he didn't do or say any of those things. He reached over for Carolyn's hand and said in a low voice, "Thank you for being honest with me, Carolyn. You're right, you know. I don't have to be perfect." In the dim light from the streetlamps, the back of the careening taxi was an intimate hideaway that shut out everyone else in the world. Brett's face shone with something like anticipation. "It's more fun to be human," he said. "Human, and not alone."

They did not stay long at the enormous, smoke-filled, noisy Palace Nightclub. Only long enough for the elaborately dressed *mama-san* to persuade the surprise celebrity to sing two numbers with the band.

Brett established keys with the bandleader and sang one standard from the fifties and one tune from his first album. The enthusiastic response from the jam-packed audience must have been music to his ears. Dominating the small stage, tiredness erased from his movie-idol face, Brett was in full possession of himself and he had never looked or sounded better. Nor had he ever exuded such an aura of confidence. He owned the club and everyone in it.

At the close of his first song, a ballad that was familiar to everyone present, he winked at Carolyn. From the stageside table to which they had been ceremoniously escorted, Carolyn winked back. And when he rejoined her, with applause still reverberating through the room, he whispered facetiously, "Who says I'm not a god?"

They stayed only long enough to finish one round of drinks and to show polite attention to an attractive Japanese torch singer. Brett's applause was stronger than the young woman's talent.

Somehow, this night was not one for doubts or questions. When they reached Carolyn's hotel room, Brett's need for her, and Carolyn's need for him, had been tacitly agreed upon. Her heart was doing flip-flops as the door was locked behind them. Brett might forget about her again tomorrow, but she wouldn't think about that now. Tomorrow was tomorrow. Tonight he belonged to her.

They were in each other's arms almost instantly, pulled together by an irresistible magnetic force. Brett's kisses were hungry tonight, and he murmured, "I've been parched for you, Carolyn. Why do you make it so difficult for me?"

Difficult for *him?* Carolyn didn't understand the words, nor did she ask for an explanation. It was enough that Brett was holding her closer, ever closer, imprinting the hardness of his body against hers, moving so that no contact would be missed in his strong embrace.

A while later, it seemed that they reversed the roles that had been set the first time they had made love. Brett was exhausted, but not too tired for desire. He undressed first, stretching out on the blue-flowered sofa, his arms folded behind his head as he watched Carolyn slip out of her clothing. She felt strangely unselfconscious with his eyes fixed upon her. There was a delicious excitement in revealing her body to him, in having him admire her with his eyes and then, when she knelt down on the carpeted floor beside him, with his hands, his darting tongue, his lips.

They were both as comfortable as if they had been together this way all of their lives. And because Brett was in a relaxed mood, seeming to float with the soft string music Carolyn had turned on before she came to him, there was no hurry this time. "Be good to me," he said softly. Then he was lying back against a pillow, his eyes half-closed, letting Carolyn discover for herself that she was capable of being the aggressor. She learned then that despite her inexperience, she knew instinctively what to do to bring him pleasure.

"Carolyn . . . oh, Carolyn!"

His moaning words inspired her to be more daring, to discover the ecstasy her fingertips could produce with the most delicate caress. She had lost her inhibitions somewhere along the way. Brett's reactions were like the applause to which he himself responded when he was performing. "Don't stop. Carolyn . . . honey, don't stop." Her imagination and Brett's encouragement had helped her cross a barrier of shyness, so that she was not shocked when Brett said quietly, "Make love to *me* tonight, darling. Let me teach you how."

It was like the slow but moving symphony that poured from the stereo speakers, sweet and beautiful, a union as perfectly orchestrated as the emotion-stirring sounds to which this dance of love was performed. There was even the rumble of drums, like thunder in her heart, when the music reached its climax and Brett clasped her tightly against him, their bodies shuddering as one in the most exquisite crescendo ever dreamed of by the music's composer.

She was breathless when she cried out, "Brett. Oh, *Brett!*"

Carolyn lay against him for a long time, his arms enfolding her. And when they finally found the cramped sofa too uncomfortable, Carolyn got up silently, leaving a slow, lingering kiss on his lips.

He rested, eyes blissfully closed, while Carolyn made her way to the bathroom. She had expected him to fall asleep, but she was not too surprised when Brett came into the steaming bathroom. She was rinsing herself off in the sunken tile tub, which she had filled with hot water and a handful of crystals from her toiletry case.

"You have the best ideas," Brett said. "Soak away the day's aggravations while you think about the night's miracles. All right if I join you?"

Carolyn's hand patted the billow of pale pink bubbles. "You're my guest. It wouldn't be polite to say no."

They laughed and held each other in the oversized tub, reveling in the luxury of their surroundings. The water was tepid and the bubbles had all but disappeared before they got out of the tub, dried each other off with fluffy towels and returned to the bedroom.

"Are you sleepy?" she asked him. "You must be. You gave so much of yourself tonight."

Brett smiled. "You were the one who truly gave of yourself."

Carolyn felt a rush of warmth to her face. "You're going to embarrass me."

"Carolyn?" He had walked over to hug her gently. "Don't ever be embarrassed or ashamed of making someone as happy as you made me tonight."

"Someone?" Carolyn felt her body grow rigid. "Someone? Do you think I could have . . . that it would have been the same with just . . . anyone?"

"Unfortunate misuse of the language," Brett said in a surprisingly solemn voice. "Me. Me, Carolyn."

She nodded vaguely and moved away from him. "You probably want to get dressed so you can go to your room and get some sleep."

"It's funny the way people claim a hot bath makes you sleepy. It's had just the opposite effect on me. I could do with some coffee. You?"

"Well, I . . ."

Brett was at the telephone. "They probably won't have anything to eat at this hour, but we can try. Cross your fingers that I can make myself understood."

Brett not only made himself understood but also managed to have the kitchen opened and a tray of tiny sandwiches brought up so quickly that they barely had time to make themselves presentable before there was a knock on the door. "My celebrity status," Brett joked. "We're going to get out of these stupid clothes as soon as I've taken care of this young man. And we're going to have a picnic. But this time we won't spoil it with petty squabbling."

They ate ravenously, sitting cross-legged on the carpet, talking and laughing quietly. How strange he was, Carolyn thought. When they were together like this, it was as if no one else in the world existed. Yet she knew that there was another Brett Wells whose circle she could never enter, a Brett Wells who didn't make her laugh with playful games; a Brett Wells who could reduce her to painful tears.

When the coffee had grown cold, Carolyn repeated her suggestion that Brett go to his own room. "You only think you're not bushed. You'll be alseep the minute you hit the pillow."

"No chance," he argued.

"Well, you can't stay here all night. Gavin will be up early and—"

"To hell with Gavin," Brett said firmly. "If you're worried about what he'll think, if you really *want* me to leave, I'll go." He looked at her intently. "But I don't want to go, Carolyn."

She held his meaningful gaze for as long as she could. And then she whispered, "I don't want you to go."

"We'll talk for a while," Brett told her. "Prop ourselves up in a decent bed and talk for a while."

"Watch television?" Carolyn meant it as a mischievous joke.

"Sure, why not? Snuggle up and watch television." He drained the last of his coffee, made a wry face and said, "It's cold." Then, as brightly as if he had just gotten up from a long, sound sleep, Brett said, "There's bound to be an old movie on. When we get bored with not knowing what's being said, we'll shut it off. And this time, it'll be my turn."

It took Carolyn a split second to understand what he meant by "my turn." Somehow, the old samurai movie lost its appeal long before the sun came up. And Brett's turn made it a night, Carolyn thought, that she would never forget.

Chapter Thirteen

Carolyn could not accuse Brett of neglect during the weeks that followed. Whenever he could spare the time, they had breakfast or dinner together. He checked in at the office between his time at the film studio and nightly rehearsals with his band or sessions with Tony Hanniman. Wardrobe fittings, interviews arranged by Carolyn and business meetings with Gavin took up his hours away from the movie set. Nights, he closed himself in his suite to study his lines for the next day's shooting. Brett was on a killing schedule.

Yet he never failed to remember Carolyn with small reminders of his affection for her: flowers for her desk, a celadon tea set to take home with her, a slim volume of *haiku* poetry. And there were nights when her telephone rang while she was lying awake in her bed hoping for just such a call; nights when he said, "I'm too wired up to sleep," or, "The script is beginning to blur before my eyes," and Carolyn would invite Brett to walk the short distance that separated them from each other.

Always, in the sweet rapture of their lovemaking, Carolyn waited for three words that would make her feel that she really meant something to him. His kisses said, "I love you," but the words never came from Brett's lips.

Carolyn decided that was not enough one afternoon when she and Gavin visited the sound stage in Akasaka. Verne Damian was directing Brett and Sadi Hayashi in a love scene. The chaise longue on which they embraced was reminiscent of the cramped sofa in the Hiroshima hotel room, and as she watched Brett's smooth, totally believable acting, Carolyn recognized every mannerism, every expression on his sensitive face.

Between takes, Gavin nodded his approval. "Brett never ceases to amaze me. He's a fantastic actor."

But Carolyn saw the scene from another perspective. The electricity that crackled between Brett and the beautiful Japanese star had everyone on the set entranced. It was too painful to watch, and Carolyn stayed away from the set after that. She also found herself turning Brett down the next time he wanted to invite himself to her room for another middle-of-the night tryst. Brett did not take the refusal lightly, becoming still more angry when she would give him no explanation for her action.

She had cause to regret her aloofness, however, when Brett began to spend almost all his free time with Sadi Hayashi, even meeting with her on Sundays, ostensibly to work on their lines. Carolyn's emotional agony began to take its toll on her sleep and on her work.

Once, after she had flared out at him over some

minor misunderstanding, Gavin gave her a long, sad look and said, "You weren't going to get hung up, remember?"

"I don't know what you're talking about!" Carolyn lied. But she knew that her nights with Brett could not have escaped Gavin's attention. And he must know that Brett's free hours were now spent in more dazzling company. Gavin was feeling sorry for her. Carolyn turned their discussion back to the mistake she had made in dating a press release, and later said with an airiness she did not feel, "I've got to write to my folks and to David. They worry when they don't hear from me often enough."

She must remember to mention David more often, Carolyn thought miserably. Brett's manager was beginning to view her as he viewed Lisa Westerbrook and the countless women whose adoring letters to Brett filled a cardboard box on her desk. If she had, indeed, joined their ranks, her pride would not tolerate Gavin's knowing it.

Carolyn decided to spend the next day catching up with requests for Brett's photograph. It was a task that was normally handled by a staff of clerks in the Macklin-Durham offices back home. Here, the requests were only from local fans, but they had accumulated during the past few weeks. With a supply of eight-by-ten glossies and a stack of manila envelopes, Carolyn tackled the job.

Gavin had flown to Matsuyama that morning on business. Brett would be at the studio all day; there was no possibility that he would stop by. Dressed carelessly in the oldest and least flattering pantsuit she had brought with her, her makeup worn off by noon, Carolyn thought about how ironic it was that she felt the need to look her best only when Brett would be likely to see her. She turned the photographs over so that she would not be looking at him while she slid them into the envelopes she had spent several hours addressing. At a quarter past one she decided to venture to the lobby to check on the day's mail.

She was stepping out of the elevator when she saw the crowd of tourists, some apparently American, but mostly Japanese. They had formed a semicircle and were busy clicking away with their cameras. A second glance revealed the subjects of their interest. Brett looked like the smiling, resplendent idol he was, and by his side stood Sadi Hayashi, immaculately groomed and dressed in a clinging white sheath dress that had Oriental overtones but had undoubtedly come from the atelier of some noted Parisian designer.

Carolyn stopped in her tracks, her breath suspended. Then she took several steps backward into the elevator cage, grateful that she had not been seen. What was Brett doing at the hotel at this hour? It didn't matter. What mattered was this terrible hurt, this knowledge that whenever she saw him in his element she felt excluded. Her racking jealousy extended far beyond the gorgeous star with whom Brett had been posing so familiarly. It encompassed his success itself—Brett's popularity, his physical impact upon all women, the democratic way in which he shared himself with everyone who admired him. Yes, he had enjoyed a few physical interludes with Carolyn. He called her his friend. But it was not enough. It would never be enough.

Carolyn, nevertheless, stopped at her suite to do what could be done to improve her appearance. Just in case, she told herself. An hour later, savagely ramming Brett's photographs into the brown envelopes, she felt ready to explode. Brett had undoubtedly had lunch with his co-star and returned to the studio without bothering to stop by the office. Why would he? Why should he? With Gavin out of town, there was no reason for Brett to drop in.

She was wrong. Another half-hour or so later, Brett walked through the doorway. He was alone. And he could not have missed seeing Carolyn's furious motion as she slammed one of the envelopes down on her desk. He had materialized like an apparition, catching her off guard.

"Carolyn. Hi. What's wrong?"

Her nerves threatened to snap like frayed violin strings. "Nothing. I'm . . . just . . . doing a little busy-work."

"You look as though you're mad at the world." Brett had stationed himself on the opposite side of her desk. Carolyn didn't look up, but Brett's voice told her that she was being studied with a concerned look. "Are you sure nothing's wrong?"

"No, there is nothing wrong!" She wished the denial had sounded less shrill. "I'm just doing routine work and starting to get a little bored with it."

"Oh. Well, in that case, why don't you knock off for the afternoon? Go somewhere, do something."

Carolyn glanced upward to give him a glance that said, "Like what?" What she actually said was, "I work here, remember? Maybe you don't appreciate all that Gavin and I do, but you didn't get your picture on two Japanese magazines this month because I was out sightseeing."

"I'm very well aware of how much you've done," Brett said quietly. "But maybe it's not how *much* work you've been doing but the dull nature of it. You're a talented, creative person. It kills me to see you sitting here stuffing envelopes. We can hire a schoolgirl to do that. Maybe you haven't been getting out enough. I wish I could squire you around, but you know I can't. Still, there's no reason why you can't get out and do something productive with your free time. Pick up the phone. You have a limo to take you anywhere you want to go. Come down to the studio. Maybe there'll be some time for us to talk between takes. Or . . . or . . ." Brett had started his pacing of the office again, a typical reaction to something that irritated him. "Go to a ceramics class, take a language course. Stop being a flunky, sitting here feeling sorry for yourself!"

She was fighting back those aggravating tears again! "I'm not feeling sorry for myself!"

"Then why are you so edgy?"

"Why are *you* so edgy?" Carolyn threw back at him.

"Because I . . ." Brett stopped his pacing across the room. "Carolyn, maybe it's because we . . ."

His hand touched her shoulder and Carolyn made a violent jerking motion to free herself of the contact. It was a reflex action that she regretted immediately, but Brett didn't wait for her to tell him she was sorry. Or that, more than anything else in the world, she wanted him to touch her, to hold her, to *love* her.

"Maybe," he said in a chilling tone, "it just *may* be that you're frustrated. Missing your boyfriend back home."

"Maybe." Carolyn got up from her chair and walked to the filing cabinet, pretending to search for some elusive piece of paper. With her back turned to him, Brett wouldn't see that she could not hold back her tears any longer.

After a short silence Brett muttered gruffly, "The desk clerk handed me a bunch of mail. Everything is addressed care of the production company. I think there's some personal stuff for you." Carolyn knew he was at the door when he said, "I thought, since I have some unexpected time free, that we could have lunch, but I can see that's out."

"I'd only be in the way," Carolyn said. "Don't you have someone waiting for you downstairs?"

"Waiting for me? No. Sadi shared a limo with me this far, and then we got roped into posing in the lobby for some tourists from Osaka. Just happened to be members of her fan club, so she couldn't refuse. But she was in a hurry to visit someone at a hospital nearby." Brett's reasonable tone changed abruptly. "Why the hell am I explaining to you? We don't have a contract! I just thought I'd invite a friend to lunch, and I get all this . . . all this . . ." Brett didn't bother to find the right words for his disgust. "I'll see you," he said. And then Carolyn heard the door close.

She needed to cry, but now that she was alone, she couldn't. Carolyn crossed the room to the refectory table near the door. Brett had left a large pile of mail there. She might as well process his fan letters while she was at it, instead of letting the photo requests accumulate again.

There were several personal letters for her on top of the stack—one from Jennie, another addressed in her mother's curlicued hand. Next to them was a picture postcard showing the framework of some sort of heavy machinery with what Carolyn soon determined were the Northern Lights in the background. She turned the card over to read: "Hello, Cousin Carolyn. Sure am surprised to hear from you after all these years. Thanks for all the hotel circulars. Here's a picture of where I am." The message, printed in large letters with a black felt pen, was signed "Your long-lost Cousin David."

Carolyn felt a wave of nausea. Brett wasn't likely to read someone else's mail, but the printed message on the card could not have escaped his attention as he carried it up in the elevator. If he *had* glanced at it, the signature alone would have told him that the sender was no pining lover. Then she had a vague memory of David and his parents visiting in Escondido once, when David was about nine. He was a spoiled child, and Carolyn had wondered why her mother insisted that he be taken along to a softball game they were all planning to attend. Brett would have remembered that; he'd complained about it for days afterward. My God,

Carolyn thought, he's probably known all along that I was lying. Maybe he's told Gavin, too. She wanted to die of shame.

She tried to console herself by reading the letters from home, but the incriminating card sat on her desk, filling her with guilt and embarrassment and regret. After a while, she tore it up and tossed it into the wastebasket next to her desk. The angry action helped to release a little of the searing emotion that raged inside her. She heard herself cry out aloud, *"Damn him!"*

Was she damning her boorish cousin for exposing her lie? David could not be blamed for being puzzled by correspondence from her. Brett, then. Yes, Brett, for having made her love him, for letting her know that he might rouse her to uncontrollable passion, might laugh with her, reminisce with her, lavish gifts upon her and call her his friend. But he would never love her the way she wanted him to love her.

Before she left the office suite, Carolyn ripped to shreds a dozen or more of Brett's theatrical photos, leaving the pieces behind her.

Chapter Fourteen

Carolyn awoke from a fitful sleep which had calmed her anger with herself. *Herself.* Before she had finally dozed off the night before, she had realized that all of her misery could be laid squarely on her own doorstep: the foolish lie about a man in Anchorage who loved her, the jealousy she had displayed before Brett, the very stupidity of having hoped that coming here would somehow make a romantic childhood dream a reality.

She had gotten over her explosive fury, but it had been replaced by a dull leaden feeling that was not dispelled by a cold shower or fresh makeup or an attempt to rearrange her unruly hair. Carolyn was not even cheered by the sleek fit of a new teal-blue dress that she had bought specifically for this trip. Would having her hair done help her morale? She was thinking about making an appointment when she stepped into the coffee shop and saw Gavin sitting alone at his customary table.

When Carolyn greeted him, he smiled and said, "Good morning. You're looking surprisingly well, considering."

He had gestured for her to join him, and Carolyn sat down opposite Gavin at the table. "Considering what?"

"I saw the shredded photos." Gavin stirred his coffee. "Good for you. I usually throw ashtrays. Sometimes, if you own one, it helps to kick the cat."

Carolyn knew that her face matched her lipstick as she apologized. "I didn't mean to leave the evidence, Gavin. You don't miss a thing, do you? If I had known you were coming back so soon . . ."

"Matsuyama's only six hundred and fifty kilometers from here. And we *are* in the jet age." After a swallow of coffee, Gavin said, "I got back last night. Brett wasn't around. Neither were you."

"I was in my room," Carolyn said. *"Alone."*

"I wasn't sure, so I didn't disturb you. And it didn't take a psychologist or a detective to tell me why you'd converted all those pictures of Brett into confetti. I've felt it coming, Carolyn. It's a familiar pattern."

"You don't have to worry about me, Gavin. I had a few . . . good times with Brett, sure. And yesterday he made me mad as hell. It was over a trivial thing, not worth discussing. But I've known him a lot longer than you have and, believe me, I don't place Brett on a pedestal. He's just a friend."

Gavin seemed to believe her. In another moment he would be congratulating her on her loyalty to David. Carolyn was sure that he hadn't pieced together the card she had left in the wastebasket; she couldn't imagine Gavin doing something like that. But she was sick to death of all the subterfuge, all the fake letters to

Anchorage and the contrived references to how much she missed her boyfriend. Between the time that she placed her order and the time her chilled melon balls, French toast and coffee arrived, Carolyn had told Gavin the truth. All of it, except, of course, that she was in love with Brett and probably always would be.

Gavin was facing her with a melancholy smile when Carolyn finished her confession. "You went through all that malarkey just so I'd hire you?"

"It was a great opportunity," Carolyn said. "I didn't know how else I could convince you I wasn't going to fall in love with Brett and create a lot of uncomfortable scenes."

"And anyway, it was Jennie's idea," Gavin recalled. "You just went along with it. Why'd you decide to confess now?"

"Because I hate lying to you," Carolyn told him. "I respect you and I like working with you. You've been a friend. Like a brother to me. And it feels good to have you know the truth."

"Well. Win a few, lose a few." Gavin sighed.

"I don't understand."

"For a minute there, with Brett out of the way, and David turning out to be just a cousin, I thought I might make my bid. But that 'brother' business put me back on square one." Gavin shrugged his shoulders. "It was a very brief hope, Carolyn. But don't worry. I'm not going to make you uncomfortable with any declarations of love. Part of my policy—don't indulge in emotional involvements on tour. My assistant's *or* mine."

Gavin didn't have to elaborate on that subject, either. Carolyn had suspected for a long time that Gavin was fonder of her than she wanted him to be. He was free to tell her so. But he must have known that she could offer him nothing but friendship, and he had saved her the awkwardness of having to spell it out.

It was strange, though, that Gavin seemed to have no other romantic interests. Jennie had told Carolyn only a little about the man; he had suffered through a traumatic divorce some eight or nine years before. Ken Macklin had seen him through that rough time, and ever since then, apparently, Gavin had devoted himself almost exclusively to his work. But his lack of female companionship seemed odd, and Carolyn dared to mention the fact. "You're a very interesting man," she said. "And you're an important man, too, in a field where . . ."

"Where I could promise aspiring young singers their big break?"

"I didn't mean that, Gavin. You have a lot more to offer than . . . than that old casting-couch attraction."

Gavin signaled a waiter, indicating that he wanted a refill of his coffee. "Maybe," he said wearily, "maybe I've been waiting for the same thing Brett seems to want."

Just the mention of that name always stopped Carolyn's heartbeat for a moment. "What does he want?"

"Someone who loves him 'as is.' Not because he's a big star, because he's damned good-looking or because he can move them into that glittering world they've only read about. For himself. For who he is, not what he is." Gavin had gotten more sentimental and philosophical than ever before, and apparently he decided that the role did not suit him. He laughed shortly and said in his more typical, Hollywood-smart way, "Understand, I'm not making a comparison. Not with this face and my voice . . . you ought to hear me sing 'Danny Boy' in the shower! But I suppose I'd be very appealing to some young hopeful who thinks I'm an open sesame to success as a rock star." Gavin leaned forward. "I've had those opportunities, Carolyn. Girls with stars in their eyes, usually with about as much singing talent as I myself could muster. And even a few who had what it takes. But I've never . . . It wouldn't *occur* to me. Believe that?"

Carolyn nodded. "I believe that, Gavin."

"Hell, Brett's young. He can wait for that honest-to-God kind of love we incurable romantics all want. Brett, you, me. Maybe every single person in the world. But it's time I got realistic. When you get as close to forty as I am, you start losing a few delusions. And I'm not complaining. I love what I do for a living, love the process of taking a raw talent and developing it to . . ."

"To where Brett is now," Carolyn finished for him. "He owes you a lot. And I know he's grateful."

"A lot less than I owe him," Gavin said. "He's a one of a kind, Carolyn. A great performer and a terrific human being. He'd never let you know it, but he worries over what he does to women. The Westerbrook woman is a case in point. She's been calling him off and on for a year, sometimes even threatening to commit suicide in front of the stage he's working on at the time. He's told me he doesn't know what to do. If he's decent to her, which he'd like to be, she'll take that as encouragement and it'll only prolong the agony. If he tells her to leave him alone, he feels guilty afterward, afraid she might carry out some of her threats." Gavin made a disparaging sound. "Sorry. I didn't mean to get into all that. I was just trying to explain the one thing Brett and I have in common. Wanting that old 'they fell in love, got married and lived happily ever after' illusion that isn't too likely in our business."

"Brett's said he wants that?"

It was a mistake to sound so interested, so eager. Gavin was looking at her with a doleful, knowing expression. "Sure. He talks to me the way you've been talking to me this morning. Like I was his brother. We've talked about love a lot of times." His eyes were looking directly into Carolyn's when he added, "Every time your name comes up in the conversation."

"*My* name . . . ?"

"But don't get your hopes up, little girl. That song he wrote—that 'mistress' number that he sang in Hiroshima—wasn't just an idle lyric. Music *is* what counts in his life. Keep remembering that and you won't get hurt."

For the rest of the time they spent at the breakfast table, they talked about less personal and less painful subjects, as though they had both exposed too much of themselves and wanted to stay clear of the subject of Brett Wells. "They have something here called controlled-temperature farming," Gavin said, nodding toward Carolyn's nearly empty fruit dish. "I don't know how it works, but isn't it great to have melons in April? Fresh fruit always in season. Terrific."

"Terrific," Carolyn echoed. They were on safer ground now. They had each said all they were going to say about Brett.

Chapter Fifteen

Carolyn had hoped that Brett would find time for her on Sunday. He didn't. She learned from two of the band members that he had scheduled an all-afternoon rehearsal with them. And Gavin, who was going to spend another day with Mr. Yoshinaga on Shikoku island, let it be known that Brett intended to devote the evening to working with Sadi Hayashi. Left to her own devices, Carolyn decided to follow Brett's advice and go out on her own.

She remembered Billie Watanabe's invitation. And it seemed ridiculous to order a limousine to take her to Harajuku, where traffic would be snarled as usual and the streets would be jammed. Carolyn dressed in jeans and a T-shirt, took a cab to the Ginza Eki train station, and learned from obliging passersby where and how to insert several coins into a vending machine to secure her ticket on the orange Ginza line.

She moved along slowly, boarding the train. It was so crowded that all she had to do was get into the right line and stand still; inevitably, she was pushed inside the train by the insistent press of humanity.

It was her first adventure on her own, and Carolyn felt a small surge of pride in accomplishment when she managed the fifteen-minute wait at the Ueno station and transferred to the Yamanote-line train for her destination.

There was even a certain excitement in getting lost during her ten-minute walk to the shopping area. She should have phoned Billie and gotten more specific directions, Carolyn thought. Still, it was fascinating to wander the narrow, shop-lined streets of Harajuku, window-shopping, exchanging smiles with the thousands of other people who hurried past her. And she experienced a little thrill when, finally, she discovered the Watanabe family's fabric shop.

Its sign, of course, was incomprehensible. But the street number was right, and through the window she caught a glimpse of a smiling woman who might be Billie Watanabe.

And, happily, it was. Carolyn introduced herself, was greeted like a long-lost old friend, and was introduced to two dignified but friendly people who smiled, bowed and welcomed her with *"Ita shai mase."* She felt, from their warm and sincere greetings, which were repeated in English, as though she had been gone for a long time and had finally come home.

Billie, a short, broad-faced, plumpish woman who had apparently been born with a smile on her face and had found no reason to erase it, apologized, "As soon as I finish helping my parents drape this mannequin, we will all show you the proper hospitality. Our window looks so bare without her. And this heavy brocade refuses to drape."

Carolyn was intrigued by the project at hand. The

object was to swathe the realistic-looking, rather haughty dummy in yards of a silver-shot heliotrope-colored fabric, to achieve the effect of a formal gown without cutting into the material. "From China," Billie's tiny mother said respectfully. "And, oh, the price is so high!"

Carolyn became intrigued with the challenge. But as she made a cursory inspection of the countless bolts of fabric in the shop, her imagination was caught by a bolt of delicately colored chiffon in a complementary shade. "I don't think you'll ever get that fabric to fall into a graceful sleeve," she said. "But if you combined this, as an overdrape for the brocade, you'd be showing off two beautiful fabrics. And you'd get a soft, see-through effect."

A moment later, feeling as though she had been created for this very task, Carolyn was fashioning a seamless evening gown with straight pins and enthusiasm. When she had finished, apologizing for her intrusion, the Watanabes surveyed their mannequin and applauded. "She could be going to a queen's coronation," Billie said. Her father only smiled and nodded his approval repeatedly. Mrs. Watanabe reached out to squeeze Carolyn's hand.

When the draped figure was set in its place facing the passersby who were walking past the window, Carolyn gave her attention to the wealth of beautiful fabrics the family offered for sale. Every rich gold lamé, every colorful cotton gauze from India, every pliant silk produced in radiant colors here in Japan, excited her creative impulse. And the trimmings! Embroidered edgings and sequined flowers vied with yards of tassels, pom-poms and intricate metallic borders. There were even pastel-hued samplings of marabou and egret feathers, delicate netsuke buttons fashioned from ivory and exotic woods. "I could go crazy in your shop,"

Carolyn told Billie and her parents. "I could spend hours here!"

They allowed her that opportunity as Carolyn began a bolt-by-bolt recital of what she would like to see done with the fabrics from every corner of the globe. Billie, who was no stranger to theatrical costuming, caught Carolyn's fervor. "Mama-san . . . a pad of paper and a pencil? Carolyn must not forget all these ideas. Please."

Mrs. Watanabe scurried into a back room and reappeared with a block of stationery and an assortment of ball-point pens.

Billie and her mother and father waited on customers, only occasionally peering over Carolyn's shoulder to see her quick, inspired sketches. No one at the art school in San Francisco had told her there were fabrics like these! She could not have imagined more flaming reds or more flowerlike lilacs. The sea was captured in myriad shades of blue and green and all the hues in between, and where the beautiful colors ended, the textures began. Carolyn lost herself in delightful self-expression. When she had finished, the counter was heaped with an assortment of drawings, not one of them mundane.

Billie's round face lighted up as she examined them during a break between customers. "These are wonderful, Carolyn! So original, so imaginative! Look, Papa-san . . . Mother, just *look!*"

"They're just quick sketches off the top of my head," Carolyn said. But her modest statement covered up an inner excitement. The ideas *were* good. If properly developed, they would show off her flair for the fantastic.

"Guido must see these," Mr. Watanabe said, tapping a finger on the collection of roughly executed designs. "Oh, so beautiful!"

Guido, Carolyn was told, owned a boutique specializing in high-fashion formal wear. He had shops in Rome, London and on Rodeo Drive in Beverly Hills, besides the one just down the block from the Watanabes' shop. "But he is in Italy now," Billie said. "And I would much rather show these to Sadi. May I do so, Carolyn? Take them to my employer and friend?"

"I'd rather work on them some more," Carolyn said.

"But she will understand that. Please," Billie insisted. "I will tell her they were whipped out in minutes and that you didn't even have a proper drawing pad and colored inks or pastels." Billie rolled up the sketches, securing them with a rubber band. "Trust me, Carolyn. You have been wasting your time working for Mr. Wells."

Brett had said the same thing. *Brett.* She never got far away from him; he was almost always in her thoughts. But it was a joy to have forgotten about him while she was letting all those fabulous bolts of cloth stir her visions. It was good, too, to be welcomed here for herself and not as an extension of a famous performer. She made another disparaging remark about her hasty sketches, but assured Billie that they were hers to do with whatever pleased her.

They retired to the back room, where a small area had been set aside for tea-drinking and conversation, but there were too many interruptions; at least two of the family members had to be in the store taking care of business. "We have so many things to talk about," Billie insisted. "You must stay and come to my parents' house for dinner. Then we can really get to know each other."

While she waited for the Watanabe family to close their store, Carolyn visited other shops in the area, her head spinning with fashion ideas. She could not have designed a suit for business wear if she had tried; her sketches always featured full or flowing long skirts, the bodices were always lacy and rich with the sparkle of gemstones, the sleeves always extravagantly shirred or puffed or drawn to resemble the wings of exotic butterflies. At an art-supply shop she bought a box of pastel chalks and a sketch pad. Brett lingered in the back of her mind, but she tingled with the prospect of *doing* something, something that was her very own.

It was after nine o'clock before the Watanabes' shop was closed and Carolyn was driven to their house nearby. It was a structure of the old wood-and-paper type, highly impractical in a climate that could become bitterly cold. Sparsely furnished, it had a spacious feeling that was enhanced by the use of rice-paper screens that divided one room into many areas. Carolyn was enchanted.

Billie prepared a dinner that included *shiro maguro*, or albacore, a delectable clear soup with tiny mushrooms and pink pounded rice, and a salad that included bamboo shoots cooked previously in *soya* and *mirin* vinegar along with a chilled vegetable that resembled asparagus but was called *fuki*. The rice bowls were treasures in themselves, and so were the little hand-painted plates on which the *tsukemono*—sour plums and flower-cut pickled vegetables—were served.

How could one person have prepared such an intriguing artist's canvas of a meal in such a short time? They sat on silk cushions around a low, red-lacquered table, the conversation pouring from them.

The Watanabes wanted to know about remembered places in San Francisco, about the mango, macadamia nut and cherimoya trees Carolyn's parents raised in Southern California. Did it ever snow in Escondido? And how had she come to Japan to serve as a publicist when she had spent a year studying dress design?

Carolyn had questions, too. She learned that the work week in Japan was five and a half days long, and that Japanese people who could not pay their debts at the New Year presented their creditors with small token gifts. Mr. and Mrs. Watanabe joined in the laughter when their more cosmopolitan daughter said, "Remember that, Carolyn. If you ever find yourself unable to make a car payment, send the Bank of America a lovely little jade-green bowl."

After the leisurely dinner, Mr. Watanabe showed Carolyn his collection of *kiseru,* Japanese tobacco pipes. She marveled over another display of antique *nurimono,* Japanese lacquerware, and learned that the *kim-makiye* pieces, examples of gold lacquerwork, were the family's pride and joy. There was a scroll Carolyn admired, an unframed painting of a *miya,* a Shinto temple delineated in only a few understated strokes of a brush. Carolyn learned, to her dismay, that her interest in the painting had been too pronounced. When, at last, it was time to leave, and Billie insisted that she would drive Carolyn to her hotel, Mrs. Watanabe made a discreet disappearance and returned with a long, light, gift-wrapped package and said softly, "It is a humble thing. A worthless gift. But please accept it anyway."

Carolyn knew what the package contained. She felt tears rising in her eyes as she started to unwrap it. But Billie stayed her hand, whispering, "No, no, no. Our tradition is that you do not open a gift in the presence of the giver."

Carolyn thanked her for the advice and expressed her thanks to the elder Watanabes, thanking them, also, for having taught her more about their country in a few hours that she had been able to absorb since her arrival. It had been a memorable day and evening.

As Billie's small brown Toyota carried them to the New Otani, Carolyn asked a few tentative questions. She learned that Billie had never married and that she was totally devoted to her family and to the famous actress she served as wardrobe mistress, personal secretary and companion. "Miss Hayashi and I are staying at the Akasaka Prince Hotel during the Tokyo filming," Billie said. "When she is not working, we live in her house in Matsuyama. You must come to visit while you are there, Carolyn. You and my dear friend share a common interest in beautiful trees and beautiful gowns. I cannot wait to show her your sketches."

There was no more to be learned about Sadi Hayashi from her admiring employee. Carolyn sensed that the actress's private life was a closed book, not to be discussed. Carolyn was tempted to ask why there was a ban on publicizing a romance between the two co-stars of the musical film, a promotional gimmick that was almost automatic in the movie industry. But something about Billie's manner told her that this subject, too, was forbidden.

Billie dropped her off in front of the hotel after a mutual agreement to see each other again soon. Carolyn was walking toward the glass doors when a taxi disgorged Rusty Johnson and Jerry Badler, Brett's bass player. They had apparently been out on the town, and Jerry had obviously had a few too many drinks. They greeted Carolyn expansively, Jerry linking her arm through his and saying, "Know what I'm celebrating? A pretty little waitress at one of the clubs broke all the rules and, know what? She slipped me her phone number with my bar bill tonight."

"Thinks he's died and gone to heaven." Rusty laughed. He took Carolyn's other arm and they marched her into the lobby, Jerry singing in a loud, happy voice, "Tonight, she told me that she likes me; Tonight she told me that she cares!" He was making up the words and tuneless melody as the three of them marched unsteadily into the lobby. They were almost at the elevators when they came face to face with Brett Wells.

Brett looked from one to the other with an icy stare.

Addressing Carolyn, he demanded, "Where've you been?" His face was livid. "Where in the hell have you been until this hour of the night?"

His question sounded ridiculous even to Carolyn. "I went shopping. I had a nice evening with friends."

Brett glared at his musicians. "I see. You could have left a note." Then, glancing at Carolyn's gift-wrapped scroll and the two small packages of art supplies, he said, "It didn't take you all day and half the night to buy *that*."

Rusty and Jerry hung back, suddenly sobered and silent.

"I did what you told me to do," Carolyn said. "I got out and . . . *did* things."

"While everybody here was worried sick about you? Gavin flew back to Matsuyama. I phoned him there, thinking you might have gone with him." Brett was angrier than Carolyn had ever seen him before. "Now he's worried, too. Dammit, I have the *police* looking for you!"

"I'm sorry you were worried," Carolyn said.

"Never have to worry," Jerry chimed in. "Streets in this city are lots safer than back in L.A."

"When I want your opinion, I'll ask for it," Brett gritted.

Jerry took a few steps backward, mumbling something unintelligible.

"Didn't you realize I'd be worried about you?" Brett demanded, turning his attention back to Carolyn. "I phoned your room before noon. Nothing. All day long, wondering where you could possibly be. By eleven tonight I was positive something terrible had happened to you. Do you know what time it is? Out carousing with . . ." Brett's eyes shot a scathing look at his two band members, then flashed back to Carolyn. "I don't give a damn what you do with your time, but you have no right to worry me this way!"

Carolyn decided to let him make whatever assumptions he wanted to make. She didn't tell him that she had met Rusty and Jerry outside the hotel entrance; it was, in fact, rather pleasurable to see him experiencing jealous resentment. "This was my day off," Carolyn said stiffly. Brett's own words flashed in her mind and she paraphrased them. "I don't know why I'm explaining to you." She lifted her head. "We don't have a contract!"

For a few seconds Brett just stared at her as though he didn't believe what he was hearing. Then he said, "I shouldn't have been concerned about you." He shot another glance toward Jerry and Rusty. "I was afraid you were out somewhere *alone.*"

Brett spun around and walked in the direction of one of the lounges. Whether or not his musicians followed him to explain that Carolyn had not been out with them, Carolyn didn't know. She stomped to the elevator, anxious to reach her room and sort out her thoughts. Brett *did* care about her. But she had enjoyed a beautiful day without him. Perhaps his dictatorial attitude and her newly activated interest in her own vocation would free her from her slavish devotion to him. Certainly, after what she had just said to him, Brett would want no more to do with her. Fine, Carolyn told herself. Good. She was free. This afternoon she had made a new beginning; and if she had also ended her relationship with Brett, that was probably all for the best.

Chapter Sixteen

Although the ache did not go away, Carolyn had less time to think about Brett during the next three days. Even though her work kept his name before her almost constantly, she found refuge in her private quarters when she crossed the hall at quitting time. Her costume ideas and fancy ball gowns had a strong Japanese influence now, yet each design showed Carolyn's flair for the romantic, the unique, the fantastic. Working in color was more than stimulating; it was therapeutic.

She was toying with bird themes—snowy egrets, flaming cardinals and lustrous peacocks—on Friday evening when her telephone rang. Gavin, perhaps, wanting company in one of the lounges. Not Brett. She had no hope that it would be Brett.

It was Billie Watanabe. "Are you busy, Carolyn?" she asked, and then apologized for not having called earlier. "We just got back from the studio and I wasn't sure Miss Hayashi would be coming here this evening. If you have other plans, we can make it another night, although time is very important."

We? Carolyn didn't press for details. "I'm not busy at all. Would you want me to meet you somewhere?"

"No, we're at Trader Vic's. We've just finished dinner, and since Sadi has an appointment here at the hotel at eight-thirty, we thought, if you don't mind, we'd just come up to your room."

They were in the hotel, then. Carolyn said, "Of course. Come right up." Surely they were not here to pay a social call!

Carolyn ran a brush through her hair, put on some lipstick and wondered why she was so nervous. She was reflecting on Billie's odd habit of alternately referring to her boss as "Miss Hayashi" and the familiar "Sadi" when there was a knock on the door.

Billie was like an eager child bursting with a happy secret. The actress was more serene, but she was also eager to explain the reason for their visit. Stunning in a fitted red silk tunic and black satin trousers, she declined Carolyn's offer of something to drink and came directly to the point. "I was very impressed with your sketches, Miss Chandler. Billie has told me how quickly they were made. With time, with swatches to work with, I can imagine that your work would have been even more exciting."

Billie's attention had gone to the drawings of bird-inspired designs Carolyn had propped on her desk. "Oh, look! Sadi, just look at this gown!"

Their praise could not have been more extravagant or more sincere. Minutes later Brett's beautiful co-star was saying, "You may have heard that I have been very unhappy with my wardrobe for the musical. I can, with some adjustments, accept the kimonos for my earlier scenes. The ones I have worn so far are from my personal wardrobe. However, I have been terribly disappointed in what I have seen of the costumes for the dream scene, which will be filmed at the Dogo Hot Springs in my home city. They look . . ." The actress made a fluttering motion with her ivory hands. "How can I explain? They look as though they were left over from a very poor and very old party scene in a low-budget film." Her black eyes took on a dreamy cast as she visualized the important fantasy sequence. "I am totally removed from reality. My heart has been broken, but I dream of my lover's return to a beautiful garden filled with flowers and graceful dancers and romantic music." She reached for the drawing on which Carolyn had used a dark green background to make the elegant white plumed egret stand out. "And lovely birds," Sadi Hayashi said in an awed, hypnotic voice. "Birds! Oh, Billie, think of it! Not ball gowns or showgirl costumes. I'm a pure white egret in a garden filled with colorful birds!"

Her exuberance was contagious. Carolyn found herself pouring out fresh ideas, grabbing a chalk to illustrate how the theme could be developed. Billie smiled her delight and clapped her hands as the three of them planned, in the film star's words, "a fantasy to end all fantasies! Beautiful, beautiful, *beautiful!*"

When the meeting came to an end, Carolyn had been told that it wasn't necessary to get approval from the producer. "My contract gives me control over my wardrobe and that of the chorus," the actress said. "There is only one problem now, Carolyn. May I call you Carolyn? And will you do me the honor of calling me by my first name, too? There is the problem of time. We will be going to Matsuyama in less than three weeks. I know that you are employed and no doubt quite busy. To get so many individual costumes made, they would have to go into production . . . when, Billie?"

Billie rolled her eyes and groaned. "Last month."

She giggled and gave Carolyn a quick, joyous hug. "But Carolyn can do it. I know she can."

Sadi's expression was quizzical. "Three people have been working for months on designs for the dream sequence. We are asking for a miracle. Can you work a miracle, Carolyn?"

Carolyn swallowed hard. "I'll go to Harajuku tomorrow. Mr. and Mrs. Watanabe will be my genies."

"With measuring tapes instead of magic lamps!" Billie exclaimed.

It couldn't be happening, Carolyn thought. But it *was* happening. And Sadi was saying, "Something opulent for Mr. Wells, too. But not *too* outstanding. He is already too eye-catching, and I do not want to fade into the scenery by comparison."

At the door, Sadi turned a gentle smile toward Carolyn. "Perhaps with an expression for your amazing talent you will be happier in my country. Mr. Wells . . . Brett has been worried about you. And it is bad for artists to be either bored or worried." She reached out to press Carolyn's hand. "I hope that Brett will not be unhappy because I am interfering with your work for him."

Carolyn felt a sudden panic. "I'd rather . . . I'd rather he didn't know." She couldn't explain her fear of appearing a failure in Brett's eyes. What if Sadi's initial enthusiasm were not justified? Experienced professionals had not met the star's standards. What if Carolyn couldn't handle the actual execution of her fanciful ideas and the costumes proved disappointing? She was already pitiful enough in Brett's eyes.

Fortunately, Sadi understood the request differently. "You want to surprise your friend and employer. Of course. I promise to say not a word. And in any case, he has too many things to think about now. I already occupy too much of his time with a personal project."

It had been a thrilling meeting. Carolyn Chandler,

fresh out of design school, had been asked to design the costumes for the most important scene in a major musical! She could not have conjured up such a possibility in her wildest dreams. But, once again, her senseless love for Brett put a damper on her joy. The "personal project" became painfully understandable when good-nights were exchanged and it was clear that Billie Watanabe was going to their hotel while Sadi Hayashi, looking at her delicate gold wristwatch, noted that it was past eight-thirty and she was late for her "appointment." "Mr. Wells will be impatient with me."

She wouldn't be too late, Carolyn thought miserably. Sadi had only a few steps to go. She was knocking on Brett's door before Carolyn closed her own.

Chapter Seventeen

With the help of the Watanabe family, Carolyn's birds soon began to exist in the real world, as well as in her fertile imagination. Each design outdid the explosion of fantasy that had produced the one before it. Given free rein, no budget restrictions, and constant enthusiasm from Billie, the elder Watanabes, and Sadi Hayashi, Carolyn was indeed able to perform miracles.

She had told Gavin about her great opportunity, also swearing him to secrecy where Brett was concerned. She heard through Sadi that the film's producer was ecstatic with her efforts. And with the office pressures reduced, with Gavin shooing her back to her drawing board and insisting that he could manage alone, Carolyn spent her afternoons and evenings in her hotel room, which was now filled with colored renderings, swatches and bolts of fabric, mounds of plumes, and notebooks full of instructions to seamstresses. The last of the eighty costumes was in frantic production before the final day's film shooting in Akasaka.

Both Gavin and Billie insisted that she must be there to watch filming of the scene in which the hero sings a parting love song to the naive Japanese dancer who has been his lover.

Brett's band had been kept in Tokyo, at no small expense, to back him up when he sang his "Don't Remember Me with Tears" ballad to Sadi. But they were joined by an orchestra of strings as Brett held the brave and beautiful little figure in his arms and sang with a heartrending sincerity that brought tears to Carolyn's eyes. Was she crying because she identified with the heroine? Because Brett had only waved at her when she came into the sound-stage area? Because she empathized with the actress who was portraying the heroine, wondering if she, too, would be left in tears when the movie was ready for editing and Brett went on to other challenges? Carolyn didn't know why she should be saddened by the scene being played before her eyes. Logically, she should be glaring at Sadi, fuming with jealousy, resenting Brett. But how could she hate an always considerate woman who had given her the chance of a lifetime? How could she be angry with the man who had whispered, "You're beautiful, Carolyn. Beautiful."

And, along with Billie, who was seated between her and Gavin, Carolyn let her tears flow unchecked when the petite heroine was left alone, and only then let the loving smile fade from her face. Sadi did not have to rely upon glycerine tears applied to her face by a makeup expert. Her tears were genuine, tracking across her exquisite face as the music rose to an agonizing crescendo and a camera silently dollied in for a close-up.

When Verne Damian shouted, "Cut! That's a take,"

Gavin let out a low-keyed whistle. "That lady is one hell of an actress. She'd have to be, to cry like that." Even he looked misty-eyed.

Billie usually showed her approval with a childish clapping of her hands. This time she turned away and said softly, "Miss Hayashi has had much practice." A little while later she was hugging the actress and laughing. "Great, Sadi! Wonderful, wonderful." It was as though Miss Hayashi, the taskmistress, and Sadi, the cherished friend, were two different people.

A farewell gala was to be given by the studio the next day. Carolyn spent the morning in the office wondering, along with Gavin, what song had been recorded on the gift record that would be given out to Brett's fans. The completed jackets had been delivered the day before. Carolyn hoped that Brett would stop by to see the seven-by-seven-inch covers and interpret the gold Japanese letters which were imprinted next to a color photo of Brett with microphone in hand, a pagoda and cherry tree forming the background. "It was my idea, and I wrote the bio for the back," Carolyn complained. "You'd think I'd know what it says on the front."

"It's just a general greeting," Gavin said. "He's been very secretive about the record he cut with the band. How'd you like to be his *manager* and not know?" But this was a strictly local promotion, Carolyn was reminded. A nice P.R. touch, but not carefully monitored by the experts in Los Angeles, who spent staggering sums on advertising Brett Wells.

"I only know it's not the 'mistress' song he'd originally planned to use," Gavin told Carolyn.

Brett wasn't going to stop by. Carolyn learned that he and his band members were already at the studio, rehearsing the songs they planned to play at the party. "You'll have to settle for me as escort," Gavin said. Had he noticed that she had been glancing expectantly toward the door all morning?

Then there was the plaguing problem of what to wear. If she arrived in jeans and a T-shirt, would she discover that this was a dressy farewell bash? Carolyn had a friend, now, to call on for advice. And Billie said, yes, these end-of-the-shooting studio parties were usually quite elegant. Reluctant to wear the ensemble that had embarrassed her at the first party, Carolyn used six yards of transparent crepe from India to wrap herself in a sari that exposed one shoulder. Against a heavenly shade of pale blue, tiny white and yellow flowers, set less than half an inch apart, had been hand-embroidered over the entire length of the cloth. It had been a gift from Mr. and Mrs. Watanabe.

It was an extravagant party, and this time, with Billie and Gavin and the band members around, Carolyn felt less isolated. Brett was busy conferring with Tony Hanniman at the piano. Sadi was nowhere in sight. When asked, Billie said, "She had to get back to Matsuyama. I stayed behind just to pack."

"I'll be forever closing up the office and trying to pack all the gifts and things I've bought into my luggage," Carolyn said. "We're leaving tomorrow. I'll have to buy more suitcases."

She felt ashamed of herself for a quiver of pleasure over the news that Sadi Hayashi had gone home. Knowing that she had never looked better, feeling glamorous in the East Indian-style dress that had been assembled without a stitch, Carolyn sipped a cocktail and stood near the piano as Brett stepped up to the microphone. He began by thanking the cast and technicians, the producer, writer and director, who had made his first appearance before the cameras so enjoyable. He thanked everyone, but when he sang, his eyes remained focused in her direction. His intensity, his expression as his eyes looked into hers, must have been obvious to everyone in the room. When Brett put his mike down, bowing to the applause of his co-workers, Carolyn was shaking inside.

Gavin had wandered off somewhere, and Carolyn looked around for him, remembering that he had said there was a lot of work to do if they were going to make their flight the following morning to Matsuyama. Several free-standing flats, painted with Japanese rural scenes, were obscuring some of the guests. Carolyn had wandered behind one of the high partitions, only to discover that there was no one there in the semidarkness. She was turning to retrace her footsteps when she heard Brett say, "Carolyn? What are you doing back here?"

Flustered by his sudden appearance, Carolyn muttered a barely coherent explanation.

"I wanted to congratulate you."

"On what?"

"I was a little hurt that you didn't share the secret with me, but then I remembered that I enjoy surprises, too. Your costumes. They're wonderful, Carolyn. Sheer dynamite."

She was pleased with the compliment, but she also felt betrayed. "Sadi promised she wouldn't tell you."

"She didn't. How long did you think it was going to be a secret with me going in for fittings? The dressing room has been full of sketches with your name signed on them and seamstresses talking about 'the wonderful new American designer.' I'm so proud of you, Carolyn. Maybe now you'll stop feeling you're not 'somebody.' You'll stop getting hurt because of . . ."

Brett had hesitated. "Because of what?" Carolyn demanded.

"Because I'm who I am and my life is what it is. You're a part of it now more than ever." Brett's hands reached out to close over Carolyn's shoulders, the warm contact stirring her need for him. "We've been acting like idiots, honey. Touchy, oversensitive, avoiding each other. You know that's not right. We've got one last night in Tokyo. Let's make it another night to remember."

Carolyn shook herself free of his touch. "Because you're temporarily alone?" She didn't mention Sadi by name; Brett would know exactly what she meant. "I'm not a stand-in, Brett. I'm not somebody you reach out for when you don't have someone more interesting to jump into bed with!"

He was furious. "You really think a lot of me, don't you? I don't know what that was supposed to mean, but I won't put up with your petty, possessive jealousy."

"And I don't want any part of your overblown ego. You think you can snap your fingers and have any woman you want. Well, I may be inexperienced and naive, but—"

"For a beginner, you manage pretty well!"

A rush of heat inflamed Carolyn's face. He was referring to the night when she had made love to *him*, reminding her cruelly that she was not an innocent little victim of his seduction. "That's about as . . . as rotten a thing as you could possibly say to me." She was shaking, too humiliated and angry to go on. They could stand here and rail at each other, trading insults, or she could choose to brush past him and run—hurry out of the studio, out of his life.

Carolyn chose the latter, and Brett was apparently too incensed to stop her. In less than an hour Carolyn was throwing her possessions into her suitcases, taking her rage out on every item she hurled at the open luggage lined up on the bed.

Chapter Eighteen

*I*t should have been one of the most wonderful mornings in her life. And in spite of her leaden feeling, the realization that her love for Brett was a hopeless emotional burden from which she had to free herself, Carolyn was not immune to the excitement of their departure. After boarding the plane at bustling Haneida airport, she watched the huge towers and ships and mountains disappear as the plane soared through a swirling white blanket of clouds.

Minutes out of Tokyo, Gavin evidently grew tired of Carolyn's listless conversation. He sat across the aisle, trading music-business anecdotes with Tony Hanniman and Carmen Battaglia during most of the flight, returning only when the soft voice of the stewardess announced that they would soon be approaching Matsuyama.

Over the years, Gavin had visited the Shikoku island

city many times, and he was anxious to point out its landmarks during the approach. "It's a growing city," he was saying. "You can see that it still has room to grow." He pointed out the intricate pattern of the coastline, the hundreds of small islands scattered like confetti over the bright blue water. Carolyn had expected a small village; the size of the city and its mass of tall rectangular office buildings rising toward the sky astounded her. She wished that this new adventure were not being clouded by her dismal mood. Brett was on this plane with her, but he might as well have been a million miles away. Carolyn did not see him until the plane had touched down. Even then, predictably, the airport terminal was crowded with wildly enthusiastic fans, jumping up and down excitedly at the first glimpse of the American star. He was enveloped in an adoring mass of humanity, while Gavin helped Carolyn into one of the waiting limousines.

"How did they know he was expected?" Carolyn asked. Her voice betrayed her weary resentment with this public ritual. "Brett's not doing a concert here."

"Not his own concert, no," Gavin told her. "But he'll be featured at a big charity extravaganza tomorrow night."

"Oh?" Carolyn's resentment was a professional one now. "I didn't know about that."

"You were busy, and this was something I worked out with Mr. Yoshinaga. We're expecting to pack a fifty-thousand-seat stadium. There'll be bands, big-name television stars. Brett, of course. And the local girl who made good, naturally."

Sadi Hayashi. Carolyn turned her attention to the ring of green-covered mountains visible from her car window. She was barely listening when Gavin went on to rave about the philanthropic industrialist who owned, among many others, the hotel at which they would be staying. "You'll like him immensely. Important man, but very affable, always smiling. You'd never guess he's juggling a dozen new projects in his head every minute. He has one of those faces you look at and think, if this man were a surgeon, I'd trust him to remove my appendix in the backseat of a taxi. Solid. He's done a lot for me, for Sadi Hayashi, for a lot of people."

Carolyn wished she could share Gavin's enthusiasm. She wished she could rise above her jealousy. But it consumed her, deadened her interest in everything and everyone who separated her from Brett.

Still, it was hard not to be impressed by the sleek white Matsuyama International Hotel. The cosmopolitan atmosphere began with its marble lobby and extended to a glassed-in Japanese garden that brought the beauty of the country to where it could be admired during all seasons by guests who chose to remain indoors.

Gavin, Tony Hanniman, Carolyn and, presumably, Brett were assigned rooms on the ninth floor, a distinct privilege, Carolyn learned. The entire floor was usually reserved, not for paying guests, but for Mr. Yoshinaga's personal friends. Her own room, spacious, with clean modern lines and simple blue-and-white decor, opened upon a breathtaking panorama of mountains splashed with colorful blossoming hedges and trees. For a moment, knowing how difficult it would be to describe this beauty to her parents, Carolyn felt a surge of homesickness, a longing for the familiar trees of the Chandler Tropical Tree Nursery, familiar voices that spoke in a language she understood, familiar faces that looked at her with deep affection. Then, as she unpacked, berating herself for the hasty, angry outburst that had made a shambles of her wardrobe the night before, Carolyn also berated herself for her negative attitude. She was seeing sights that most people could only dream about. She could hardly say there were no

kind and loving people here; the hospitality was touching and warm. Only an ingrate would forget the
Watanabe family, the friendliness of the people she
worked with, the courtesy shown her by every Japanese
stranger who had welcomed her to a shop, given her
directions when she was lost, made her feel comfortable when she was forced to pantomime her simplest
wants. An out-and-out *ingrate,* Carolyn thought. For
there was only one flaw in this fantastic adventure. It
was her stormy relationship with Brett Wells.

And even that miserable situation was her own fault.
Brett had never promised her anything more than his
friendship and the sharing of good times when his work
allowed it. The hours he had chosen to spend closed up
in his suite at the New Otani with his beautiful co-star
might rankle, but how could she have expected the two
of them *not* to be attracted to each other? And how
could she have fumed inwardly at the mere mention of
Sadi Hayashi's name? The actress had opened a door
that had been barred to Carolyn on her home turf. She
had assured Carolyn that once the film was released,
with proper credits, there would undoubtedly be offers
that would launch a brilliant career in costume designing.

Carolyn had bathed, a rumpled beige linen suit had
been whisked from her room and returned neatly
pressed, and her morale had improved with her appearance by the time Gavin escorted her to a palm-studded,
white-paneled Japanese-style restaurant. Skylight pan-
els, white screens and blond-wood tables and chairs
added to the room's air of serene simplicity. Everyone
was there except Brett, who had been detained at the
airport and was still changing upstairs.

It was during the specially prepared luncheon in the
Iyo restaurant that Carolyn was introduced to their
host. And Gavin's description had been perfect. Mr.
Yoshinaga was a mid-fortyish, impressive, confidence-

inspiring man, his black hair short and as immaculately groomed as his conservative hand-tailored suit. Where his English failed him, his gracious manner took over.

Proud of one of his newest hotels, Mr. Kozo Yoshinaga personally escorted his guests on a tour of the Tokiwa, a grand banquet room in which one sank into rich red carpeting figured with a pattern of geometric designs. Crystal chandeliers produced a gala effect. They inspected another, smaller banquet facility called the Rikyu, richly paneled with gleaming mahogany, and Carolyn marveled over a wedding-ceremony room and another devoted to the tea ceremony. How gracefully the old and the new had been blended here by the architect! Both rooms were modern in feeling, yet they were imbued with the Japanese spirit. Or perhaps it was only that the stark simplicity of uncluttered rooms had looked "contemporary" in ancient times. The brilliant colors in one room, the soft avocado monotone of the other, were a delight to Carolyn's eyes.

While they were admiring the cozy Kokusai restaurant, where natural brick, cone-shaped fixtures containing balls of soft amber light, and a dark, shining tile floor created a countryside-inn atmosphere with, again, a futuristic look, Mr. Yoshinaga was called away to a business appointment. Along with his sincere *"ira shai mase,"* the inevitable welcome, he apologized that time did not permit his escorting them to the Chinese restaurant and cocktail lounge that were evidently his pride and joy. However, nighttime would provide them with a rewarding view from the Starlight Lounge that evening. And they would be his dinner guests at the adjoining Chinese-style restaurant after dark.

Chapter Nineteen

*T*hey had dined lavishly on delicacies from around the world, Gavin and the band members insisting that Carolyn must try the abalone in oyster sauce, the shark-fin soup with shredded chicken, the exotic *beche-de-mer* with shrimp eggs. While the musicians took advantage of the seemingly endless dishes and potent drinks, their host sat at the head of the long table with Brett Wells, the guest of honor, at his side. In spite of the language barrier, they communicated easily and Mr. Yoshinaga's sense of humor had kept not only Brett but also everyone else in his company in a festive mood.

Brett's laughter turned to serious attention when the party moved into the beautiful Starlight Lounge after dinner. Carolyn only glimpsed his expression. Her eyes, like those of everyone else in the plush sky-view room, became riveted to the tall, strikingly handsome

American entertainer who seated himself behind a white concert grand piano that dominated the lounge. He was an attractive blue-eyed man with curly gray-sprinkled hair. His face, too youthful to make the distinguished gray in his smartly styled hair seem anything but premature, was an aesthetically pleasing combination of strong, well-defined features, self-assurance, and pleasure in finding himself in good company. The audience, mostly well-dressed Japanese businessmen and their chic wives in expensive Western-style dinner dresses, was apparently familiar with the entertainer; he was greeted by a welcoming round of applause.

Careful not to be overheard by Mr. Yoshinaga, Rusty Johnson whispered, "Just what the world needs. A blue-eyed Brett Wells."

Jerry Badler, starting to feel his fourth gimlet, quipped, "Yeah, but five gets you ten he can't sing."

Gavin hushed them. Their loyalty to Brett was no excuse for bad manners.

The entertainer, in keeping with the elegant decor of the lounge, was wearing a tuxedo that had been molded to his lithe frame. Diamond-studded cufflinks flashed from his wrists. Imposing, Carolyn thought. Even Brett did not command the respectful silence that followed the initial applause. And if there was such a thing as a performer "owning a room," the poised stranger owned this one.

Another glance at Brett. Oh, he was always polite, but it was clear that he envied the ease with which the man behind the piano smiled, leaned into his micro-phone and said, *"Mina-San, Komban-wa! Watashi-wa Tommy Carlough desu."* Brett's face remained impassive. The phrases were translated as the entertainer addressed the American guests. "Good evening, ladies and gentlemen. My name is Tommy Carlough." Then he added, "On behalf of the management and staff of the International Hotel, I want to welcome you to Matsuyama. We're honored by your company and I'm sure everyone here tonight joins me in hoping you will enjoy your stay with us." When everyone seated around Mr. Yoshinaga applauded, he added, "I understand most of you are from California. When I've finished my first show, I hope you'll let me join you for a drink and the latest news from my native state." He gave his attention back to the rest of his audience, speaking in rapid-fire Japanese, undoubtedly translating what he had just said, for the local patrons looked toward the American entourage and applauded their welcome.

"I'll be damned," Carmen Battaglia whispered. "Funny. He doesn't *look* Japanese."

A few strong piano chords quieted Carmen. Tommy played the introduction to an old-time favorite, and when he eased into the song, it was as though every word of the lyric had a deep and special meaning to him. He blended into one old American standard after another, interspersing these heartfelt renditions with more recent songs, sung in a baritone as rich as Brett's, but possibly even more polished. A few years older than the superstar, he had apparently been singing for a long time, so at ease with his talent that one number followed another in a succession interrupted only by warm applause.

Carmen repeated his earlier comment: "I'll be damned." And while the singer acknowledged requests from people who were obviously regular patrons, Carolyn turned to Gavin. "He's great, isn't he? Have you heard him before?"

"A number of times," Gavin said. "Every time I've been here during the past year."

"Year?" Most foreign entertainers stayed in Japan for a matter of weeks. "He's been here a *year?*"

"And he worked in Tokyo and other cities before

198

that. Why not? He's built up a tremendous following. He does TV shows, acts as disc jockey on an English-language rock show. The guy likes it here, and you can see the people love him. I'm surprised Sadi didn't tell you about him. She even wears T-shirts advertising his radio sponsor."

"Did he know Brett was going to be here tonight?"

"Of course he knew. He and Mr. Yoshinaga are drinking buddies after hours." Gavin paused. "If you mean why isn't he impressed and nervous, give me one reason why he should be. This guy's great, and he's on his home turf."

Just how much Tommy Carlough was on his "home turf" was proven a few minutes later when he said, first in Japanese, then in English, "Ladies and gentlemen, I don't have to tell you that we're privileged to have a great international singing star with us this evening." He went on to extol Brett's successes in the concert and recording fields, finally announcing that Mr. Wells would be adding a musical motion picture to his list of credits, part of which would be filmed at their own suburban Dogo Hot Springs. He stood up, applauding, as he completed the introduction and then urged the audience to join him in encouraging Brett Wells to come up to the piano.

"Brett's been champing at the bit," Rusty said *sotto voce*. "He doesn't have to be encouraged."

It was true. As supposedly secure as Brett's fame had made him, he wouldn't have been human if he had not wanted to show off his own considerable talent. There was a brief whispered conversation between Brett and Tommy. They arrived at a choice of songs both knew, one of them Brett's first hit ballad. And with Tommy replacing Tony Hanniman, who usually served as accompanist, Brett took the microphone.

"I've been fired," Tony muttered, pretending he was hurt. "Good. I'd rather sit here and drink than work."

It was Brett who worked. Competition must have inspired him; he had never put more of himself into his own love song or the currently popular rock number that followed it. But was it loyalty to their house entertainer, the age of the audience, or some inexplicable reserve that rewarded Brett with polite but hardly thundering applause? His accompanist's songs had been followed by excited, sustained ovations. Applause for Brett had faded by the time he rejoined his friends.

Carolyn wanted to cry for him. It didn't help when Carmen said, "Terrific, boss." Or when Tony said, "You keep reminding me why 'Saving My Kisses' took off the way it did." Carolyn's compliments and Gavin's were brushed aside with a curt "Show some manners, people. You don't talk when an artist's performing."

Nor did it lessen the tension of all the people who knew Brett best when Tommy silenced the room with a few gentle chords and sang a lovely Japanese ballad that he graciously translated in an English recitative with his own moving piano accompaniment: " '*Daremo ina iumi, Ima owa mo-aki daremo.*' I walk on the beach. The crowds are all gone now and I am lonely because you are gone. Yet, like the memory of the sunshine and the summer, you are always in my heart."

Brett listened intently, but no more so than the Japanese people who filled the lounge. Carolyn was touched by the song, and found herself fighting back tears.

Brett's musicians were becoming too obvious in their comments. Their efforts to bolster his morale came through sounding patronizing, even to Carolyn: "Figures. These are mostly people past forty. And they can understand those lyrics."

It wasn't deliberate, Carolyn knew. The other American singer was simply doing what he did every night—filling requests. It just seemed like a nose-thumbing gesture when he closed his show with a foot-stomping number. Few of his loyal fans could have understood the lyrics, but he brought the house down just the same.

Gavin leaned to whisper in Carolyn's ear, "That's what you call one-upmanship without malice. And so much for the theory about the age of the audience. Just look at this jumpin' crowd!"

Carolyn felt resentful of the other singer's popularity, but, as it had been with Sadi Hayashi, it was impossible not to like him. Tommy Carlough made the rounds of the Starlight Lounge, stopping to trade a few words with people at every table, laughing at friendly exchanges, then came to their table and reached out his hand to Brett. "Great performance!"

Tommy shook hands with everyone in the party, laughing when Tony commented on his Japanese, and saying with believable modesty, "It's just past the 'hello, how are you' stage."

Mr. Yoshinaga nodded, ribbing him. "Terrible. Terrible Japanese. No class."

"You should have heard me a year ago," Tommy said. "I knew one sentence. *'V.O., mizu wadii kudasai.'* Still one of the lines I couldn't live without."

"Meaning?" Carolyn asked.

"'May I have my favorite booze and water?'" the singer explained. "Which reminds me . . ."

He sat with them during most of a fill-in set by a long-haired American blonde who sang current top-forty songs in English and was warmly received. But it was apparent that the crowd was nursing drinks and waiting for Tommy's next show. He shared Mr. Yoshinaga's hospitality with them, exchanged a few quiet words with Brett and then excused himself. Mr. Yoshinaga rose, too. They were going to have a brief conference about the big charity concert, Gavin explained after their host had made certain that glasses were filled and the party would go on in his absence.

They were free to speak openly now, and Brett's band members had not learned their lesson. Even Katsumi, who had joined them late, but in time for Brett's two numbers, chimed in with what was undoubtedly meant to be a supportive comment. "Tami-san sings okay. But you were great tonight."

Brett's fist smashed down on the table. Glasses rattled, and like everyone else present, Carolyn gave a startled gasp. "Stop!" Brett commanded. "I blew it tonight. I didn't reach these people, and Tommy did. But he's *worked* to build up the kind of support he's got here. He's a fantastic talent and he deserves the kind of reception he gets. I don't want to hear anyone else build me up at his expense."

Then he turned his angry gaze to Carolyn and said in a quieter tone, "And I don't want to be treated like some big-time star, a figurehead. I'm totally aware of reality. I just wish my friends were, too. I wish they would accept me as I am—human, fallible, and deserving of a little more honesty!" Brett stood up and stalked away from the table, leaving a deathly quiet behind him.

"I've seen it coming," his arranger said in a barely audible voice. "Brett's under tremendous pressure."

"So tonight wasn't one of his better nights," Gavin replied. "He's tired. Got up at the crack of dawn, got mauled by fans at the airport. A little humility isn't going to shatter him. Tomorrow night—"

"Tomorrow night," Tony Hanniman cut in, "he's going to be doing what he did tonight in front of fifty thousand people. Following the same act he followed here." Tony was like a musical extension of Brett. No one worked with him more closely or was more finely attuned to his strengths and weaknesses. "Carlough's the number-one performer in this city, and Brett's right. He's hot. That crowd's going to be *his*."

Gavin was shaking his head dolefully, knowing that what the calm, bespectacled pianist had said was true. Then he was Brett's high-powered manager again, faking a dismissing laugh. "Oh, let's all come off it," he said. "Brett's the biggest name in this business today. Are we going to sit here and worry about a one-time benefit on an island nobody in New York or L.A. could find on the map? Brett's here to make a *film*. Drink up and forget it."

They drank up, but while they listened to the young woman who strolled to their table with her guitar singing a mellow ballad about unrequited love, Carolyn knew that no one in their group was forgetting it. All of their livelihoods depended upon Brett, but they wanted to demonstrate their high regard for him for more personal reasons, too. And they had failed tonight, because they didn't really know him at all. The way I don't really know him, Carolyn thought dismally. If she really understood him, she would not have destroyed their friendship. And Brett's friendship, since she could not aspire to his love, was a precious thing, unbearably painful to have lost.

The young singer at their table was deserving of her full attention, but Carolyn's mind was elsewhere. When the female vocalist had been applauded and chatted with, Carolyn pushed her drink away from her. "I think I've had enough," she said. "If you'll excuse me, I'm going upstairs."

"Want me to see you up?" Gavin offered.

"Oh, I think I'll manage to find my way."

Gavin and the musicians seemed to be geared up for a late-night session. But Tony Hanniman got up from his chair when she did, saying, "All right for you young guys to party till dawn. Me, I've got to get some sleep if we're rehearsing for the concert tomorrow." He and Carolyn started out of the lounge together.

"I don't know why I went into this business," Tony said. "I'm a *day* person." He was clearly worried about Brett and knew that Carolyn was, too. As they made their way to the exit, he put his arm lightly around her waist, guiding her.

Carolyn had assumed that Brett had gone to his room. Or out into the night, seeking a boost at some other club, where sitting in with the band would create a sensation. Or to the home of Sadi Hayashi, where he could lose himself in the beautiful actress's embrace. She was wrong. Near the end of the crowded bar, she saw Brett sitting on one of the stools, turned so that his face was seen only in profile. He was swirling the tall drink in his hand and listening with rapt attention to Tommy Carlough.

A group of Japanese men, much younger than most of the other patrons in the lounge, had just arrived. They were not boisterous, but they seemed to have made several stops at other watering holes before they reached this oasis. It took a few moments to thread their way past them. Long enough for Carolyn to hear Tommy saying, ". . . language thing is secondary. You know enough to get by. But keep in mind this was a crowd that grew up with American pop songs during the occupation. You know the era. Okay, tomorrow night you'll have a mixed crowd. Tons of kids, but it's for charity, and the price of tickets is steep, so what I'd sing if I were you . . ." He stopped, noticing Tony and Carolyn. "You're not leaving? Stick around for my next show and maybe we can jam. You really burn up a keyboard, Tony. After hearing you on that last album, I wanted to chop up my piano for firewood."

There was more musician talk, more compliments were traded. Then Tony apologized for the interruption of what was undoubtedly a productive conversation.

"I'll catch you after the concert tomorrow, Tommy. Every chance I get while we're here. Right now I can't wait to hit the sack."

Tony's arm, casual and barely making contact, was still circled around Carolyn. And no one who knew Tony, or knew that he had exchanged no more than a few lines of small talk with Carolyn since they had met, could have misconstrued his words.

Yet Brett managed to do exactly that. He gave Carolyn a long, searching look that spoke volumes. "I can imagine," he said.

Before Tony started steering her out of the busy Starlight Lounge, Brett had turned around on his barstool and was saying, "You know my repertoire, Tommy. What would *you* open with?"

Chapter Twenty

To Carolyn's surprise, instead of being resentful of Tommy Carlough, Brett used the latter's long experience with local audiences to his own benefit.

Four hundred thousand people lived in Matsuyama. Thanks to Mr. Yoshinaga's efforts to organize and promote the charity concert, one-eighth of them poured into the coliseum that was usually the scene of bicycle races. And every top-notch entertainer on Shikoku island was there, along with a nationally famous television star who had flown down from Tokyo to serve as the master of ceremonies.

Carolyn sat in the front-row area reserved for VIP's and the press, occasionally glancing at Mr. Yoshinaga's proud smile as one performer after another brought cheers from the packed bleachers. They had special affection for an exciting jazz trio headed by a superb pianist named Hiroshi Igaue; the group had taken an

American art form and given it their own distinctive stamp. Tommy Carlough, as Gavin said during the singer's introduction, was a shoo-in. With the backing of Mr. Igaue's trio, he sang several jazz arrangements, then reached back for an old standard that had his fans clapping wildly. He returned for two encores, finally bowing off to introduce "a dear friend." And of course, the highlight of the evening was the appearance of Sadi Hayashi. She joked with the M.C., looked kittenish and sexy and sophisticated all at once during a disco-style dance number, and left the stage to a standing ovation. She returned to lead Brett Wells onto the stage, asking the audience to give a hearty Matsuyama welcome to her co-star in the musical film that would put their beloved city on the map. Carolyn held her breath. If ever there was a hard act to follow . . .

Following the advice of Tommy Carlough, Brett confined himself to songs from the occupation years, standards that were familiar to the older members of the audience. With that segment of the crowd safely in his pocket, he responded to shouted requests from the young fans, singing two of his own album hits. He was his magnificent self again, and he brought the mass of wildly delighted people to their feet.

Most stirring of all was the closing number, during which the entire company sang together, arms around each other's shoulders, their respect and affection for each other encompassing everyone in the enormous stadium. Rusty and the drummer with the Igaue trio outdid themselves with drumrolls, a spectacular fireworks display lighted the sky, and Mr. Yoshinaga quietly murmured, "Very good. Very good. *Class!*"

There was more music to celebrate the success of the event when Tommy's midnight show in the Starlight Lounge became an impromptu jam session and the hotel's owner played to the hilt the role which seemed to please him best. Jerry Badler led a toast to Mr.

Yoshinaga, "our super-host." For Carolyn, it would have been the most sparkling party she had ever attended, except that there was no time during the festivities when she exchanged a single word with Brett or even came within fifteen feet of him.

During the next few days, while the film crew was setting up at the nearby health spa, another host took over. Tommy Carlough insisted that Brett and his band members see the outstanding sights of a city that was like a second home to him. Carolyn was included in the singer's invitation, as was Gavin. But Gavin had visited Matsuyama many times before and said he had work to do. Carolyn's offer to stay at the hotel and help him was dismissed. "I'm just going to be catching up on correspondence," he said. "And anyway, there's no point in your being a publicity trainee. From what I've been hearing about your costume designs, you're launched on a different career. Don't miss seeing all you can see of this beautiful island."

That morning they were chauffeured to the foot of a tree-covered hill in the very heart of the city, where an aerial tramway took them up to an enormous feudal castle that had been twenty-six years in construction after the first stone of the massive supporting structure was laid in 1601. There were no spires, such as those Carolyn associated with fairytale castles. The rocks curved in sweeping lines to be topped with pagodalike tiers, the overhanging gray tiles forming a rickrack pattern around the upswept rooftops. Massive wooden gates led from one area of the sprawling, segmented castle to another. And the view from Matsuyama Castle took in the entire width and breadth of Ehime prefecture.

Carolyn had ridden to the summit with Carmen. Leaving the national landmark, however, she found herself crowded next to Brett, their stiff silence awkward as the cable car lurched downward. Near the end of the ride, Brett, concentrating on the scenery, said, "Quite an improvement over that view we used to rave about. Remember when we'd bike up to that big house on Marion Lane?"

Was he remembering that the hilltop back home was where he had held her hand, helping her down a rocky incline? No. Brett wouldn't remember that; he had just been helping her, as he later helped Jennie. "That house could have fit in a corner of one of the rooms we just saw," Carolyn said. "And it didn't have a moat."

She waited for an extension of the dialogue, but there was no more. Yet Brett was endlessly talkative during the rest of that day. The trouble was that most of his words were addressed to their volunteer tour guide. Incredibly, the two vocalists had struck up a warm friendship. Or maybe it was only incredible to Carolyn, who had expected two equally attractive, equally talented men with similar voices and styles, to view each other with cold, competitive eyes. The opposite was true. They talked endlessly about "gigs" they had played, club managers who had "driven them up the wall," audiences that had pleased or irritated them.

At one point, Tommy told them he had "served time" in a club near their hometown and had, out of sheer boredom in the afternoons, taken a course in macrame at an Escondido craft school. It was like old home week when they discovered that their paths had nearly crossed, or when they discovered that they both knew this piano-bar man or that tenor-sax player. Brett's musicians could join the repartee, which at times sounded like a class reunion. But Carolyn could not. More than ever, she felt left out of Brett's life. Now, when Brett and his newfound friend talked about riffs and diminished chords and arpeggios, she could more easily have communicated with aliens from Andromeda. She began to realize that it was not merely Brett's fans, Brett's female acquaintances, Brett's success that made her feel small and unimportant. She was now disturbed by a language and camaraderie that shut her out. She was even beginning to resent Brett's happiness at finding someone else he could communicate with.

Tommy Carlough became a male Sadi Hayashi; as much as Carolyn rebelled inwardly at the amount of Brett's time and attention he was taking up, she could not help liking the man. That afternoon, standing before one of the enormous inscribed boulders that dotted the city, Tommy went out of his way to explain to Carolyn that the columns of engraved Japanese letters were *haiku,* the seventeen-syllable poems, usually describing the beauties of nature, which were dear to the hearts of the Japanese people and especially to the residents of Matsuyama. "There are more than two hundred monuments like this scattered throughout the city," Tommy said. "And they get a lot of attention." He flashed a smile that was reflected in his aqua-blue eyes. "There are actually *haiku* buffs, the way we have . . . well, we don't have 'ode buffs.' What's a reasonable comparison?"

"Crossword-puzzle freaks," Carolyn told him. "I'm one."

Tommy stuck out his hand. "Join the club. I have a friend back home who sends me American crosswords, but I use them up faster than she can get them to me."

While they were shaking hands, Carolyn remembered that she had brought a book of puzzles she hadn't had time to touch. "Brett's sister thought I might get bored on the plane trip. She gave me a whole book of puzzles. Anyway, it's at the hotel. I'll see that you get it."

"All *right. Arigato gozaimasu!*"

"*Do-itashi-mashite,*" Carolyn replied. "And that's about the extent of my vocabulary—'thank you' and 'you're welcome.'"

"But that's great," Tommy cried. Then he pointed a finger at her sharply. "Capital of Ghana, five letters."

"Accra."

"Make lace, three letters."

"Tat."

Tommy laughed. "You're a real pro, Carolyn. Like mine, your head's probably stuffed with words that don't appear anywhere outside those addictive little squares."

Brett had been standing nearby under a tree. He came closer to them now. "This . . . ah . . . Shiki Masaoka you mentioned, Tom. You said he was the master *haiku* writer. Were any of his poems set to music?"

Tommy shook his head. "They're not lyrics, Brett. How many choruses could you wring out of seventeen syllables?"

"There's a disco number on the charts right now with only *two*. 'Do it,' " Brett countered.

Everyone laughed, and Brett's uninformed question about the *haiku* was forgotten. They were talking their exclusive musician talk again and Carolyn retreated from the conversation.

On their next few excursions, Carolyn admitted to herself that Brett, Tommy and the band members were not being deliberately rude. It was just that she *was* an outsider among them. She made an effort to enjoy the sights and to appreciate the fact that she had been included at all. And one morning, when a launch took the group to a postage-stamp-sized island, where the white sandy beach was all their own, Carolyn made an attempt to be more outgoing by leading the conversation. "I bought a new bikini for this trip," she told anyone who cared to listen. "I just assumed, from all the pictures of silk kimonos and fans and parasols, that it's always warm in Japan." She had tested the water with her toe and decided it was too cold for a dip.

"A few months ago," Tommy said, "this island was

covered with snow. You have no idea how cold it can get here, even in the south."

Brett seemed irritable this morning. "Weather. That's what you talk about when there's absolutely nothing else to discuss."

It was a snide reminder that Brett took a disdainful view of people who had no interests worth talking about. But, dammit, she *did* have interests beyond the weather. Was she expected to talk about the jewels and feathers that trimmed the egret costume Billie was expecting from Tokyo this morning? Talk about her consuming interest in the very man who had just silenced her with his sarcastic words? Amuse Tommy and Rusty and Carmen and Tony with anecdotes about her unrelenting need for Brett Wells, or the love that was sometimes, as it was at this moment, hard to distinguish from hatred? Carolyn pretended a search for seashells and wandered down the beach alone.

Her gloom seemed inescapable, even the next day, when Tommy arranged for box lunches, called *bento,* from the hotel's Kokusai restaurant, and they were driven to a spectacularly beautiful gorge at the foot of Mt. Ishizuchi. Crystal-clear water tumbled over enormous moss-covered boulders in a tranquil wilderness setting that would have defied an artist's brush. Brett was entranced, thanking Tommy for bringing them to such a peaceful place.

"I knew you didn't need a tour of the local nightspots," Tommy said. "You can see those back home." But when he noted that there was just time for him to return to the hotel and dress for his first show, he urged everyone to join him in the Starlight Lounge, and the invitation was eagerly accepted.

Carolyn didn't join the party that night. Not even when Gavin knocked on her door and urged her to do so. "Tired from too much hiking?" he asked. "Come on, a little music will perk you up."

"I don't want any more music!" Carolyn spit out. She was startled by her own vehement tone. She might as well have said "musicians."

"What's wrong, Carolyn? You didn't back off from the grand tour of Tokyo."

"It was different there," Carolyn admitted glumly.

Gavin fixed her with a knowing look. "Because you had the tour guide all to yourself?" He didn't wait for a hot denial. Gavin turned toward the door. "I know the feeling, and it's slow poison. I lost my wife over it. And, you know, it took me a long time to realize this, but jealousy is the ultimate form of selfishness."

"I'm not jealous!" Carolyn protested.

Her lame protest was ignored. "When you start being eaten up because someone you care about is having a good time with other people, you're being possessive. You're only thinking about yourself. If you'd expand your own horizons—develop your own capabilities for leading an interesting life—you'd be able to share the person you love without being miserable." Brett's name wasn't mentioned, but it hung between them like a palpable presence. "And maybe you'd be more appealing to that person than a self-pitying—"

"Gavin, when I want somebody's corny philosophy, I'll start reading trashy supermarket magazines!"

"Okay, I'll be quiet." Gavin had been standing in the open doorway. Now he turned his back on her. "Just thought I'd stop by and see if you could use an escort. Brett won't be in the lounge tonight."

"I don't *care* where Brett is," Carolyn fumed.

Gavin turned for a moment. "If you're going to play the martyr, stay in your room and suffer, you might as well have something worthwhile to stew about. Brett's having dinner at Sadi Hayashi's house tonight. I doubt he'll be back in time for Tommy's midnight show."

Rage, blind fury, humiliation! Carolyn added Gavin

to her list of people to love and hate at the same time. Worst of all was her awareness that he was feeling sorry for her. He might as well have given her a lecture on why a woman was a fool to fall in love with a handsome superstar, and how to live with her misery if she did.

Nor did it help the next afternoon when Carolyn's night-long agony was intensified by physical evidence that Brett was still very much intrigued by his co-star.

Billie had dropped Carolyn off at a shopping mall, where an arched glass covering enclosed rows of intriguing shops and protected the inevitable crowd of shoppers from a persistent drizzle that had started during the previous night. Preliminary work was supposed to have started at Dogo Hot Springs today. Carolyn assumed that Brett and his band members had reported to the outdoor location. Sadi Hayashi had left her house at five that morning and Billie was to join her on the set around noon. It was a day, Carolyn thought, for being alone.

Strolling the narrow street, occasionally glancing upward at the high domed ceiling, Carolyn was completely unprepared for the sight which met her eyes. She would have fled, if Sadi had not seen her, too, and called out a cheerful greeting.

The actress was seated at a small table in a patio coffee shop, her film script on the table which separated her from Brett. Dressed for a solitary shopping tour in the rain, Carolyn felt like a bedraggled old crone as she was greeted by the two stars, both of them glamorous in spite of their casual wet-weather clothes.

Brett had gotten to his feet. Carolyn avoided his eyes, uncomfortable under an inspection that was only sensed.

"What a lovely surprise!" Sadi was beaming. "How will I ever convince friends who have never been here that Matsuyama is not a very small town?" She gestured at one of the two empty chairs facing the table. "Please join us, Carolyn. We are like children who have been let out of school. Verne Damian is tearing out his hair, but we can hardly test camera angles in this weather."

What made her stab back at Brett? "I try not to talk about the weather," Carolyn said. "People find it so dull."

Brett paid no attention to the barb. He repeated Sadi's invitation to join them, but it sounded unconvincing to Carolyn.

Carolyn nodded at the papers on the table. "Thank you, but you're working. I won't interrupt you."

"We are doing nothing that won't wait," Sadi insisted. "And I've been wanting to talk with you. I want you to see how beautifully my costume fits. And it suits me so perfectly. Since I'm small, I didn't want to be overwhelmed. You managed that perfectly!"

"It's a great design," Brett acknowledged. He remained standing, the perfection of his face clouded by an untypically melancholy expression. "I saw it last night, and it's fantastic."

Carolyn shifted awkwardly on her feet as Sadi said, "It's hanging in my bedroom closet at home. You must come see how well it's turned out, Carolyn. Later today? Yes, you must come to have lunch with me. I'm going home in a few minutes, and you can come with me. Or if you have plans for the rest of the morning, we can try to locate Billie and she'll drive you out."

"I . . . have some important errands to run," Carolyn said. She couldn't think of a way to elaborate or explain the urgency of her missions. "I'll take a cab out," she said.

"If you're going back to the hotel, have the desk clerk call for a limo," Brett put in. He didn't have to tell her that she *should* go back to the hotel. Carolyn was hardly dressed for lunch at the home of a prominent film star. "You won't need directions. Everybody in this city knows Sadi's estate."

Brett was resuming his seat when Carolyn hurried away, feeling more than ever like a pitiable fifth wheel.

She devoted the rest of the morning to making herself as attractive as possible, and when the limousine driver whisked her from the hotel to Sadi's doorstep, Carolyn was actually looking forward to the luncheon date. Her painful encounter with Brett that morning was not erased from her consciousness—he was forever at the edge of her awareness—but it would be exciting to write home and describe a visit to the fabulous home of a famous film star. And seeing the costume she had designed for Sadi would be the culmination of one of her cherished dreams.

A tiny, smiling maid met her at the door and ushered her into a spacious, glass-walled living room decorated in almost unrelieved white. Like the garden that fronted the low, clean-lined stucco-and-glass house, this room conveyed a feeling of opulence by its very simplicity. The architecture and furnishings were modern, but the white-carpeted room still retained an indefinable Japanese aura. Perhaps, Carolyn thought, it was the flowerless sculptured garden visible through the mammoth glass wall. White-gravel pathways led from a natural rock waterfall to a charming teahouse and then to a sparkling turquoise swimming pool so naturally tucked into a meandering enclosure of twisted trees and boulders that it might have been a woodland lake.

Carolyn was inspecting the room's foot-high white lacquered tables and sumptuous white silk floor pillows when she was surprised by the entrance of Billie Watanabe.

Billie was lavish in her greeting, considering that they had seen each other only that morning. She hugged

Carolyn, welcomed her to the house, and waving at the white expanse of the room, said, "Do you like it?"

"I've never been inside a house anything like it," Carolyn said with honesty.

"Miss Hayashi has beautiful taste. What a shame we cannot have our lunch outdoors. The garden is her special pride."

Carolyn had walked closer to the window wall. "It's like a life-size dish garden. Everything so perfectly harmonized and natural and understated."

"You see? You are an artist," Billie said approvingly. "You understand that a Japanese garden is like a *haiku* poem. Or a scroll on which the picture is created with a few simple strokes of a brush. Miss Hayashi loves flowers, but bright colors would destroy the serenity of this garden. She works with nature and the confines of the space allowed to her. When she is not working, she finds her solace in her creation out there. Hers, and that of the nature spirits."

"Solace?"

Billie seemed to be as embarrassed by the word as Carolyn was, suddenly, in asking the question. "I meant peace of mind," Billie corrected hastily. "Her work is very demanding, as you must know from working for Mr. Wells. People in the public eye must have their moments of privacy, in which they find themselves."

Carolyn sensed an evasiveness and warned herself not to pry too closely into Sadi's guarded personal life. She was wondering where her hostess was, when Billie said, "You must forgive me, Carolyn, for talking so much and not conveying Miss Hayashi's deep apology. She was called away a few minutes ago. We both regret and hope you will not be offended because she cannot be here to welcome you."

Carolyn hid her disappointment. Strange that she

should feel let down because the woman who was consuming all of Brett's attention would not be here for lunch. Billie continued to elaborate on her apology, anxious to let Carolyn know, without actually using the word, that her employer's absence was occasioned only by an unavoidable emergency. Strange, too, was the way Billie, who usually talked in the carefree manner that reflected her schooling in San Francisco, had lapsed into the exaggeratedly polite, almost archaic manner of speaking that typified the formal Japanese. Perhaps it was this house. There was something in the atmosphere of this cloudlike white room that demanded soft speech, traditional courtesies and gentle dignity.

It was impossible to pinpoint why Carolyn's feeling persisted; there was an enigma here; nothing was exactly as it seemed. There was the tour of rooms, one more inspired than the next, each a perfect example of the philosophy that had dictated the *haiku*-like garden. And there was the moment, before a white sliding panel that Carolyn knew must lead to the actress's bedroom, because it was the only room they had not inspected, when Billie said, "*Sumi masenan*. Please excuse me. I will bring your beautiful creation to the sitting room for you to see." It was an unspoken, polite way of letting Carolyn know that she was not to enter Sadi's intimate quarters, and she could not help wondering bitterly if, last night, another stranger *had* been admitted. She returned to the white room to wait for Billie.

Handling the feathery white costume as though it were a priceless gem, Billie held the hanger high over her head to make sure that the plumed train did not touch the floor tiles. Now she was more like the laughing, hand-clapping friend Carolyn had known before. And the gown was, indeed, a wonder to behold. It was the first time Carolyn had seen it complete. The seamstresses in Tokyo had been working on it up to the last moment. She wanted to be modest to counteract Billie's praise, but it would have been dishonest to deny that she had captured the grace and the beauty of the egret without forgetting the slender human figure it was to enhance. Carolyn had not produced a literal bird figure. She had caught the exotic bird's spirit, and the result filled her with pride.

"Sadi cannot wait to wear it," Billie said as she carried the costume back to the bedroom closet. "When she tried it on for me, I thought she never looked more divine."

Carolyn, left alone for a moment, closed her eyes. Sadi was too beautiful *now*. When Brett saw her in the white fantasy gown, he would be breathless with admiration. There was a painful irony in the fact that she was helping to beautify her own rival.

In the sparsely furnished dining room, which also seemed part of Sadi's garden, Carolyn and Billie were served by the same quiet little maid who had admitted Carolyn to the house. Considering Sadi Hayashi's Americanized work dress, Carolyn had expected the meal to be casual and typically Western style, too. It was not. Sitting on thick square cushions at a table no more than a foot high, they were presented with small portions of artistically arranged foods, delicately flavored. The food was as varied in color and design as the fragile porcelain dishes in which it was served.

"At home," Carolyn said, "when I was young, I always wondered why our china had to be perfectly matched. This is so much more interesting."

"Yes, my mother was shocked, in California, to learn that mismatched plates indicated that you cannot afford a proper set of dishes. Here, we enjoy the experience of many different colors and shapes and designs."

Carolyn laughed at her awkwardness in using chopsticks to eat the *chawan mushi*, a steamed custard which began the luncheon. She was fascinated by cornucopias of fried bean curd stuffed with a tempting mixture of fish, rice and shredded vegetables. *"Inari-sushi,"* Billie called the crisp stuffed horns. "We always include them in our picnics. However, Sadi ordered them today because she wanted you to enjoy something truly Japanese."

Carolyn was also introduced to *wakame,* a type of dried seaweed that had been marinated, cut into dainty pieces, and served with flower-shaped slices of cucumber and rice vinegar. Like the vegetable dish that had preceded them, the small *fukashi manju,* bean-paste cakes that accompanied the tea, were a joy to the eye as well as the palate.

While Billie was serving their green tea from a fragile white pot decorated with a charcoal-colored bamboo-leaf design, Carolyn recalled that she had seen an almost identical teapot at the home of Billie's parents. When she mentioned the fact, Billie explained that she had made both pots.

"For the gift-giving one New Year, I painted one like this for my parents and one for Miss Hayashi. Had the gifts come from a stranger, I am sure they would have hidden their teapots from sight. But of course my family loves me and Sadi has been my friend ever since she was quite young and I sewed dresses for her mother. I knew the Western styles, you see, and that lovely lady was devoted to fashion."

The remark seemed to loosen Billie's self-imposed restraint concerning her friend's personal life. "Miss Hayashi's people are of the *shizoku* class. The military, or what the British would call the landed gentry." Billie went on to explain that in spite of postwar democracy, among the older generations there was still the distinction between the *kuwazoko,* or nobility, and the *hei-min,* or common people. "The *shizoku,* such as Sadi's family, are usually wealthy, prominent families, but they are not titled and are not likely to be invited to the Imperial Palace for tea." Then, reverting to her childhood days in Fresno, Billie said incongruously, "They fit smack-dab in the middle."

She joined Carolyn's laughter at the contrasts in her speech, and the stiff, formal atmosphere was eased in a discussion of local customs and manners. "We women socialize this way, talking about our lives and our problems. Here, perhaps more than in the United States. There, it is not often that the wife stays home without complaining while her husband socializes with his male friends. Here it has always been accepted."

"Even if the companions are *not* men?" Carolyn asked.

Billie pondered the question for a moment and then evaded it gracefully. "Times are changing," she said. "Many of the traditions, both the good and the bad, have already changed. An electronics executive does not go to his offices in a ricksha."

It had been a pleasant conversation, Carolyn thought when it was time for her to leave. Yet it had somehow seemed more like a guarded exchange than the sort of talk she might have had with Jennie or another woman friend. While Billie had skirted around the subjects she deemed too personal, Carolyn had been cautious, too. She had wanted to learn what Billie knew about Sadi Hayashi's relationship with Brett. Billie lived in this house. Had she been here last night when Brett had come to dinner? She must know how much time they spent together, must know that two such attractive people would be drawn together. If Brett had spent most of last night here, Billie knew about it, but clearly she had no intention of disclosing that knowledge.

Chapter Twenty-one

It was not an egret, but a white heron with an injured leg that, according to legend, had discovered the curative powers of the Dogo Hot Springs more than three thousand years ago. It was now the most famous spa in Japan, so celebrated for the healing effects of its mineral waters and its sylvan beauty that special rooms in the rustic-looking but luxurious inn had been set aside for the exclusive use of the Emperor.

Carolyn thought the place worthy of an emperor as she sat one morning in a green grotto watching her creations come to life under the bright sunshine. The dancers in the dream sequence did not seem to dance at all. They fluttered and soared, a blaze of brilliant-colored feathers and iridescent silks. Under Verne Damian's direction, and that of a noted Japanese choreographer, the fantasy ballet scene portrayed a woodland filled with graceful flying birds. Sadi Hayashi was a floating vision in white as she danced her solo. And when the returning hero appeared, resplendent in a gold-shot emerald brocade samurai costume, to take the egret into his arms and sing his assurance that he was real, Carolyn was swept away by the sensual beauty of the scene.

Verne had the scene shot not once but three times. Yet it did not lose its grip upon the senses of those who were privileged to watch the filming. When the director shouted his final "Cut!" there was a brief silence and then a loud cheer from the cast and technical people. There was applause for the director, the stars, the writer. Then, unbelievable to Carolyn, the cast was looking directly at *her* and applauding wildly.

Careful not to crush her precious white gown, Sadi came to give Carolyn a cautious hug and a kiss on the cheek. Her smile dazzling, the actress addressed her co-workers in Japanese, and then translated for her American friends: "I have made twenty-two films. But this is the first time I have been upstaged by a *dress!*" There was laughter and another round of applause.

They had, in Verne's words, "a surefire winner in the can," and that evening, on a terrace in front of one of the huge pagoda-topped inns that surrounded the hot springs, there was a party to celebrate. Press arrangements had been made by the studio, leaving Gavin and Carolyn free to mingle with the guests. And what guests they were! Sadi's co-stars from past movies were there, along with important figures from the film industry, as well as other visiting celebrities who had flown down from Tokyo. It was a gala event at which the drinks flowed faster than the gurgling waters of the crystal-clear hot springs, and everyone was already intoxicated with the joy of finishing a job and knowing it had been well done.

Carolyn enjoyed the compliments of a seemingly endless parade of people, glowing in the director's introduction: "Carolyn Chandler, our fabulous costume designer." But the praise of strangers began to leave her feeling hollow. Some of the guests had already left the party, and Brett, usually with Sadi at his side, was still the center of attraction on the far side of the terrace, talking with nightclub stars and producers, signing autographs for lesser members of the cast, posing for countless photos.

For Carolyn, the feeling of being isolated in this glittering company had returned. Today she had launched a promising career, but she would have gladly gone back to hacking out descriptions of weddings and shower parties for a small-town newspaper if there could be another nine days in her life like those she had shared with Brett, another night like those in which he had taught her the ultimate expression of love. And she loved him now with a poignancy, a depth, a hopelessness that was like a burning stone under her breast—inescapable, always painful.

Once again she was looking for Gavin when Brett finally broke free of the crowds that had been surrounding him all evening. He walked directly to where she was standing at the edge of the lantern-lighted terrace. His samurai costume had been exchanged for a smart white suit, and tonight, flushed with success, he looked almost too dazzlingly handsome for Carolyn's misty eyes.

"I haven't had a chance to congratulate you," he said in a solemn tone. "I've been bragging when people rave about your work, telling them I knew you way back when."

Carolyn couldn't bring herself to look up at his face. She stared at the stone flooring as she mumbled her own congratulations. "You're an actor now, too, Brett. A polished, convincing actor."

Brett slipped his arm through Carolyn's. "Let's get away from all this chatter and talk."

Carolyn let him lead her down a fern-bordered pathway to a secluded garden in which the Dogo-Onsen waters sprang from an ancient stone fountain. It was a balmy night, starlit, and lacking only a full golden moon to provide the most romantic setting imaginable. They came to a stand of strangely twisted trees, strung for the occasion with painted paper lanterns. For a long time they were quiet, Carolyn's heart pounding, Brett probably absorbed by the beauty of the garden. Then he turned to her and said, "This hasn't been right, Carolyn. Nobody here is as close to me as you are, and we've hardly been speaking to each other."

"You're an important star," Carolyn reminded him. "You have to spend your time with important people."

"Important people!" Brett had reached out for her. "Don't tell me who's important to me, Carolyn." His arms pulled her harshly against him and his kiss was like a devouring flame.

Carolyn did not respond. Her body ached for him, but her heart told her this was impossible. He let her go and she said, "You'd better get back to the party, Brett."

"Why? So I can spend more time with important people?" He repeated her words angrily. "Carolyn, when are you going to start realizing that you're *somebody*? The reception you got today, not from a public audience, but from people in the industry, was fantastic. When are you going to stop putting me in one category and yourself in another? Your talent's being recognized, the way I always knew it would be. I'm just another guy doing a job, a guy who got a lucky break. Hey . . ." He placed his fingers under Carolyn's chin and lifted her face upward so that she was forced to look into his eyes. "I'm your *friend*, Carolyn."

Friend. The word was like a dagger gouging her heart. "Thank you," Carolyn said stiffly. "There were a couple of nights when I was very *friendly*, too." She had placed a scathing emphasis on the word. "You've since found another 'friend.'" She jerked herself free of him, crying, "Let me go! Get back inside. Your little white egret's waiting for you!"

Brett stared at her, dumbfounded. "Sadi? You're talking about *Sadi?* I know you have a great imagination, but even you wouldn't imply that I'm having an affair with . . . you're accusing me of . . . ?"

"Yes, Sadi, Miss Hayashi, whatever it is you call her when you're alone together!" Carolyn spun around and started running down the stone path, headed for the terrace. "It's none of my business. I don't care what you do, just . . . stop treating me like a yo-yo. *I don't want to be your damned friend!*"

Brett was right behind her. "You're so wrapped up in feeling sorry for yourself, you don't even make sense!" he accused. "It seems to me you've found plenty of distractions for yourself. Rusty, Gavin—I couldn't believe it, even Tony Hanniman."

Carolyn stopped in her tracks, whirling to face him. "Are you low enough to read something into . . . into every innocent conversation I've had with another man?"

Brett had halted his pace too, fixing her with an angry stare. "You didn't even waste time finding common bonds with Tommy Carlough. When the two of you were doing that ridiculous crossword puzzle bit the other day, I couldn't believe it. What a basis for grand rapport! The capital of Ghana, five letters. See you in my hotel room later!"

"You're insane!" Carolyn heard herself shrieking. "He was being a gentleman because he knew I'd been left out of the conversation for days."

"Are you finished?" Brett asked. His fury more than matched Carolyn's. "Because if you are, I think I *would* like some saner company."

"Go!" Carolyn shrilled at him. "Go! I don't ever want to see you again!"

"That goes both ways!"

They were within earshot of the noisy revelers on the terrace when Brett fired his parting shot. "You're even resentful of my *job*. That's as stupid as if your mother made a scene because your father spent some time repotting a . . ." he searched for the right comparison, ". . . mango tree!"

"My mother," Carolyn was shouting indignantly, "wouldn't worry if he spent a month on a desert island with a movie star. My mother knows he *loves* her!"

Chapter Twenty-two

"I don't understand the delay," Carolyn was saying. She looked up from the menu of the International Hotel's first-floor Kokusai restaurant. "Why are we staying?"

Their waiter appeared, and from the long list of available entrées, printed in Japanese, French and English, Carolyn ordered a hamburger steak.

When Gavin had made a gallant effort to order *aiguillette de canard aux basilic*, mangling the pronunciation when he could as easily have asked for the breast of duck with basil sauce, he gave Carolyn a wan smile. "When Americans start ordering hamburgers from an otherwise gourmet selection, it means they're homesick. You want to know why we're staying?"

"Yes. There aren't any more concerts scheduled. The film's ready for editing. We've even seen the rushes. Why another four days in Matsuyama?"

"Something I think we owe Mr. Yoshinaga," Gavin said. "He's cooked up a big event, and Brett, for one, wants to be part of it. So does Sadi, for that matter, but then, she lives here."

"Another concert?"

Gavin shook his head. "No."

"Brett doesn't need another farewell party. The four of you have been having one every night."

It was true. Gavin, Brett and Mr. Yoshinaga, joined by Tommy Carlough after his last performance in the Starlight Lounge, had spent every night out on the town until dawn. Maybe Brett was spending his daylight hours with Sadi, but Carolyn knew that he was doing his late-night socializing with strictly male companions.

Still hurt by Brett's stinging words, regretting the ugliness of the words she had hurled back at him, Carolyn turned her wrath onto the people who absorbed Brett's time. She made a derogatory reference to "expatriate glamour boys," naming Tommy. And to "bar-crawling millionaires who inflate their egos by picking up the tab at expensive nightclubs." "Maybe he should fly the three of you to the Copacabana in Tokyo," Carolyn went on. Her predinner cocktail was loosening her tongue and she had chosen Gavin as sounding board. "There's a one-hundred-dollar-per-person cover charge there. Dollars, not yen. When I think of all the unfortunate people in the world, extravagance like that just turns my stomach."

Gavin heard her out, eyeing her with more sadness than annoyance. "You can fault me for partying with Mr. Y.," he said calmly. "My excuse is that I'm very grateful to the man. When Ken and I were struggling with a new booking agency, he gave us our first contract to provide entertainers for his hotel chain. Besides, I enjoy the man's company. And you have your own quarrel with Brett. I don't even want to get into that.

Tommy's a long way from home and he works damned hard at that piano. He deserves to get out of this hotel and have fun. But I'll tell you something, Carolyn. When you start on Mr. Yoshinaga's case, you lose me. Have you ever looked around this hotel? Really looked?"

Carolyn's face began to burn. "Looked . . . at what?"

"Blind people. Crippled people. People who couldn't possibly find employment elsewhere. He's *invented* jobs for them. Come to one of his factories someday. There are so many handicapped people working in them, it's got to be a hiring policy. That concert he gave here raised a ton of money for charity, and he not only paid the expenses, he matched the profits, yen for yen." Gavin's look was not critical. It was more like that of a father looking at a child who has disappointed him. "So if he chooses to host a friend he doesn't see too often—that's *me*—and if he takes a little time from his harried business world to spend with two bright, talented, interesting entertainers, that's his privilege."

There was nothing she could say that would erase her embarrassment. She had even turned Gavin Durham against her. And maybe her attitude had communicated itself to their host. Miserable, hating herself for having made a mess of a glorious opportunity, knowing that Brett was through with her once and for all, Carolyn spent the rest of that week waiting for a party invitation that did not come.

She told herself that she was "partied out." She thought about how out-of-place she had felt at previous parties, where Brett's popularity only emphasized her insignificance in his life. She thought about how shallow the conversations were, the dropping of names and hypocritical compliments, the kisses aimed at the air to preserve professionally applied lipstick. She despised those superficial gatherings. But she watched the preparations for Mr. Yoshinaga's big gala and waited for a word, a printed card, a call to her room. None came. And her feeling of rejection and isolation intensified.

Carolyn was alone while she watched the hectic preparations for Sunday's big farewell event. The band members were like teenagers let loose in an expense-paid paradise. She seldom saw them. Brett was practically invisible during the day, and she knew he was seeing Sadi. Gavin had let that slip, and Billie had confirmed it. Lonely, homesick, and tired of faking cheerful letters to her friends and family, Carolyn wandered through the deluxe hotel seeing the grand banquet room converted into a tropical Eden. Potted palm trees banked the walls. Hawaiian decorations were being strung from the chandeliers. The big party was apparently going to be a luau. She didn't have to worry about shopping for a muu-muu or a grass skirt. She was obviously excluded.

Running into Tommy Carlough at the coffee shop, she was able to confirm her guess about the Hawaiian theme. "Mr. Yoshinaga's probably driving the chefs crazy," he said. "The island food's got to be authentic. Nothing but the best."

They would be flying back to California on Monday. Carolyn concentrated on last-minute souvenir-gift shopping and organizing her purchases. But she could not dispel the feeling of gloom that had settled over her. She was on the verge of tears as she packed her suitcases Sunday morning. At two o'clock Mr. Yoshinaga's party would begin and she had not been asked. Carolyn felt like an uninvited child watching a birthday party on the lawn across the street. *Brett . . . Brett. Tomorrow we're going home. Tomorrow will be the end.*

She blotted her eyes hurriedly when the knocking at her door persisted at a quarter past one. Carolyn admitted Gavin, colorful in a Hawaiian print shirt, a flower lei around his neck. He glanced at Carolyn's robe, then her somber face. "You don't look too ready, but there's still time. The guests won't start arriving until two."

"I'm not going," Carolyn told him. Her voice was flat and unemotional.

"Not going?" Gavin scowled. "Hey, that's the ultimate in bad manners, Carolyn. I don't think Mr. Yoshinaga deserves that from you."

"I don't go to parties to which I'm not invited!" Carolyn spoke sharply, emphatically, her voice rising. "And I haven't been invited to this one."

"Nobody from our group was invited," Gavin shot back irritably. "Brett wasn't, the band members weren't, *I* wasn't. If you had bothered to communicate with people, you'd know we invited ourselves because we want to help."

"Help publicize the hotel with Brett's name? That'll be another nice ego trip for Brett."

"This hotel doesn't need to be publicized," Gavin thundered. "Carolyn, what's happened to you? This party's almost a *secret.*"

"All right, so he'll be promoting the film. Mr. Yoshinaga's one of the angels." Carolyn spoke with less certainty now. "I'm not interested. I have packing to do. I . . . I can't wait to get home."

Gavin shrugged his shoulders. "Suit yourself. I know Brett's going to be very disappointed if you don't show. And I'm beginning to think Brett is right. The people who really care about you . . . *love* you, like the two of us, can't get past that wall you've built around yourself. How the hell can you love other people when you think so little of yourself?"

Gavin left her with that undeniable truth to torture her. Every word he had said was true, and the result of her stupid insecurity was a loss that would torment her for the rest of her life. Carolyn shoved a suitcase to the floor. It fell from the bed, spilling its contents. She threw herself across the space it had occupied and let the sobs rack her entire being.

She was still lying facedown on the bed, still crying, when there was a second knock on the door. Carolyn glanced at her watch. Ten minutes before two. She could not have gotten herself presentable now if she *had* decided to go. When the knocking was repeated, she called out, "I'm sorry, Gavin. *I'm not going.*"

There was quiet, and Carolyn assumed he had gone. She got up from the bed and started to check the door, not sure she had locked it after Gavin's first visit. She was reaching out to check the lock when the door burst open, nearly knocking her off her feet as Brett stalked into the room. Carolyn gasped.

"Okay, tell me you don't want to be seen because you look like the devil!" Brett shouted. "As a matter of fact, you do. There! Are you satisfied? Feel belittled enough? I've been working on a surprise for you for months. This is my one chance to show it to you. And if you don't care about yourself, you're not going to embarrass Gavin by missing this party. You're not going to embarrass me! I've got to be ready to go on in just a few minutes. I want to be there to greet the guests. And, damn you, Carolyn, you're not going to spoil this last day in Japan—not for me and not for yourself. You've got about eight minutes to get yourself down to the banquet room!"

He had been yelling at her, so angry, so authoritative, that Carolyn could only stand listening to him with her mouth agape. She made a feeble protest: "I can't make myself presentable in eight minutes, Brett. I . . . My eyes are all . . ."

"Red. Okay, you'll look like a rabbit, but you're

going to *be* there." And suddenly he took matters into his own hands. He grabbed Carolyn's wrist, dragging her toward the bathroom. He held her in a viselike grip, running cold water over a washcloth he had thrown into the basin with his free hand. She struggled to get free, but the cold cloth was held against her face. "Cold water. That'll do it."

"Brett, stop!" He was sloshing water all over her, splashing his Hawaiian print shirt, nearly getting the drops on his immaculate white pants. "I'll do it myself," Carolyn promised. "Please, Brett. You're going to be late yourself."

That reminder stopped him. He tossed the dripping cloth into the basin. "Wear sunglasses. They'll think you're a movie star. Slap on some lipstick." He was hurrying to the door, skirting the pile of clothes next to the bed. "Find something in that mess and put it on. I'll see you in the Tokiwa. That's the big banquet room. *Be there!*"

Carolyn didn't take time to protest his imperious command. She was splashing water on her face when she heard the door close behind Brett. And then she was rushing to follow his orders, slipping into a flowered print that could be construed as Hawaiian, putting on lipstick, giving her hair a flick with a brush. Brett wouldn't have raged at her like a lion if he didn't care. He said he'd been working on a surprise for her for months. What surprise? Why? Because maybe he did love her? Wasn't that what Gavin had said?

Carolyn was in the elevator before the allotted time had elapsed. She hardly looked glamorous enough to compete with the luminaries who would no doubt be attending, but Brett had already seen her at her worst. And he had said, *"Be there!"*

Carolyn was there, at the entrance to the banquet room, in which tables for at least three hundred were decorated with masses of flowers. She was there, wanting to die of shame for the harsh words she had spoken, as the guests began to arrive. They were greeted in the broad doorway by Mr. Yoshinaga, by hotel employees dressed in Hawaiian garb, by six of the lovely girls who had danced in the fantasy scene with Sadi, and by Sadi herself, all of them wearing the fabulous costumes they had worn in the film.

They handed each of the guests a beautifully wrapped gift, and one of the gold-imprinted envelopes with Brett's picture on it, the record that had been her idea and which she still had not heard. And Carolyn's eyes, hidden behind sunglasses at Brett's suggestion, flooded with tears again as the happy arrivals were ushered to their seats at the banquet table.

They were in their Sunday best, their faces shining with pleasure, though they were wizened and brown, wrinkled with years. Some were in wheelchairs, others leaned on canes and walkers, some walked stooped over, and some, fragile and small, walked aided by the gentle people who formed the reception committee.

Tommy was standing beside her, his smile offering a warm welcome, the expression in his eyes one of tender affection. "There's not a cab available in this city today," he said. "Special vans were ordered for those in wheelchairs. And did you ever see such beautiful, beautiful people? Last year, I got so choked up, I could barely sing."

"Last year?" Carolyn repeated.

"Mr. Yoshinaga does this every year. At all of his hotels. Makes it a big day for the senior citizens to look forward to. And look at the way those girls are guiding people in." He indicated one of the young dancers who was laughing at some private joke with a tiny old woman in a dark, probably long-worn kimono. She led her to her chair with slow steps, as gently as if the old woman were made of delicate porcelain. "The respect they have for old people here," Tommy was saying. "The reverence. It's such a privilege to entertain them."

"A privilege?" Carolyn asked. "But since you work here, doesn't Mr. Yoshinaga *expect* you to sing?"

"No. This is his personal party. He wouldn't demand that I sing here. It's not part of my job. This year, like last, I offered my services. And he was elated. When I corralled Brett and his band, he was overjoyed." Tommy exchanged greetings with an old couple passing by. "*Konnichi-wa. Konnichi-wa!*" he exclaimed, bowing as he wished them a good afternoon.

I could have been helping at the door, Carolyn thought. If I hadn't locked myself up in my room and avoided people, I could have been saying "*Konnichi-wa*" to these dear old people too.

A hush of anticipation fell over the banquet tables when all the guests had been seated. Rusty, his glittering drums half-surrounded by potted palms, rolled a call for attention. Carolyn watched, standing near the door, while a madcap master of ceremonies came bounding onto the small, low stage. Manuel, one of the waiters who worked in the hotel's Chinese restaurant, and who spoke Japanese, English and Filipino Tagalog with equal fluency, let Carolyn know that the M.C. was one of the country's top television comics. "But you don't have to know what he's saying to laugh at him."

Manuel was right. The old people were seized with giggles at the mere sight of the comic. He rattled off a few words and Carolyn found herself laughing with the rest. She looked from the television star to his audience, touched by the sight of wizened faces and dancing eyes.

Tommy was introduced. Many had apparently heard him before, and when he addressed them in Japanese, the love that flowed between performer and audience was something you could almost reach out and touch. Brett's musicians accompanied Tommy through two lovely Japanese songs, one of them the sentimental ballad that looked back, now that the beach was gray and deserted, to days when the sun had shone. *"Daremo ina iumi,"* he sang in that rich baritone that was strangely similar to Brett's. Like the memory of that sunshine, he was telling them, like the memory of summer, they would always be in his heart. And then, because the old people would not let him go, Tommy sang, in keeping with the party's theme, "The Maui Waltz" in English.

Through the enthusiastic clapping, Carolyn wondered what Brett could possibly do to win so much affection when he came on. But she suspected that Tommy would have coached him on his selections. They weren't competitors, they were friends.

Billie had joined the small group clustered near the door. She smiled and squeezed Carolyn's hand. "Beautiful no? If only there had been room for the entire chorus."

She was talking about the mini-ballet that followed; Carolyn could see Sadi and the six dancers behind a screen that served as a theater wing. Mr. Yoshinaga had taken his place near the door, too, his distinguished features radiant with the ever-present smile. He managed to look elegantly dressed even in a shirt emblazoned with palm trees and surfboards. When Billie went on to say that the six performers had been selected in a drawing, and that the losers were disappointed, Mr. Yoshinaga told her, half in Japanese, half in English, that there was not only a limitation in space, but in time. Old people tired easily. The program could not be too long, for there was still the dinner.

There were rapturous sounds of "Ohh!" and "Ahh!"

when the white egret and her company of brightly plumed birds appeared. Sadi Hayashi was *their* celebrity. Why, they might even see this beautiful star walking into one of Matsuyama's shops, or run across her in their lovely parks! A shortened version of the closing scene in the film had been choreographed. This afternoon, Sadi showed her love for the eager-eyed old people for whom she danced. She *was* the incomparably lovely white egret.

And how those sweet, shy, awed and smiling people returned her love!

"They know," Mr. Yoshinaga said in a tone too sad to match his appreciative smile. "They know. They think of how they are old, and they see her dance. And her husband is young, still so young, and cannot be with us—will not ever see her dance."

Billie's face had turned scarlet. Her whispered admonition was respectful. "Mr. Yoshinaga, Sadi does not want anyone to know."

"The public," he replied. His eyes were fixed on the stage, to which Sadi was returning alone. "The *public*, because she does not want to capitalize on her tragedy." He gave Billie a gentle smile. "But we who are her friends, how can we not know?"

In the next moment, there was no doubt that Carolyn had to be included among Sadi Hayashi's friends. She was addressing the three hundred or more people seated at the long, flower-bedecked tables. Carolyn could not understand her words, but the mystery was cleared up when Sadi extended a hand in her direction, then led the applause that followed.

"She has told them you are the designer of these beautiful costumes," Billie whispered. "They are applauding your work!"

Carolyn bowed, knowing her gesture was awkward, wishing she had given this event the time and respect it deserved. Hastily dressed, red-eyed, hiding behind incongruous dark glasses in an indoor banquet room! She had to look foolish. Yet, Brett's words came back to her. How could she love anyone, love *him,* if she did not love herself? She lifted her head, bowed again, and knew that she had never felt prouder in her life, in spite of her tear-swollen eyes.

"Yes, you are her friend," Billie said softly. "And Sadi is yours." She tugged at Carolyn's sleeve. "We can miss the comedy routine. Please. I feel so ashamed for not having told you. Can we talk for a moment outside?"

They slipped out of the room into the thickly carpeted hallway outside. Peals of delighted laughter, rising in pitch at the end of each joke, could be heard even through the thick pale wooden doors. Billie reached out for Carolyn's hand. "There is no shame, except mine for not having told you, Carolyn." And Carolyn listened to the story of a beautiful, gifted girl born into a wealthy, loving, but rigidly traditional family. They were fiercely protective of their class, determined that their only daughter would marry a highly respected, equally wealthy man of the *shizoku* stature. Acting and dancing were part of her training as a young lady, but not to be considered as a profession.

Sadi had done worse than choose the wrong career. During the filming of her first movie, she had met and fallen insanely in love with a young, struggling actor. Sadi had made a heartrending choice between a family she loved and respected, and a man she knew she could not live without. A child had been born, but the grandparents would not come to see it. Sadi was disowned, she had disgraced her family by dancing before the cameras in skimpy clothes; she had sullied the family name by marrying an impoverished actor.

"Her baby lived only a few months. An inherited

disease, Carolyn. I do not know the name in English, but it destroys the nerves, muscular control, wastes the body."

Carolyn could think of no words that would express what she felt.

"It struck Sadi's husband in later life, but not too long afterward. She has worked to see that he has the best possible care. When she worked in Tokyo, a special plane brought him to the hospital there, so that she could visit him. Now, the trips, even in a stretcher, will be too strenuous for him, the doctors say. It is torture for Miss Hayashi to visit him, and it breaks my heart to see her sitting alone in the garden when she comes home from the hospital. Sitting, meditating. Perhaps she thinks a curse was visited upon her poor Shiro because she disrespected her parents' wishes. That is hard for you to understand, perhaps, but, as you have seen today, our older generations are highly honored in this country."

"She can't believe it's a punishment of some sort," Carolyn said. "Devoting herself to a man the way she has . . ."

"She loves him, Carolyn. I am no longer allowed to visit, but I know he must be a living corpse, totally without control over his movements. He was a dashing young man. Strong, active, full of good humor. Sadi does not allow anyone but me to enter the room where she keeps his pictures. I don't know what she thinks, but I know she has never looked at another man. Mr. Yoshinaga has tried to reconcile her with her family, but they are adamant. Their hearts have been broken, their daughter is dead. And it would be a mercy if her beloved Shiro could escape his tortured body."

Carolyn blinked back her tears. "I remember, on the set in Tokyo, when she cried before the cameras. You said she'd had practice . . . much practice. But every time I've seen her, she's been smiling, laughing."

Carolyn felt a stab of guilt. "Always saying nice things to people, doing kind things for people. Just think what she's done for me!"

Billie nodded. "And for me. I have never found love, Carolyn. Think how empty my life would be if I did not have my work with her, and Sadi's friendship. Yet she envies me, I know, because on Sundays I am with my mother and father." She brightened. "No more. You understand now, and I am sorry I did not confide in you sooner. It's just that Miss Hayashi does not want to be pitied by her fans. Or have them come to see her films because of a family scandal or a tragedy. And Shiro's care has been costly. She must work to maintain the house that she built for him when she still believed he would someday come home. And to be a successful star, she must always be vivacious, always smiling."

There was a happy shriek from the senior citizens behind the door. Carolyn placed a kiss on Billie's forehead. "Thank you, Billie. For telling me. And for being who you are. My friend."

They embraced hastily, and Billie said, "Now, soon, you will see what Sadi has been doing for Mr. Wells. Preparing a surprise for his audiences, yes, but mostly, he has told me, because it was something *you* wanted."

They made an unobtrusive entrance, unnoticed because the comic M.C. had joined a trio of Chinese jugglers on the minuscule stage and was being buffeted about, pounded with hollow ninepins, sent sprawling as he tried to join their act. Rusty was emphasizing each head bump and pratfall with precisely timed thumps and rolls. A mere three hundred elderly people could not possibly be filling this huge room with so much laughter; there had to be a thousand.

The jugglers bowed at the close of their spectacular finish. And the master of ceremonies, breathless from exertion, was talking to the audience.

"He's telling them that the record each was given at

the door was made by a famous American singer they have probably seen on their television screens," Billie translated.

Manuel joined in the explanation. "He just said that the singer is going to do the song that's on the record."

"And that he hopes they will join him in the second chorus," Billie translated.

Mr. Yoshinaga held a cautionary finger to his lips. "Shhh!"

They were quiet, and Carolyn didn't have to be told what was happening. After a long, enthusiastic barrage of Japanese, she heard the popular comedian say, *"Brett Wells!"*

In a happy frame of mind, the audience would have clapped enthusiastically for a bellhop, Carolyn thought. For the man who had given each of them a special souvenir recording, they cheered like teenagers at a football game. What could he sing? How would he equal Tommy Carlough's intimate rapport with these lovely old people?

Brett didn't give her long to wonder. He blew a kiss to his audience, bowed, and took the hand mike from the M.C. *"Arigato gozaimasu,"* he said.

A faint suspicion had been creeping into Carolyn's mind during Brett's introduction. Something *she* had wanted him to sing? She had loved all of his songs, even the one that had been poorly received at the concert in Hiroshima. There had been no special requests from her. Unless, of course . . .

Tony Hanniman played a few soft introductory chords. And then she knew. At the *ha-na-mi* in the park, the cherry-blossom festival after which they had made love for the first time, she had told him how much she loved the ancient song. She had hummed the melody in the elevator, wondering if he would take her into his arms at last. She had thought of the short-lived blossoms many times since then, equating them with the most wonderful days and nights she had ever known—days and nights that had passed too swiftly.

A ripple of happiness that was tinged with awe ran through the banquet room. Softly, more tenderly than Carolyn had ever heard him sing, Brett was crooning:

> *Sakura, sakura*
> *Yayoi no sara wa*
> *Miwatasu kagiri,*
> *Kasumi ka kumo ka.*

What were they thinking, these poor, crippled, time-worn and perhaps lonely people? Were they realizing that there would not be many more *ha-na-mi* for them, with friends and food and drink and folk songs under the cherry trees? Were they thinking of the cherry blossoms themselves, the brief time when the blossoms were perfect and perfume filled the air all around them? Thinking that life, too, was beautiful, but finite, lasting too short a time? They did not appear depressed by the song that was closest to every Japanese heart. They listened with rapt attention, as if they had never heard this thousand-year-old melody before, their suddenly youthful faces shining with love for the music and, by extension, the golden-voiced stranger who was singing it just for them.

Through it all, Carolyn knew in her heart he was singing to her. Not even when he had looked directly into her eyes when he sang about love had the message been more personal. Brett did not glance in her direction. He may not even have seen her in the room. Or he may have seen her leave it just before he was introduced. Did he know that she was here, that she remembered the night they had listened to the touching strains of this song, would never forget that later that night he had taught her to love with her body as well as her heart?

When Brett began the second chorus, he didn't have to encourage other voices to join him. Trembling old voices, strong voices, soft, sweet voices, voices sadly off-key, voices mostly old, but some young enough to sing the haunting song many more times in the years ahead, every voice in the room rose to praise the "Cherry blossoms, cherry blossoms, Like a cloud in the morning mist . . ."

Nioi zo izaru,
Izaya, izaya
Mini yukan.

Then it was over, and Brett was bowing again. If there was a dry eye in the banquet hall, it escaped Carolyn's attention. No one seemed ashamed of the tears. Carolyn reached up to remove her out-of-place sunglasses. Billie's face was streaked with tears. It was a moment to seal in memory, along with the cherry blossoms Carolyn had pressed in her guidebook—a moment she would never forget.

Waiters had sprung into action. The luau delicacies were arranged on long tables for a buffet. Plates were carried to those who were less mobile, drinks carried to performers, dancers and musicians. There was an excited hubbub, everyone talking at once. Billie was explaining to someone that it was a recognized tradition that women did not drink *sake,* and Sadi appeared, still in her white costume, but less cautious now as she and Carolyn hugged each other. And Brett was at Carolyn's side, with Tommy Carlough saying to him, "Helluva note. I do three numbers and you only do *one?* The star only does *one?*"

"Can you think of another song to follow *that* one, buddy?" Brett retorted.

"No way."

"By the way, thanks for letting me do the honors. You could have done it a lot better yourself."

Then Mr. Yoshinaga, his perfectionist eye watching every move made by his hotel staff, somehow found time to invite Billie and Sadi and the Californians to yet another party: a farewell party in the lounge where Tommy performed, so that it was not necessary to say good-bye now. Carolyn shook Mr. Yoshinaga's hand. "Thank you. I wouldn't miss it for the world." Then she added impulsively, "You're beautiful, Mr. Yoshinaga. *Domo arigato!*"

Brett had heard her thank-you. He watched her smiling and nodding at the people at a table nearby. He saw her laughing at a private joke with Billie and heard her assure Tommy that when she got home to California she would send him a bale of crossword-puzzle books, even if the postage left her without money for gasoline.

"It took me a long time, but I learned your song," Brett said when they found themselves alone near the door. "I didn't forget your request, Carolyn." He was pinning her with that intent gaze that always seemed to probe her very soul. "You may think so, but I haven't forgotten anything. *Anything.*"

"I hope you'll forget the way I've acted, Brett. I should have tried to understand your work. I was so jealous . . . I never guessed that you were planning a beautiful surprise for me."

"Maybe I was jealous, too," Brett admitted. "Maybe, at the hot springs, when you said there was a difference between the two of us and your mom and dad, I should have stopped right there and told you that's not true."

"You've never told me that you love me, Brett," Carolyn said. "Not once, even when we were . . . like one person."

"Oversight to be corrected," Brett said. "I would have sworn I was making it obvious. From about age fourteen."

Her heart was fluttering like a caged bird. "Couldn't you have *said* it? Stopped me from almost hating some of the greatest people in the world?"

Brett leaned to plant a soft kiss on her forehead. "Later," he said. "I've got to circulate now. Later."

Carolyn lingered for a moment, not wanting the otherwise tempting food because her stomach felt suddenly tied in knots. And this time Carolyn wasn't doubting herself or questioning whether Brett felt exactly as she did. He *did*. She was *somebody*—an applauded designer who would soon be getting offers, the woman Brett Wells loved!

When she was leaving the banquet room with Gavin shortly afterward, Carolyn saw Brett circulating. He leaned down to kiss a shriveled old woman, and made another blush with a big bear hug.

"Can you handle that?" Gavin asked as the elevator took them to their floor. "I know they're old people, so maybe it doesn't bother you this time."

"It won't ever bother me again," Carolyn told him firmly. "If they were all young, gorgeous, famous and madly in love with him, it wouldn't bother me. He loves people. Loving people who adore him is part of his job."

Gavin's face took on a startled expression. As the elevator doors hissed open, he said, "You're learning. You're getting there. Maybe you've already arrived."

"He can stay there all day if he wants to," Carolyn went on. She felt free—free and confident and bursting with anticipation.

"He won't stay there longer than good manners dictate," Gavin said. He made an elaborate pretense of studying his watch. "I'd say ten minutes at the outside."

Gavin had been close enough, Carolyn guessed, to hear what she and Brett had been saying to each other. "I owe you a lot of apologies, too," she said.

"Some other time." He grinned and walked her to her door. "Another time when you aren't expecting company."

Brett did not knock at her door for nearly half an hour. It had given her time to shower, apply fresh makeup, and slip into the silk tie-dyed coat Brett had bought for her. Struggling into the tight black jumpsuit would be a waste of time, she decided. Playful, excited, she replaced it with a tiny bikini bottom. The coat just barely covered it. She broke the seal on a bottle of heady perfume bought in Harajuku as a gift for one of her mother's friends.

There had also been time to slip on her only pair of spike-heeled sandals. When she crossed the room to answer the door, Carolyn felt very sexy, and the feeling was delicious.

When Brett came into the room, he looked her over before he spoke. Then he said, "All that just for me?"

"I wasn't expecting the members of your band," Carolyn teased. "I don't do this for just anybody."

Brett's hand reached out to touch her face, stroking her cheek with his fingers. It was a tender touch, as soft as the adoring look in his eyes. "Only for the man who loves you? That's what I came to say, Carolyn. Something I've always felt, and thought you knew. I love you." He let a tender half-smile light his face. "And while it's very exciting to know that you wanted to look sexy for me, I want you to know that sex is . . . well, it's not *un*important. But when it's good, it's only a small percentage of what people who love each other share. With you, there's so much more. Knowing you're a friend as well as a lover."

She was starting to get misty-eyed again. "I kept

being hurt because that was all I was to you. Your friend."

"But don't you see that friendship is the most important aspect? In a relationship . . . in a marriage, just knowing that somebody's going to *be* there, no matter what? You're my Rock of Gibraltar, honey. My roots. The one person who can look beyond the image and see . . . and see the man."

It was a compliment she would always cherish, but right now she wanted much more than friendship. Their love demanded physical expression.

Brett didn't kiss her; they kissed each other, their ardor equal in a long, lingering meeting of lips that had longed for each other. So hungry was she that Carolyn didn't care if she ever drew another breath; she only wanted this glorious sensation to go on forever.

They held each other for a long time, their kisses growing in fervor, Brett's hand pressing against the small of her back until Carolyn was swept away by a desire to rid herself of the wisp of fabric that separated her from him. She wanted Brett unclothed, too, so that she could see him in all his sense-intoxicating perfection, touch him, kiss him, know the ecstasy of being one with him. Between the now-ravaging exploration of their tongues, Carolyn whispered, "Brett, we've wasted so much time. Let's not waste any more."

They made their way to the bed without letting go of each other. Before they had dropped into a fervent embrace, the bright silk *boumake* coat and the bikini bottom formed an unceremonious heap on the floor, along with white trousers, shorts and a garish Hawaiian shirt.

Entwined in each other's arms, it was as though they had just made the discovery that their bodies were made for lovemaking. She would never be able to rain enough kisses on Brett's face, his neck, his chest, never have enough of his hands caressing her every curve.

Brett's breathing was irregular, his words now as passion-stirring as the heat of his embraces. "I love you. Why didn't I know you wanted to hear me *say* it? I wanted to hear it from you, too. I love you."

She wanted to laugh and to cry and to repeat the words over and over, hear them over and over. "I love you, I love you, I love you. Oh, Brett, how I love you!"

Then the precious words blended into a single emotion in which Carolyn opened her heart and her mind and her body in one rapturous moment as she felt him take possession of her. She let out a little gasping cry and tightened her arms around his warm, naked body. "Love me, Brett. Love me, love me, love me. Now!"

He loved her. In every way there was to love, Brett loved her. They moved together until the electric quickening of their bodies rivaled the startling clap of thunder outside.

Then they were peaceful, their breathing slowly returning to normal. Carolyn lay still, Brett's arm supporting her head, nuzzling her face against the hard pillow of his chest. "It's raining," she heard Brett say in a languid manner. "Did you hear that thunderclap a while ago? That's the way I feel inside. Like a raging storm."

From their bed they could see the heavy rain pelting the broad window wall. "Funny," Carolyn said. "It feels like the sun is shining."

"It will, darling," Brett said huskily. "It always will, if we can be together like this." His free hand was caressing her breasts again, the touch almost worshipful. And then he was talking about the sunny tomorrows he wanted to share with her, projecting himself into a future in which each of them would pursue their careers but never to the extent that the work that kept them creative and interesting to each other interfered with the kind of life they wanted to live. "Fewer tours for me," Brett was saying. "Maybe one film a year, if the first one clicks. One album a year. And you—maybe just enough assignments to keep you happy doing what you enjoy doing and do so well. That should leave enough time, wouldn't you think?"

She knew what he was saying, *hoped* she knew what Brett was proposing, but it was still too unbelievable. "Time, Brett? Time for what?"

"For each other. For our home together." He brushed Carolyn's forehead with his lips. "For the kids we're going to spoil rotten. We're going home tomorrow morning, darling. As soon as we recover from jet lag, we're going to City Hall and get a piece of paper that makes this marriage legal. So far, it's only been approved by heaven."

Electric-blue lightning flashed through the room. It reminded Carolyn that tonight would be doubly exciting. From the three glass window walls of the Starlight Lounge, the city lights would seem diffused, like feathery circles of color filmed by a camera out of focus. The lightning would be a spectacular sight to watch while they enjoyed their last night in Matsuyama. Along with the thank-yous and good-byes and *sayonara, sayonara,* which meant not just "good-bye," but literally "If that be so, we shall meet again," she and Brett would steal the sky's thunder with the wondrous announcement of their love.

Silhouette Special Edition

MORE ROMANCE FOR
A SPECIAL WAY TO RELAX

Six new titles are published every month. All are available at your local bookshop or newsagent, so make sure of obtaining your copies by taking note of the following dates:

APRIL 15

MAY 20

JUNE 17

JULY 15

AUGUST 19

SEPTEMBER 16

May Special Editions
Available Now

Tender Deception by Patti Beckman

After the crash, memory gone and
appearance altered, Lilly Parker began to search
for her identity and found Kirk, her husband . . .
who had fallen in love with the woman
she'd become!

Deep Waters by Laurey Bright

Dallas fought her attraction for anthropologist,
Nick, from the steaming jungles of Enigma
Island to the moon-silvered beaches . . . but
where he was concerned she knew she would be
easily conquered.

Love With A Perfect Stranger
by Pamela Wallace

One night aboard the Orient Express they
met—and carried away by romance, Torey
gave her heart. Now, trip over, Peter West
would leave her life forever . . . or would he?

May Special Editions
Available Now

Mist of Blossoms by Jane Converse

Singing star Brett Wells was tired of being
chased by women. So how could Carolyn tell him
of her love when he insisted that they remain
just friends?

Handful of Sky by Tory Cates

Shallie had to make her way in rodeo, a man's
world, and Hunt McIver's help was invaluable.
But the man himself remained a mystery . . . one
she longed to solve.

A Sporting Affair by Jennifer Mikels

Alaine's heart never had so much as a sporting
chance of escaping unscathed once she met
ballplayer Doug Morrow, the charismatic
pitcher who made it clear he would have
things his own way.

Silhouette Special Edition

Coming Next Month

After The Rain by Linda Shaw

One man had already hurt Patrice Harrows
and she was not yet ready to trust Madison
Brannen. But there was one thing the lady
lawyer couldn't argue away: her love for him.

Castles In The Air by Tracy Sinclair

Mike Sutherland was determined to buy Morgan
Construction but the owner, Sam Morgan, to his
surprise was a woman—all woman—and equally
determined not to sell!

Sorrel Sunset by Gena Dalton

Dynah Renfro and Reed Harlan struck a bargain
to be co-owners of a race horse . . . but Reed
soon had full ownership of Dynah's heart
and her future.

Coming Next Month

Traces Of Dreams by Jane Clare

Art historian Pia Martell and photographer
Jules d'Archachon seemed made for each other.
Would love be strong enough to hold them together
when jealousy threatened to tear them apart?

Moonstruck by Christine Skillern

Until Caroline Conal set sail with Jake
St. Simon she had never known real work—or
real love. Beneath the starry Pacific sky they
lost themselves in a love without regrets.

Night Music by Kathryn Belmont

Carla Santucci tried to remind herself that
Harrington Bates was her boss—but on one special
evening she saw a side of him that refused to
leave her memory.

Silhouette Special Edition

95p each

43 ☐ ALL SHE EVER WANTED
Linda Shaw

44 ☐ SUMMER PARADISE
Laura Eden

45 ☐ LOVE'S TENDER TRIAL
Maggi Charles

46 ☐ AN INDEPENDENT WIFE
Linda Howard

47 ☐ PRIDE'S POSSESSION
Jeanne Stephens

48 ☐ LOVE HAS ITS REASONS
Olivia Ferrell

49 ☐ A MATTER OF TIME
Brooke Hastings

50 ☐ FINDERS KEEPERS
Dixie Browning

51 ☐ STORMY AFFAIR
Brenda Trent

52 ☐ DESIGNED FOR LOVE
Tracy Sinclair

53 ☐ GODDESS OF THE MOON
Leslie Thomas

54 ☐ THORNE'S WAY
Joan Hohl

£1.10 each

55 ☐ SUN LOVER
Sondra Stanford

56 ☐ SILVER FIRE
Pat Wallace

57 ☐ PRIDE'S RECKONING
Carolyn Thornton

58 ☐ KNIGHTLY LOVE
Billie Douglass

59 ☐ THE HEART'S VICTORY
Nora Roberts

60 ☐ ONCE AND FOREVER
April Thorne

61 ☐ TENDER DECEPTION
Patti Beckman

62 ☐ DEEP WATERS
Laurey Bright

63 ☐ LOVE WITH A PERFECT STRANGER
Pamela Wallace

64 ☐ MIST OF BLOSSOMS
Jane Converse

65 ☐ HANDFUL OF SKY
Tory Cates

66 ☐ A SPORTING AFFAIR
Jennifer Mikels

All these books are available at your local bookshop or newsagent, or can be ordered direct from the publisher. Just tick the titles you want and fill in the form below.

Prices and availability subject to change without notice.

SILHOUETTE BOOKS, P.O. Box 11, Falmouth, Cornwall.

Please send cheque or postal order, and allow the following for postage and packing:

U.K. – 45p for one book, plus 20p for the second book, and 14p for each additional book ordered up to a £1.63 maximum.

B.F.P.O. and EIRE – 45p for the first book, plus 20p for the second book, and 14p per copy for the next 7 books, 8p per book thereafter.

OTHER OVERSEAS CUSTOMERS – 75p for the first book, plus 21p per copy for each additional book.

Name ....

Address ....

....